Angels AND Atheists

Angels AND Atheists

Jay Carp

River Pointe Publications
Saline, MI

Angels and Atheists

Published by
River Pointe Publications
Saline, Michigan

ISBN: 978-0-9848103-2-1

Interior design and composition by Sans Serif
Cover design by Barb Gunia

Printed in USA

DEDICATION

Humans think of angels as supernatural messengers who can protect and guide them in their times of need. Because angels are interwoven throughout the fabric of religion, humans assume that angels exist only in holy form.

Since there are no formal rules, regulations, or instructions defining angels, each person has to decide the shape, the substance, and the power of their own angel. These options, along with the belief that angels are ethereal, make it hard to convince people that there are human angels who live among us. This is their mistake. They are not aware that mortal angels are as close to heavenly angels as frosting on cake.

During my adult life, I met three such angels. Each had a strong love of life; each believed in goodness; each had a different personality. What they did have in common was that the three of them blessed me with their love. Before I became a three-time widower I was fortunate to have married and shared my life with each angel. This book is dedicated to these angels.

Now, I have only my memories to connect me with them. And I do have many happy memories. I will be sleeping and a dream will get me chuckling and I will wake up laughing over something that happened in the past. These are the memories I want to remember.

Occasionally, I dream about something that penetrates my sleep deeper than a dagger and is so painful that I wake up in a panic. These are the memories I want to forget.

I try to follow the same beliefs that my angels embraced. Virginia, Ruth, and Hazel wanted the world to be a better place for everyone on this earth. Bar none. My hope is that, someday, all angels, both earthly and heavenly, will prevail and that happiness, love, and freedom will be as much a part of every person's life as is sunrise and sunset.

This should please my angels and it would also please me.

Books by
Award Winning Author Jay Carp

Jay Carp Fish Tales 2011

Loneliness 2011

The Patriots of Foxboro 2009

The Gift of Ruth—Large Print 2008

Cold War Confessions 2007
USA Best Book Awards, 2007 Winner

CHAPTER 1

Bill Bruckner wanted to put a hand over each ear and block out the conversation that he was overhearing. His two guests were eating breakfast and bragging about their past sexual experiences. Both were in their mid-sixties. These rusty and raunchy roosters, plumped out in their vests of body fat, were cawing about make-believe details to prove they were once extremely virile. Bruckner certainly didn't want to hear descriptions about their fictitious teenage conquests. He thought, "My God, they're making up stories about things that happened fifty years ago." Their eagerness to prove they were still potent disgusted Bruckner.

However, despite his irritation, Bill didn't cover his ears. He just stood in front of his guests, glancing out the window and shaking his head. He hoped they would quickly finish their breakfast and go about their business. Bruckner had opened his restaurant early this particular morning so they could eat and then begin their drive to northern Michigan for the opening day of deer season.

Until last week, he had completely forgotten that the hunting season was about to begin. It was only after a phone call from both hunters, Gil Oldham and Barney Black, that he remembered that he and his best friend, Sam Cutler, made the same journey last year. Bruckner only accompanied Sam because Sam wanted him to cook for a group of hunters in a club that Sam had joined. Since that last hunting season, Sam Cutler had died under suspicious circumstances, and his death weighed heavily on Bruckner.

During their call, Oldham and Black had asked him two questions: was he going up north and cook for the hunters this year, and would he open his restaurant and make breakfast for them so they could get an early start? Bruckner had absolutely no intention of cooking for them, but he didn't tell them that. Instead, he said that he would think about the trip and answer their questions in a day or two.

Bill Bruckner was in his mid-fifties. He was tall and thin with a shock of curly white hair. His black eyebrows brought attention to his blue eyes. His facial expression rarely changed. He looked stern, but when he did smile, he radiated pleasantness.

That evening, sitting in their living room, he told his wife about the phone call he received and the requests that were made. Maribeth Bruckner had been Bruckner's wife and business partner for almost thirty years. She wore her hair short and did not tint her gray hair. She had a lithe figure that she kept by exercising daily. She was a handsome matron whose looks still drew admiration. Maribeth listened to her husband and asked, "What are you going to tell your hunting friends?"

"I definitely am not going hunting with them. I won't kill a live animal and I won't touch a gun. Last year I went only because Sam asked me. We cooked for eight hunters. All we did was cook and clean. Sam may have hunted in previous years, maybe he didn't. I don't even know why he joined their club; he hated guns. I guess he wanted friends. Although we were physically close to the hunters while we were there, I didn't make particular friends with any of them. They did their thing, Sam and I did ours.

"It was a wasted trip for me because I didn't enjoy myself and Sam made it worse by finally opening up and telling me about his problems. To answer your question though, I will probably open the restaurant early the day before hunting season begins. I'll make breakfast for anyone who shows up so they can drive and be at their camp on opening day. That's all I intend to do."

Maribeth smiled at her husband's generosity. "You realize you are not obligated to do anything and that they will probably not pay you a penny for their meals? It is a freebie that they take for granted."

"Maribeth, of course I know that. I'll tell you something else. It was not a good experience for me. I had never met any of them before that trip. They were all Sam's friends and I never got a chance to really talk with anyone; they drank, swore, and never bothered to thank Sam or me for our work. I only went with him because he asked me to do the cooking.

"I'm willing to serve them breakfast because most of them are veterans and I never refuse to feed a veteran. This is a tradition that my father started when he opened our restaurant and I don't intend to break it."

Maribeth replied, "Well, you are a softy, you always have been. Do you want me to go with you to help you open early?"

Bruckner got up from his chair, went over to his wife and kissed her on the top of her head. Maribeth always made him feel good. "No, thank you, although that is sweet of you, but cooking for that small a group won't be a problem."

Later, in bed, he thought about his hunting trip with Sam Cutler. He realized that he hadn't known much about Black, Oldham, or the six other hunters in the group. He wondered why he, or even Sam, had bothered to go on that trip. He didn't have a gun or a hunting license and he certainly didn't care about shooting deer or any living animal; he had seen enough death in his life. The two of them just sat around, reminiscing about their pasts and cooking. They enjoyed their memories and the break from their normal routines but three days of cooking didn't allow much time to interact with the hunters; the eight of them were locked into a different world. Bruckner and Cutler spent most of their free time discussing Sam's problems.

In camp the hunters were more intent on drinking and discussing their adventures than in swapping stories with the cooks. Bruckner decided that his hunting trip with Sam was some kind of "senior citizen guy thing," because there was no rational reason for either of them to be there.

The next morning, following his talk with Maribeth, he called Oldham to tell him that he would cook breakfast for him and Black and anyone else that showed up so they could get an early start on their trip up I-75. He told them to drive to the back of the parking lot and come in through the kitchen; that is where they would eat, not in the dining room.

On November 14, the morning before the regular firearm hunting season, Bruckner was up and at his restaurant, the Crossfire, before 5:00. He was brewing a pot of coffee when Black and Oldham arrived. He looked at his two guests. Both were dressed in their camouflage suits along with orange hunter caps and vests with their hunting licenses; each man had stitched a patch on his left shoulder to show that he had been in military service. Black had been in the navy; Oldham, in the army. Bruckner remembered them saying that they both served in the Korean War.

They made a contrasting appearance. Barney Black was a short, wizened man with wrinkles on his cheeks and a stubble beard. He was over sixty years old and jittery. He spoke quickly, and was always fidgeting.

Gil Oldham was large, pudgy, and about the same age as Black. He was slow to speak, slow to move, and usually had an ache or a pain or some physical problem to share with his friends. They were almost exact opposites in their personalities, which made for a good friendship between them.

Bruckner filled a carafe of coffee and put it on the table. They all sat down and poured themselves coffee. Barney Black spoke first, "Bill, you don't know how glad we are that you're making us breakfast so we can get an early start. I just wish you were coming with us."

Bruckner answered him, "Well, I can't. I have an electrician coming to change a couple of circuits around here in the kitchen. I'm not sure how that's going to work out so I'm going to stay around to see what happens."

He asked them what they wanted to eat, took their orders, and left to cook breakfast. He prepared three meals and carried the plates back to the table.

To his total surprise, Black and Oldham had a bottle of Jack Daniel's sitting on the table beside their coffee; the bottle was open and was almost one-third empty. Bruckner was not pleased to see that they had started to drink. "You guys should be careful. You don't want to be stopped with an open bottle of liquor in your car or have alcohol on your breath."

Gil Oldham answered, "Well, we kind of have a problem. We ain't exactly sure who'll be cooking and me and Barney don't intend to starve. So, we brought along a few bottles of Jack Daniel's and Southern Comfort for nourishment. In fact, we've been sampling them already this morning. Would you care for a nip?"

"No, and if you're going to be driving shortly, you better lay off the booze."

Black suddenly said, "Maybe you're right." He and Oldham started to eat their bacon, sausages, fried potatoes, omelets, and toast. Bruckner just toyed with his food; he had lost his appetite.

Black and Oldham engaged in a lively discussion about how they wished there would be women at their hunting camp and what they would do if there were. This was when Bruckner wanted to put his hands over his ears. He tuned out their conversation.

When his attention returned to the discussion, both were talking about hunting. Black was saying, "Bruckner is right about drinking too much. Them goddamn state troopers are hunting us hunters. Instead of going after crooks and robbers they are waiting at 69 to give us speeding tickets. I don't know why they are not doing their job."

Oldham added, "I don't know, either. Anyhow, I hope we have snow this year. It sure is a help in tracking."

Then, he changed subjects, "Barney, do you remember when we picked up them two 'Lap Lizard Whores,' Vivian and Dew Drop, at that truck stop. We was almost too tired to hunt."

"Yeah, I remember them. We had good times back then. But, it's changing. Three weeks ago, when I was up scouting our camp, I saw a brand new pickup truck and three dark skinned guys. The truck was parked near an old deer print and they was pointing at it and screaming in some foreign language. I thought they were going to come in their pants. They don't know a deer from a donkey but, sure as shit, they'll be running around, screwing everything up for us real hunters. They ought to go back to where they came from."

Oldham's reply was sullen, "Well, they won't. And, these damn liberals will say, 'they have their rights.' Well, so did we, once; we've lost ours to people who ain't even American, like chinks, blacks, Muslims. They're all the same. They are coming in over our borders. They settle in this country, get on food stamps, and us whites have to support them." He stopped speaking, and suddenly picked up his drink and drained the liquor in one gulp.

Black added his thoughts, "That's not all. Us whites are being deprived of our rights by minorities and our Christian religion has to put up with these heathens. And that's the problem. There are too many damn minorities in this world. These non-Christian heathens are breeding so fast and so often that they're gonna change the fate of the entire world. Us Christians will end up as their slaves. Just watch and see." Barney Black tapped his fingers on the table when he emphasized his point about too much irreligious sex going on.

That pronouncement just hung in the air like the stink at the town dump on a hot day. Bruckner did not know how to respond. He knew that prejudice is not like a snow bank; there is no way to shovel a path through it. He said nothing.

Finally, Gil Oldham said, "What the hell are you talking about? We was sitting here, eating breakfast and planning our trip north and all of a sudden you come up with this screwing crap.

"Why did you go from hunting to these foreigners screwing their brains off and having more kids than us?

"I think you may have drunk too much liquor."

Black got huffy and he defended himself, "We wasn't talking just about the trip to our hunting camp. We was talking about how bad the hunting season has become. It's crowded with these minorities who don't know how to handle firearms. They get a hunting license, they drink while they carry loaded weapons, they don't care about safety. They don't know anything about hunting. We've got too many foreigners, they're dangerous; and they're not like us.

"And the world is full of these non-Christian fools. They are screwing each other and that is really going to change the world for us Christians. Ain't that right, Bill?"

He was appealing to Bruckner, who didn't want to get involved in this conversation. Bruckner decided to try and change the subject. "Maybe the three of us ought to volunteer our services and try to change those terrible odds against us?"

Black was immediately on the defensive and indignantly replied, "Bill, that ain't funny. I'm telling you that overpopulation of non-Christian countries is gonna put us in the minority. Hunting is just one place where the problem shows up. You'll see what I mean when we have so much world population that there won't be enough food. When billions of people are starving, you'll see heathen cannibals. You watch."

That thought was repulsive to Bruckner. Before he could reply, Oldham answered, "You're crazy, Barney. The world will destroy itself by blowing up thousands of them nuclear bombs long before we get around to eating each other."

Bruckner was disgusted. He had gotten up early to open his restaurant and cook breakfast for these two. He really didn't know them; he was feeding them so that they could get an early start on the deer season. He didn't mind the inconvenience, his restaurant was known throughout this area of Michigan as a place where any veteran could get a free meal or borrow a couple of bucks. What angered him was the conversation; it was nothing he wanted to hear and the level of intelligence was well below brain dead.

Bruckner's world revolved around his own life and his own problems. He never wasted time trying to solve any major world problems. He was smart enough to know that the best he could do was to keep his life simple by working on his own individual responsibilities.

As he sat and listened to the gruesome ways the world was going to end, he became curious about Black's outlandish predictions. He asked, "Barney, when did you decide that the world was going to hell?"

Black replied, "Well I never thought about it until Preacher John made me aware of the screwing that was going on in the heathen countries in the world."

Bruckner froze when he heard the name Preacher John. Until a few years ago, when Preacher John first moved to Milan, Bruckner had never heard of him. Since then, he had met him and had seen how Preacher John operated. He knew that Preacher John was an evil person and he blamed him for Sam Cutler's death. Preacher John was the only person Bruckner ever hated.

He kept his thoughts entirely to himself and asked another question, "Do you believe that your Preacher John is right?"

Black was positive in his response, "Absolutely, and as he pointed out, there are a lot more non-Christians having sex than there are Christians. Don't you agree that there is too much sex in the heathen world?"

Bruckner said, "Barney, I've been too busy to give it any thought. All I can tell you is that, if your Preacher John is correct, we are being outmanned and outgunned."

Black was in no mood to be cajoled. "Bill, this ain't funny. No politician, no government, and no religion is saying or doing anything about the overcrowding of the world by non-Christian heathens. Preacher John says that Christ has to return soon or Armageddon will surely come upon us."

Bruckner rolled his eyes; he'd had enough. Here it was early in the morning on a beautiful fall day and all he had heard so far was doom and destruction. He subconsciously tried to shoo the hunters out and on their way. To soothe his conscience, he made sure their thermos bottles were full of coffee as he walked them to their car in the parking lot.

After they left, he poured himself a fresh cup of coffee and sat down; the morning chef, along with the day manager and the waitstaff, would soon show up for work. Meanwhile, Bruckner began to think about why he felt so dissatisfied with everything and everybody. This was not like him. It seemed as if he just could not reconcile himself to the death of his friend.

Sam Cutler had been his companion for over thirty years; however, they had drifted apart and then Sam died unexpectedly. His passing bothered Bruckner. Since Sam's death, he felt that his world was much smaller. Nothing pleased him anymore. He knew that lately he was irritable and grumpy. He didn't like himself, he didn't like the world, and he was sure the world felt the same way about him. It reminded him of the way he felt when he first came home from Vietnam.

On impulse, he picked up the phone and dialed his home number. He expected it to ring a few times and was surprised when it rang only once. A familiar voice immediately said, "Good morning, Darling."

Bruckner replied, "Good morning, Maribeth, I didn't wake you?"

"No. I am sitting in the kitchen drinking coffee and making a shopping list."

There followed a long pause. Bruckner didn't say a word. Maribeth finally asked, "You did call for a reason, didn't you?"

Bruckner apologized. "I'm sorry, Maribeth. My mind is wandering this morning." He waited another short period before he continued. "Do you have the phone number of that bed and breakfast in Canada at Point Pelee where we stayed years ago?"

"You mean the Iron Kettle?"

"Yes, that's the one. How would you like to go there for a couple of nights and we could go bird watching at Point Pelee?"

Maribeth was surprised. "I thought you had to be at the restaurant to have the kitchen redone?"

"Well, there's some rewiring that needs to be taken care of but I don't have to stand around with my arms folded. The electrician knows what to do.

"I want to get away for a few days. I need to talk with you. I'll appoint Milton as commander-in-chief and I'll be ready to go."

Maribeth sighed, "I'm glad you said that. Even our kids say that you have been more than a little short tempered lately. I'll have to change our schedule around, we were supposed to go out for dinner with the Baxters tonight. I'll give them a call and get a raincheck. Going to Point Pelee will be fun. Let me call the Iron Kettle and get back to you."

The next morning Bruckner and Maribeth were sitting on a log looking at the huge expanse of Lake Erie as the sun began to rise. They were dressed warmly and had the entire view almost to themselves; only a few hardy bird watchers came out in the cooler weather. There were two long ore ships traveling on the lake and most of the migrating birds had come and gone. The beauty and quietness of their surrounding had a calming affect. They sat, holding hands and sorting thoughts.

Finally, Bruckner spoke, "Feeding those two hunters yesterday was not a pleasant experience. It only brought back memories of Sam and how he passed."

"You still miss him, don't you?"

"That's only part of it. Yes, I miss him but there is more to it than that. I know that everyone has a date to return the flame of life we have inside us. What bothers me is that I don't think that Sam had as happy life as he deserved. He lived but did he enjoy himself at the end? After what he told me on our hunting trip, I'm almost sure that he didn't. That makes me sad.

"I don't want to end up that way. I want to know that I enjoyed myself. That's why we need to talk. I want to spend more time with you, doing the things that we have always said we would like to do."

Maribeth replied quickly, "I would love that and so would our kids and our grandkids."

Bruckner looked at his wife. "Maribeth, I love you and I love my family. However, I'm sure you realize that I was married to you long before we met all those other relatives that you just mentioned. I meant it when I said I want to be with you."

She laughed and replied, "Bill, you are a nut, but I get your message. I also want to spend our time together. We can because we are really not that old yet. However, I'm sure you'll agree, we should also have plenty of time for our family.

"What will you do with the restaurant?"

"I'm thinking of complete retirement. We've been taking weekend trips but I want to turn control of the restaurant over to our son. You and I can travel the world or play golf or do whatever it is that retired people do.

"Milton is more than capable of managing the restaurant. He's a trained chef and he's been ready and waiting for years. In some ways, he is better at running the restaurant than I am. It is about time he got his chance. I will slowly back off, retire, and be available if he wants me. You and I should spend our time galloping toward golden sunsets."

Maribeth sat quietly for a while; she was bursting with happiness at their new plans. "Do you remember that National Geographic special we saw last summer on PBS about the bird preserve on the Yucatan Peninsula? It was teeming with pink flamingos."

"Yes, I think it was called the Celestun Bird Sanctuary, or something like that; I do remember that it was near the city of Merida."

"I would like to go there. I've been thinking of those thousands of pink birds that live in that area; they were beautiful. Wouldn't that be fun?"

"Can we finish our time here in Point Pelee first?"

Maribeth put her arm around her husband's waist. "Don't be such a smart-ass. You know what I mean."

Bruckner hugged her close to him. "You're right, I was being a smart-ass. That's because I feel so good about our decision. I haven't felt this happy in months. Yes, we will see the pink flamingos."

They both wanted to travel. So why not?

They marked that trip to Point Pelee as another pearl in their never ending rosary of love.

Bruckner and Cutler had first met under the worst of conditions.

Vietnam. The war aged them long before they had a chance to mature.

Bill Bruckner was drafted at eighteen. Until then, he lived in Milan, Michigan, with his father, mother, and younger sister, Alice. His family was close knit and his parents participated in both children's activities. His father owned a restaurant on Dexter Street and his mother worked there part time as hostess. As far as he was aware, he had a normal, happy childhood. His lone complaint, and it was only a small one, was that he had to work more than most of his friends. He spent much of his free time bussing dishes and clearing tables at the restaurant. These were jobs he didn't particularly like. However, he did enjoy the work when he advanced to preparing food and learning how to cook.

His parents wanted him to stay in college and not be drafted. This was not to be. After his freshman year at the University of Michigan, he decided it was his patriotic responsibility to report for army duty. Instead of asking for a deferment to continue in school, Bill Bruckner chose to serve.

Bill Bruckner and Sam Cutler met when they were sent as replacements for a platoon that was heading back to combat. They were together almost their entire tour of duty. They saw things and did things that no human being should ever have to see or do. They were helpless as their fellow soldiers died from bullets and shrapnel ripped through their bodies. They smelled the sickening odors of death and putrefaction. They heard the agonizing screams of human pain. They witnessed civilians, including children, murdered and raped. They were bitten by insects that made their lives almost unbearable. They walked over ground so hot from napalm bombs that they didn't dare touch the soil with their bare hands.

They could not tell friend from foe. Would the native walking toward them toss a grenade after they walked past him? Was the peasant who sold them fruit the same person who screamed in the underbrush at night that Americans would die the next day? They learned to shoot first and ask questions later; after awhile, they didn't even bother asking questions.

They endured all these physical hardships, along with their continuous psychological pounding, until they became animals whose only thought was to stay alive. They survived by relying on each other and their platoon brothers for the love and friendship each human needs to continue to live.

What they did not realize was that each became the other's confessional booth. They listened when the other spoke and no thoughts or ideas were hidden between them. This honesty was what kept their individual threads of humanity from breaking.

When their tour of duty was close to the end, Cutler was shot in the leg during one of their last patrols. He was helicoptered to a hospital and neither was able to contact the other before Bruckner left Vietnam. Bruckner was flown back to the States and discharged in San Francisco. As he was being processed for discharge he was absolutely stunned to find people carrying placards that called him "CHILD KILLER" and "MURDERER." He was sworn at and spat on by complete strangers and had no idea why he was the target of such hate. He had done nothing wrong. In fact, he had done what the federal government had asked him to do. He had been fighting to protect these very people who were reviling him. Why was he being treated like a monster? His shabby reception in the country for which he had risked his life and for which he had taken such a mental and physical beating left a deep impression on him. He felt bitter and antagonistic toward the very civilians he thought he had been defending.

After his discharge, Bruckner flew to Detroit to meet his family. When he landed at Detroit Metropolitan Airport, they were anxiously waiting for him. His mother clung to him, crying from happiness. His father shook his hand, hugged him, and patted him on the back. His sister, Alice, hugged him and kept saying how thin he was. They left the airport elated that the family was back together again and that their son had survived the Vietnam death trap.

Their euphoria was short-lived. Initially, Bill was welcomed with open arms. The family was so happy to get their son back alive and without any physical injuries, that he was greeted as a returning hero. Absence did make the heart grow fonder; the prodigal son had returned.

However, his father and mother soon realized that the son who had gone to Vietnam was not the same person as the son who came back from Vietnam. To his parents, that son came back both troubled and frightened. They heard him screaming and moaning in his sleep almost every night. They would enter his bedroom and shake him awake when his nightmares were extra loud and violent. He wouldn't tell them about his nightmares and he couldn't go back to sleep. He would prowl through the house for the rest of the night.

Talking with Bruckner was almost impossible; his answers were short and curt. He kept odd hours, he was moody, he drank a lot, and he smoked pot. He was back inside the family home but he was not available to the family. They couldn't understand why he wasn't like he was before he went to Vietnam. Even Alice who had clung to him and wept when she first saw him, was upset.

Within four weeks, everyone lost their composure; there were continuous arguments and disagreements. What made the problems worse was that his mother, father, and sister kept asking him what he was thinking. They were trying to understand his problems. The constant questions made him even more defensive. When he wasn't at home, there were constant whispered conversations about him and his attitude. His family began to be concerned that he could be a danger to both himself and everyone else in their household.

All this mistrust and bad feelings came to a boil during an evening meal that started normally. The trouble began when Bruckner's father casually asked him if he was interested in coming back to work at the family restaurant. When Bruckner said, "No," his father asked him what he planned to do. Bruckner blew up at that second question. He accused his father and the whole family of spying on him and not leaving him alone.

From that moment on, the atmosphere was split as if a bolt of lightning had struck the dining room table. The family's complaints all poured out in a tidal wave of wails. Everybody was crying and shouting.

It ended when Bill threw his fork on the table and shouted, "Goddamn it. Quit prying into my life. Leave me the fuck alone." He ran out of the house, slamming the door behind him.

Bruckner went to the Old Shack, a local tavern, and sat at the end of the bar. He radiated so much rage and misery that everyone, including the bartender who only approached when he was signaled, left him entirely alone. When he returned home at about 1:00 the next morning, he was slightly drunk and in a more mellow frame of mind than when he left.

As he approached the porch, he noticed his father sitting on the front steps; he was leaning against a roof post and wearing a sweater against the night chill. Without saying a word, Bruckner sat down beside his father and, after awhile, said, "Dad, you must be cold. How long have you been waiting?"

"Not too long, really. I didn't think you'd be home until late so I didn't come outside until after twelve-thirty."

These were the last words between them for five minutes or so. They both sat on the steps silently wrapped in their own personal misery. The father had something to say, but he wasn't sure how to say it without triggering an explosive outburst; the son fully expected a tirade that he didn't want to hear. Finally, his father cleared his throat. "Bill, when you were born, your mother and I believed we had the best mannered, smartest kid in the world and, as you grew up, we never changed our minds. After Alice came along, we were about the happiest family in Milan.

"Now everything has changed. Your mother is upset, Alice and I are both unhappy, and we know that you're not pleased with any of us. We don't seem to be able to talk to each other. Our family is walking around on tiptoes and whispering to avoid arguments. We don't understand you and, I guess, you feel the same way about us.

"I'm not blaming you anymore than I'm blaming us. It's just that you've changed and we've also changed. When I came back from combat after World War II, I had a difficult time adjusting, but nothing like this. Now, we don't mesh with each other and nobody is happy. We need to talk about our disconnect.

"What do you think?"

Bruckner answered his father, "Dad, you're right. This has not been a happy time for the family. You and Mom and Alice have been patient and I know that, I really do. The truth is I have problems, terrible problems. I'm still in Nam and I'm having a hard time adjusting. Every night in my dreams I see my brothers gutted and blown up and every day I see a world that doesn't give a shit about my brothers or their deaths. I can't understand that. Nobody seems to give a damn about Nam except me. I don't have much in common with anyone. I'm not getting along with my own family and I have interrupted everyone's life. No one in the family is happy. I think I need to move out and be by myself, at least for awhile."

They again sat in silence, but this time there was no tension between them; they had come to an understanding. The next day, Bruckner rented an apartment in downtown Milan and moved out of the family home. The apartment was on Main Street, on the second floor, almost directly over the Milan Bakery.

This change of lodgings, which at first seemed like a family disaster, proved to be a blessing. Bruckner had had his soul scorched by war and the burns were deep. He would never forget what he had gone through; he still had his vivid nightmares and night sweats. However, he needed to put his war experiences in perspective. How was he going to live the rest of his life? Over time, the move provided Bruckner the room necessary for his boiling emotions to surface and evaporate. Death, destruction, and hatred had to be completely exhaled before he could begin to inhale a life that had any chance of happiness.

At first, it seemed as if his move forward was a step backward. He was thrust into a society that he felt resented him; it made him even more wary. He got even with the uncaring, well-off, civilians who didn't care about him or his Nam brothers by adopting a hostile attitude toward the world. He grew a beard and let his hair get long and straggly. It was a long time before his inner tensions even began to unwind.

Bruckner got a job driving a cement truck at Gotts Transit Mix. Monday through Friday, he would begin each working day by going downstairs to the bakery for hot coffee and doughnuts. He rarely spoke because he was usually hung over from the night before. He just sat at a table, hunched over and hugging his hot coffee, keeping his sour thoughts to himself.

The man who served him was Jamie, the owner of the bakery. Jamie had a second cousin who came back from Vietnam a few years earlier with the same attitude; Jamie was wise enough to leave Bruckner alone. He didn't start conversations, he didn't offer any comments, he just gave Bruckner his order and collected his money. Eventually, Bruckner nodded at him and even spoke a little. After that, Jamie occasionally gave Bruckner an extra doughnut or a refill on his coffee. Still, he kept his distance, being only as friendly to Bruckner as Bruckner would allow. This was the beginning of bridging the gulf that divided Bruckner from peace and acceptance.

After work, Bruckner went back to his apartment to clean up, eat, and go to the American Legion bar down the street and drink. He was ignored by most of the other veterans and not considered a real soldier by a few hard asses who didn't realize that Vietnam was not fought like World War II. The older veterans had fought a war where the enemy was always in front of them and always wore uniforms. They gave no credence to a military that blended into the civilian population and that would attack from the rear at any time. They thought the Vietnam veterans were soft and pampered. He got into arguments when he was confronted and, occasionally, came close to getting into fistfights. Eventually, as a regular patron, he was able to come and go almost unnoticed and unchallenged.

Weekends were different. He would sleep late on Saturdays and then take care of his errands and personal business. In the evening, he would eat at a restaurant and then tour the local taverns to purposely get drunk.

Sundays, after he got over his hangovers, were his quiet days. He went for hikes in the many parks and wooded areas in the eastern Michigan area. For some reason, or for no reason at all, he wanted to be by himself. In time, he began to drop by the family home late on Sunday afternoon to eat dinner and be with his mother, father, and sister. At first, the meals were quiet and awkward with carefully guarded conversations to avoid confrontations. However, as family love asserted itself, the discussions warmed up and began to be lively and convivial.

Time passed and Bruckner started to pay some attention to the people who came into the bakery. He began to recognize Jamie's steady customers; he didn't acknowledge them, he was just aware of them. One Friday morning, as he hunkered over his coffee with an exceptional hangover, he noticed a man standing in front of Jamie that he thought he recognized. The man's back was to him but his six foot four inch frame looked familiar. He didn't want any contact with him, or anyone else, so he turned his face away from the counter. Suddenly the man was in front of him. He said, "Bill Bruckner, even with your beard I'd recognize you. I heard a couple of months ago that you were back from Vietnam. Thank God for that.

"How are you doing?"

Bruckner stood up as straight as he could and still was not nearly as tall as the man he was speaking with. "Mr. Tannenbaum, how are you?"

"I'm well. What are you doing now that you are home?"

"I'm driving a cement truck for Gott's."

"Do you have any plans to go back to school?"

"I'm not sure, Mr. Tannenbaum."

"Listen Bill, you were in my classes for four years. There's more to you than driving a cement truck. I know you have to unwind after what you've been through but don't wait too long before you do something with your life. Our time is not determined by us. Enjoy it, don't waste it."

Bruckner was taken by surprise. This tall, thin, serious man in front of him was not the same tall, cheerful, plump man he had come to respect and like when he was his teacher. When Henry Tannenbaum was teaching math and science he was humorous and clever; now, he seemed sober and intense.

Bruckner replied, “Oh, I won’t, Mr. Tannenbaum. I intend to do something soon.”

Tannenbaum looked at Bruckner and smiled. “Look, Bill, I’m sure you are getting more advice than you either want or can use. I’m not trying to add to the pile. I just don’t want to see you go to waste.

“I usually go fishing by the dam on Ford Lake every Sunday. If you ever want to talk, come on over. I’m a good listener.” With that, he shook Bruckner’s hand and left.

Bruckner sat back down again, confused about his meeting. Henry Tannenbaum had changed; he was much thinner physically and more sedate in his personality. Bruckner thought, “Well, I’ve changed too. So what the hell?” With that he continued sipping his coffee and forgot about the incident. The following Sunday he went for dinner at his parent’s house. Dessert was being served when he remembered his meeting with Henry Tannenbaum.

To keep the conversation going, he said, “Mom, Dad, you will never guess who I bumped into at the bakery last Friday. Would you believe that I talked with Henry Tannenbaum?”

His mother responded, “Henry? How is he? I haven’t seen or heard from him in a long time. I often think about him. He was in our graduating class at Milan High, so many years ago.”

His father added, “He is one of the nicest people I’ve ever known. He didn’t deserve the tragedy that struck him.”

“Yes, what a shame,” his mother said.

Bruckner had no idea what they were talking about. He asked, “What happened? What tragedy happened to Tannenbaum?”

His mother looked at him. “You don’t know? Well, right after you were drafted, his wife was broadsided by a drunk driver who sped through a red light and plowed into her car. She was instantly killed.”

Bruckner almost gasped at what he heard. He was more familiar with death than he wanted to be and he could understand Tannenbaum's shock. Any family member's death, especially one that was so unnecessary, so brutal and so random, would knock a person off guard. "My God, Mom, what a terrible thing to happen."

His mother shook her head. "Darling, it was even worse than that. Henry was waiting for her at a banquet that was to honor him as Michigan Teacher of the Year.

"Henry almost went mad with grief. He quit teaching and disappeared for a year. He went into a Catholic seminary and nearly decided to become a priest. He finally returned to teaching and counseling because he wanted to help young people. He counsels anyone, including the inmates here at the Federal Prison. He also ran for and won a seat on city council. He tries to help people cope with their problems. As far as I'm concerned, his tragedy has brought him close to being the most understanding human I have ever known."

Bruckner thought about Tannenbaum's suffering over the next few weeks. He kept scratching at it, as if it were a mosquito bite on his forearm. He wanted to know how Tannenbaum managed his problems and if there were any lessons that could help him deal with his demons. Finally, on a warm spring Sunday afternoon, Bruckner made his way to the spot where Tannenbaum was fishing on the Saline River. Tannenbaum sat in the shade, a plastic cooler and fishing pole in front of him; he was strumming a guitar. He waved his arm. "Hi, Bill, can I offer you a beer or a sandwich?"

Bruckner replied, "No, thanks." He sat down beside Tannenbaum and, for a few minutes, he was quiet. Finally, he said. "Mr. Tannenbaum, I've been having problems since I got home."

Tannenbaum put his guitar aside. "I gathered you had problems. You look burned out. Almost all of you Vietnam veterans come home and have problems adjusting. You saw too much and did too much without having a chance to recover from the horror. It's like a diver coming up from the ocean too fast and getting the bends. You all need time to decompress.

"What are your problems? Have they lessened in the months since you came home?"

"Well, I'm sleeping a little better but I still have nightmares. Maybe not as often. I'm nervous, mad at the world, and drink too much, along with smoking pot."

Bruckner sat quietly for a while before asking, "Sir, how do you handle your problems?"

He answered Bruckner indirectly. "Bill, do you believe in God?"

"I'm not sure."

"Then, you don't believe in God?"

"Mr. Tannenbaum, I haven't thought much about God one way or the other."

"You did when you were in combat didn't you?"

"Everyone over there prayed and thought about God. We all wanted to stay alive. Doesn't everybody? I prayed, but I'm not sure to whom. So did all my friends. Some made it home; too many of them didn't. Those that didn't are now buried in the soil. God didn't help them; no one helped them. That's part of my problem."

Tannenbaum spoke softly. "I'm sure it is. Look, I'll tell you about me but I don't know if it will work for you. You have your own fears and doubts and my answers may not be your solution. My answers depend completely upon my faith.

"I am a practicing Catholic who believes in God. I converted to Catholicism after my wife passed. I'm absolutely convinced that I will see my wife in my next life in heaven. Seeing her and my family will be my reward for being His servant. I don't argue with any of the answers that Catholicism prescribes because I believe so strongly in God. That's why I work so hard to do God's work here on earth.

"You may or may not believe in God. As a fellow human being all I want is to see you enjoy life and be happy. I hope you see the workings of the universe the same way I do, but that depends on faith. I can't prove faith, I can only assume it. I make no judgment or criticism about whether or not you have faith because, if I were you, I might feel exactly the way you do. If you don't have faith you are not a bad person; you may only be an incomplete person.

"Bill, you will have to sort all this out for yourself. Faith cannot be taught, it has to be believed. However, I will tell you one thing that is true. It has to do with life and it has nothing to do with faith. You should get yourself a helpmate, a friend, a wife. Everyone needs someone who will be by your side throughout life. There is nothing that will make the wine of life taste sweeter than someone with whom to share the cup.

"Because I lost my wife, I'm aware of that truth every hour of every day of my life. Love never dies even when it has dissolved into memories." Tannenbaum stopped speaking for a few seconds. His voice choked as he continued, "Find someone to share your dreams and lift your goals to the heavens. That's all I can tell you."

Bruckner sat beside him, thinking about Tannenbaum's words. He knew that Tannenbaum had shared his innermost feelings about love, and he agreed with him on that. However, he wasn't sure about having faith in God.

He would have to think over what his former teacher had told him about faith. The smell from the cesspool of war was still overpowering his emotions and nothing seemed right or clear to him. His faith, if he ever attained faith, would not begin until he purged himself of his negative feelings. It was a problem Bruckner was to wrestle with for years before he began to make up his mind.

On the day Samuel Cutler thought he turned eighteen years old, he enlisted in the United States Army. His enlistment was not so much prompted by patriotism as desperation; he would have done almost anything to change his style of living. Until his eighteenth birthday, his life had been one of ambiguity and anxiety. Even the day he was eligible to enlist was not totally clear. He was found abandoned as a newborn in the back of a church in Bath, Maine. The doctor who first examined him decided that he was a newborn, maybe three days old and, on that basis, the doctor subtracted three days from the day Sam Cutler was retrieved from under a pew. That date was recorded on the doctor's report. Unlike all the other men and women who joined the military on that day, Sam Cutler could have been three days older, or even three days younger, than advertised.

He was an orphan who lived in foster homes in Bath until he joined the army. By his recollection, which would not take into account his first few years, he lived with no less than five foster families. It was the first set of foster parents who had given him his name, Samuel Cutler, and he never thought of changing it.

Whatever the reasons, young Sam never found a permanent set of foster parents. Some of them had problems themselves that had nothing to do with him, some didn't warm up to him after they brought him home, some were disappointed in his personality, and some didn't feel they were getting enough work out of him. Whatever their individual discontent, they all returned him to the orphanage. As a result, Cutler grew up a shy person who was very careful in trying not to irritate or offend anyone. He clung to anyone who was kind to him.

Although he was never sexually abused or physically assaulted, he was never warmly greeted or hugged. None of his foster parents showered the waif with the most important ingredient a child needs—continuous, genuine, copious love. He grew up completely unsure of himself, always wondering what he was doing wrong and why he couldn't please anyone.

When his birth certificate said he was eighteen, Cutler joined the army to get away. The military was a revelation to him and he embraced it. He was treated no differently than his peers. Even though he was on the bottom rung of the ladder, he was not alone, his equals were also on the bottom. He couldn't sink any lower than the rest of the bottom rungers and yet he was no less respected than the others.

Cutler learned that the military had strict rules and regulations he had to follow. He also learned that, if he stayed within the confines of those rules and regulations, he was safe. He liked that feeling. He decided that he would make the military his career and stay in for twenty years.

When he went to Vietnam he was repulsed by all the brutality and death that surrounded him. If it hadn't been for the friendship of his platoon of bottom rungers, especially his good friend Bill Bruckner, he would have gone to pieces. By the time his tour of duty in Nam ended, he was having second thoughts about remaining in the army. The shock of war was affecting him. It was then that Cutler was wounded and evacuated to a military hospital. His wound became infected and he was flown back to the States where he spent months undergoing medical treatments. During this time, Sam lost all track of his platoon members, including his closest brother, Bill Bruckner.

As a result of his tour in Vietnam, Sam Cutler received an honorable discharge from the army as a wounded veteran with a pension. Cutler limped back into civilian life feeling old, cold, alone, and abandoned. He had no one he could notify that he was now a civilian. Physically and mentally Sam Cutler was in worse shape than on the day he first enlisted in the army.

CHAPTER 2

Time passed, and life started to mellow for Bruckner. Living away from his family made it easier for them to reunite. They stopped bruising each other and their Sunday dinners began to heal their wounds; the love within his family thawed his frozen emotions. Edging closer to his family and working his way through each day blunted the raw memories Bruckner carried. The constancy of routine, daily, weekly, and monthly, leveled off his periods of fear and depression. He slowly began to feel the joy of life.

One Saturday morning, Bruckner's phone brought him abruptly out of a deep sleep. He reached for it half awake and fully hungover. He wasn't drinking as often but he was still drinking heavily. He groggily answered, "Hello."

His father, in a chipper voice, said, "I'll bet I woke you up and you're hungover."

"You'd win a lot of money if you bet on that, but you didn't phone me just to get rich did you?"

"No, Bill. Really, I'm sorry that I have to call but I think this message for you is important. I just got a phone call from someone named Cutter asking for you."

"Cutter?"

"I think that's what he said, 'Sam Cutter.'"

Bruckner suddenly became alert; he immediately forgot his pounding headache. His thoughts rolled to his past when he saw his brother taken away in a helicopter. Was he coming back? "Oh no, Dad. I'm sure the name you heard was Sam Cutler."

He held his breath before asking, "What did he say?"

"Not much. He asked for you by name and when I told him you didn't live here but I could either give him your phone number or pass a message along, he said he couldn't call you because he had no money. He told me to tell you that he was at the Ann Arbor bus station and he needed help. That was all he said."

Bruckner was surprised and grateful to get a message, even indirectly, from Cutler. He often wondered about what happened to Sam and had always hoped that he was okay and doing well. Now he would see him. He told his father, "This is important. He and I lived through Nam together. We got separated and I never found out what happened to him. Dad, thank you very much; I'm going to leave for Ann Arbor right away. Thanks for calling me."

Bruckner got dressed quickly, grabbed a cup of coffee from the bakery, and drove as fast as he could to the Ann Arbor bus station. At first, he couldn't find Cutler in the terminal. Looking around, he finally spotted him on a seat against the wall. Sam Cutler was sprawled out, sleeping and snoring.

When Bruckner got close to Cutler, he was shocked at his appearance. He looked so much older than the last time they were together. Cutler had looked so small and frightened when he was being loaded into the evacuation helicopter. His leg was wrapped with a bloody bandage and he had waved a feeble goodbye as the helicopter lifted off.

Now here he was, gaunt and disheveled. His hair was long and tangled and he had a thick beard. As Bruckner got closer, he saw a bottle of whiskey sticking out of Cutler's pocket and he reeked of alcohol, sweat, dirt, and, Bruckner thought, urine. He looked and smelled pitiful.

Bill sat down beside his brother. Suddenly, he was swept with remorse and sadness. The last time he saw Sam he was on a stretcher, waiting to be evacuated. Now he appeared as unsavory as a twice-used wet Kleenex. Obviously, Cutler had not had an easy time in life.

He gently shook Cutler's arm. Sam jumped awake; he was startled and blurted out, "What?" Then he saw Bruckner and relaxed and smiled. "Oh my God," he said loudly. "Thank you for coming, Bill, I sure need your help."

Bruckner didn't answer. He couldn't speak; he choked. He had finally found Sam Cutler. It looked as if Cutler's life had gotten even worse after his Vietnam tour. Wasn't being hit by an enemy bullet enough? What other hells had his brother had to endure?

Instead of talking, he patted Cutler on his shoulder. Finally, "Good to see you, Sam. Let's get the hell out of here.

"Are you hungry? When was the last time you ate?"

"I'm not sure. Maybe a day or two ago."

"Oh my God. Come on," Bruckner responded. He picked up a dirty duffel bag at Cutler's feet and led him to his parked truck.

Cutler eyed Bruckner's faded blue Dodge pickup, fifteen years old with rusted out fenders. He asked, "Will this thing carry both of us and still run?"

Bruckner was glad for the interruption of what was going through his mind. "Sam, I got this truck for a song and I've been fixing it up for months. Mechanically, it's as good as new. All I have to do is fix the cosmetics; in the meantime, you're safe."

He drove to a McDonald's and had Cutler sit while he ordered what he asked for, a quarter pounder with cheese, a large order of French fries, and a large chocolate shake. He watched, in amazement, as Sam wolfed down the food, hardly bothering to chew. No sooner had he finished the last of the hamburger and the chocolate shake when Cutler threw it all up. Amidst Cutler's abject apologies, the two of them cleaned up the mess and left. All the way to Milan, Cutler kept thanking Bruckner. He was guilt-ridden for what had happened inside McDonald's. Bruckner didn't say a word.

Once inside Bill's apartment, he told Cutler, "Sam, you strip down and take a shower. I mean a long, hot shower. Throw all of your clothes into this garbage bag. While you do that, I'll make you something to eat."

"Bill, what'll I wear? These is the only clothes I got. I know they ain't clean but I got nothing else to put on."

"You can wear some of my clothes until we go shopping. They will be a little big for you, but, at least, they're clean. Now, get going."

While Cutler was in the shower, Bruckner phoned his father. "Dad, I went and picked up the man you talked to this morning, Sam Cutler. We're at my apartment now and he is taking a shower." He stopped speaking as he tried to gather his thoughts.

His father broke the silence by asking, "How is he doing?"

"I can't tell you how bad I feel for him, Dad. I told you we went through Nam together and I was glad to finally hear from him. But it is so sad to see him. He looks like hell, thin and beaten down. His clothes stink and he's a nervous wreck. He's had a rough time; he threw up when he ate some food, his first in who knows how long. I'm going to fix him something to eat when he gets out of the shower."

His father softly said, "You can bring him to the restaurant if you want to. That way, you won't have to cook."

"No thanks, Dad. I want to cook for him. I owe him that. I guess what I'm calling to tell you is that I won't be over for dinner tomorrow. You and Mom surely don't want to meet another castoff from Nam."

There was a pause for a few seconds before his father answered. "Bill, no one from Vietnam should be considered a castoff; you bring your friend over with you tomorrow. All your friends are welcome at our house, especially if you two went through the war together. We survived your homecoming, so your mother and I are veterans in our own right.

"You understand? Your mother and I and Alice want you and your friend to be over here for dinner around four o'clock."

Bruckner had no doubt that his father meant what he said; he was a blunt and honest person. He thanked his father and hung up. When Cutler stepped out of the bathroom in his newer, larger wardrobe, Bruckner had fixed him scrambled eggs and toast. He ate more slowly and Bruckner showed him the smaller bedroom in his apartment and told him to catch some sleep. Cutler did not wake up for almost ten hours.

Late Sunday morning, they went back to Ann Arbor and shopped for underwear, blue jeans, a long sleeved shirt, socks and sneakers for Cutler. By the time they went for dinner with Bruckner's family, Cutler looked, and felt, much better than he had on Saturday. He was scrubbed, clean, and the long sleep had calmed his nerves. He still looked like a wild man with his bushy beard and long hair, but he looked like a clean wild man. He hardly said a word during the meal; however, he did eat more slowly and did nothing bizarre or out of the ordinary.

Bruckner's mother and sister were reminded of Bill's behavior when he first came home. Cutler only spoke in answer to direct questions and his replies were brief. He made very little eye contact and he seemed nervous and uncomfortable.

Bruckner's father wondered how many of these Vietnam veterans had overcome their war experiences and resumed their normal lives? How would he have reacted had he been a Vietnam veteran instead of a WWII veteran? He thought that the Vietnam veterans were more neglected by their countrymen than any other group of veterans. He was glad he had insisted that his son bring his brother with him when he came to dinner.

Bruckner watched Cutler and he saw himself before he overcame his demons. His worst fears of what could happen to Cutler had been realized. Cutler had fallen further than Bruckner and no one had bothered to help him. That is, until now. He felt a responsibility to his brother and he promised himself that, after almost two years of not knowing what happened to Cutler, he was going to try to help him.

Sam Cutler almost couldn't believe that there were people that accepted him. He felt uncomfortable with all the kindnesses shown him; he was not used to being treated civilly and with respect. When Cutler thanked the family for their hospitality, there were tears in his eyes. The Bruckners responded by giving their son and his guest enough food to feed themselves for a week.

For those at the dinner table it was as much a communion as it was a meal. Each person left the table not only well fed but, more important, with a strong pledge to help someone in deep distress. Because Cutler had gone through the nightmare of Vietnam at Bruckner's side, he deserved to be honored and given a chance to overcome his problems.

Monday morning, Bruckner called his boss and asked for time off; he told him that he needed a week for personal business. His boss was not pleased with the request. He liked Bruckner because of his reliability, but he had a business to run. He told Bruckner that he would try to keep the job open for him but, if business dictated hiring another driver to keep up with the demand, Bruckner would have to wait until there was a new job opening. Bruckner told him he understood, thanked him for being honest, and still took the week off without pay. Luckily, when Bill called his boss on the following Monday, he was told to report for work.

During that week, he spent most of his time with Cutler; he wanted to talk with him. His plan was simple. They walked. He took Cutler to the Crosswinds Marsh Preserve, the Michigan Arboretum, and Gallup Park. They strolled for hours in relaxed, pleasant atmospheres. There was no binge drinking and not too much social drinking.

At first, Cutler was quiet. But after one or two days of outdoor exercise, Sam began to open up. It was then that they could really talk to each other.

Cutler wanted to know why Bruckner had not kept in touch with him. Bruckner told him that immediately after Cutler had been evacuated, he tried to find him. However, the army had lost track of him. They weren't sure if Cutler had been wounded or could they tell him to which hospital Cutler had been sent. Even after he got home to Milan the army couldn't answer his questions about Cutler. If Bruckner hadn't gone through a war with Cutler he wouldn't have known he even existed. He certainly wasn't able to trace him through the army's records.

Once Sam realized that Bill tried to find out what had happened to him, he felt better. He assumed that he had been forgotten and that bothered him. He needed friends to help make decisions for him. When he realized that Bill had tried to find him, Cutler opened up and told him how bad his life became since his discharge. He said that he couldn't get a job and ended up homeless, washing dishes from coast to coast. He summed it up, "Because I was a Vietnam veteran I was treated worse than pickled dog shit."

Cutler moved into Bruckner's apartment and stayed with him, taking over the spare bedroom. Cutler clung to Bruckner like an ingrown hair and Bruckner mother-henned him until some of Cutler's jitters and fears eased. They would go bar hopping at night and because Bruckner was not drinking as much as he had been, they would occasionally go to the Crossfire for a couple of beers just before closing time. His father would sit and talk with them. After listening to Sam's laments about being out of work, Mr. Bruckner offered him a part time job at the restaurant. Cutler immediately backed off, "Oh, no sir, I will starve before I ever wash another dish in a restaurant."

Mr. Bruckner laughed. "Sam, I'm not talking about washing dishes. There are other jobs that need doing: lawn mowing, floor vacuuming, moving tables and chairs, maintenance work, errand running. I could use you fifteen, maybe twenty hours a week."

Cutler accepted the job and was pleased with this turn of events. He was proud of himself. One Sunday, on a hunch, Bruckner brought Cutler over to meet Henry Tannenbaum at Wilson Park. If anyone knew about possible jobs in Milan, it would be Tannenbaum. The three of them talked for quite awhile and Tannenbaum told Cutler he would scout around for job opportunities. Within two weeks, Sam was hired at the Ford plant in Milan to work on the production line.

Cutler was happy to be working full time, drawing a regular paycheck, and keeping his part time job at the Crossfire. He began to feel useful and relevant; people relied on him. He became a little less withdrawn and more outgoing in his attitude. The ghosts of the Vietnam quagmire that had shackled Bruckner and Cutler to the past began to be just memories. They began to fit into both the present and the future.

But Bruckner's life changed abruptly a few months later when his father died unexpectedly. His dad left for work one morning, got behind the wheel of his car, and put his car key into the ignition. It was at this point, according to the coroner's report, that he departed this world and was chauffeured into the next. Isabel, his wife, found his upright body in the front seat two hours later. She had looked for him after the chef at the Crossfire called to ask where he was. The news of his sudden death shocked his family. He had shown no symptoms of illness; he was a healthy man, approaching middle age and enjoying life. Death is the eternal reply to the eternal question that no human knows how to ask or how to answer.

The family was devastated. The more a person is loved and respected, the harder it is to accept his or her passing. Losing a loved one is a bitter slice of life; losing a parent deepens the pain and the hurt. Alice came home from the University of Michigan where she was finishing her senior year. Bill temporarily moved into the house to comfort and be near his mother. He was especially affected as he and his father were just beginning to rediscover the friendship they enjoyed when Bill was growing up. He kept punishing himself for all the time he lost with his dad when he first returned from Vietnam.

Yet, life goes on for the mourners. The earth continues rotating and humans keep marching toward their own mortality. Isabel Bruckner decided that she had to staunch the flow of her grief and bind her wounds. Three days after the funeral she told her son to return to his apartment and her daughter to go back to school. They protested, then they realized their mother was right: survivors have to continue living no matter how heavily their feet drag.

Alice left early the next morning. Her son was eating breakfast when his mother returned from seeing Alice out the door. She sat at the table. "Bill, I need your help." He took the time to study her face; she appeared tired and haggard.

"Yes, Mom?"

"The Crossfire reopens in two days. Would you be able to be there when it opens and stay around for awhile?"

"I could, if you want me to, but I'm not sure I would add anything. I'm also not sure I remember anything about the restaurant business. Besides, Dad recently hired a new manager, didn't he?"

"Yes, he did; he hired her after you didn't want to work at the restaurant. Our revenue was going down. He hired someone with a restaurant background to look at our problems and build up the business. And she began to make a difference. Her name is Maribeth Punkey and your father and I like her both as a person and as a businesswoman.

"She couldn't attend the funeral but she called to tell me that she will be at the restaurant when it reopens. She is very good and I'm fond of her, but I still would feel better if someone from our family was there when we reopen. Either your father or I have always been at the Crossfire ever since we bought it. The business will be yours someday, unless we sell it, so why not start now?"

"Okay, Mom, If that's what you want. Dad always hoped I'd come back and I have no other plans. I don't know what good I can do, but I'll try." He immediately called his employer, told him he needed time off to straighten out his family affairs and that he probably wouldn't be coming back to work.

Bruckner arrived at the Crossfire very early the day the restaurant reopened. It was an old, two-story wooden building that looked more like a barn than a restaurant. It was located on Dexter Street, just off the U.S. 23 interstate exit. The building had been painted purple years ago and now begged to be repainted. The roadside sign was small and easily overlooked. The interior was divided into two large areas, one was a sports bar and the other was a dining area. As he made his way to his father's office, several of the older employees stopped working to give him their condolences.

Bruckner entered the office and started to go through the drawers in his father's desk. As he piled his dad's mementos on the desk top, he stopped occasionally when he came across a long-forgotten family photograph or an object from the past. He couldn't help feeling guilty for not being closer to his father before his death.

When he was looking into a bottom drawer, his eye caught a glimpse of blue, and he saw a young woman walking into the room. She was in her early twenties, about the same age as Bruckner. He noticed that she was dressed in a white shirt and a blue business suit and was a little shorter than the average woman. Her blond hair was pulled back into a pony tail and her blue eyes were set in a heart shaped face. Bruckner was immediately impressed by both her bright demeanor and attractive looks. He had not seen her before; she was gone for the day the few times he and Sam came into the bar in the evening.

She looked at Bill Bruckner. "You are Mr. Bruckner's son, Bill. I have only known your father since he hired me as manager, but that's enough time to realize what a fine man he was. He was so kind and gentle. I began to think of him as my second father. I am so sorry for your loss."

Bruckner had to look down as he choked out a reply, "Thank you."

After an awkward pause, the woman continued, "My legal name is

Maribeth Punkey. I changed it from our family's original Polish name, which was too long for me to spell and too hard for anyone to pronounce."

There was another moment of silence before Bruckner spoke. "Please sit down, we need to talk. How do you prefer to be addressed? By your first name or your last name?"

She sat in a chair in front of his desk and answered, "Maribeth will catch my attention every time."

"Okay, Maribeth it is. Did my father ever talk to you about me?"

"Oh, yes, he spoke of you often, actually, very often. He was disappointed that you didn't want to work here. He told me that when he hired me. He hoped you would change your mind one day and, as the two of you worked through your differences, he began to think that might happen. He was always talking about your childhood."

Maribeth stopped speaking. She sat there, twisting the leather straps of her purse and looking straight at Bruckner. He realized that she was as uncertain of her future as he was of his. He impulsively said, "Look, I understand that this is a bad time for you as well as for me. Your boss suddenly dies, his son shows up at work. You're probably wondering what's going to happen to you. Right?"

Maribeth nodded her head. "Yes, and, to be completely honest with you, I'm thinking of resigning."

"Do you have another job lined up?"

"No."

Bruckner thought carefully. He didn't want her to leave. If he asked why she was thinking of resigning, she might say something that would make it impossible for her to change her mind. "Before you make your decision, I hope you'll listen to what I'm going to say because, if part of your reason for leaving is based on my showing up in my father's place, I deserve to be heard."

Bruckner began to tell Maribeth about himself. He described working at the Crossfire as a young man and why he had left the University of Michigan to enter the draft. He was brutally honest enough to admit that he had lost his way since he came back from Vietnam and that he was still drifting.

He also told her that he now regretted turning down his father's initial request to return to the Crossfire and get back into the restaurant business. He lost the opportunity to work with his father and that was his mistake. Bruckner ended by saying, "Maribeth, I wanted you to know about me before you decide what you are going to do. I may have lost my rudder but I haven't lost my mind.

"I need your help. I haven't been associated with the restaurant for years and I'm not going to just barge in. My father and you had plans for this place. Why don't we sit down at lunch and you can fill me in on what they were? I also want to hear about you. I'm sure we can work something out. We need to talk.

"This place needs your help, more now than ever before. There are a lot of people who would be out of work if this restaurant shuts down. I'm not trying to pressure you into staying if you're determined to leave, I just want you to look at the overall picture before you make up your mind.

"I would like to make you the following proposition. Stay for about a month or so before you decide whether or not to resign. See if you think we can work as a team as you did with my father. If you still want to resign, I'll wish you the best of luck. If you think that you can work with me and we can do the things you and my father planned, I want you to stay. We will work out an arrangement for you to either become part owner or share in the profits or both. I don't care which, as long as you are happy enough to stay.

"I would like to try to work with you, as a team. Would you be willing to consider working with me?"

Maribeth visibly relaxed. "You sound as straightforward as your father. Yes, I have been concerned about what would happen if you took over for him. And, yes, I will stay awhile before I make any decision.

"However, I won't be able to meet you for a long lunch. There are too many details to take care of. Later, maybe at dinner, I'll be able to tell you what your father wanted for the restaurant and I'll describe my background and experience. Would that work for you?" He agreed that they would meet later that day when her schedule was less hectic.

They finally got together in the Crossfire's main dining room in the late afternoon. Maribeth was constantly bombarded with questions from the staff while they ate and talked; despite the interruptions, they enjoyed their conversation.

Maribeth began by telling Bill, "I was getting my Master's degree in Restaurant Management at Michigan State when I decided I knew as much in practice as I was learning in theory. That's because my mother and father ran a mom-and-pop restaurant in Hamtramck for over thirty years. I was there from the time I was born until I went to Michigan State as an undergrad; my baby bottles were sterilized on the restaurant stove. I worked every job there is in a restaurant.

"My parents both died within a year of each other five years ago. They were squeezed out of the restaurant business because they didn't attract new customers to replace their older ones. They knew nothing about advertising, competition from chain restaurants, or catering special events. They could cook, but they didn't know how to serve.

"My father was pleased that I wanted to be in the restaurant business but he was angry when I changed my name to Punkey. He said, 'What is good in Poland should be just as good in America.' He couldn't understand why I thought that the name 'Wiceniewski' would be hard to fit on a business card.

"I saw your father's ad for a manager, I called, and we set up an appointment to meet. I canvassed this entire area and ate at the restaurant a couple of times before my interview. When I talked to your father, he showed me through the restaurant and then he asked me what my thoughts were. When I told him, I was completely honest and I think I nearly blew his socks off when I listed all the obvious problems. I was sure that I wouldn't get the job."

She stopped talking to take a drink of water and Bruckner couldn't keep from asking, "What did you tell him?"

"What I thought was the truth. This location is excellent, right off the freeway. However, this location is so good that it is also a problem. Look at the number of national chains that have opened restaurants here. They are much newer and brighter, with much larger and more modern signs than the Crossfire's. Inside, it looks old and dingy. This restaurant needs a complete refurbishment both inside and out. The menu has to be redone, the staff retrained, and the bookkeeping overhauled. It reminded me of our family restaurant before we closed.

"Well, your father thought about what I said for a day or two and then he called me to come back. We talked about the best way to make changes and, after that, he hired me. We were just at the point of starting the renovations when your father passed.

"I was thrilled when he hired me. I wanted to make good for your father as well as for me. I wanted to honor my parent's memory.

"I still do."

After a long discussion, Bruckner and Maribeth agreed that, as soon as possible, she would come up with a list of individual responsibilities for each of them. They both would decide on the division of duties and would set up work schedules. Until then, Bruckner would continue to clean out his father's office and reacquaint himself with the restaurant operations.

The next week, Bruckner spent most of his time familiarizing himself with how the restaurant was run. That was more important than cleaning out his father's desk. When Maribeth arrived for work, they would have coffee together and talk about the restaurant. He would ask her questions and she would give answers. They began to lower their personal barriers as they got to know each other.

Within a month, they discovered that it was easy to talk to one another and they soon were exchanging personal confidences. He would wander through the restaurant acquainting himself with how business was handled. He talked to everyone on the staff. A few were older employees who already knew him when he had worked there before he went to college; most had been hired after he left. He was surprised at the changes now common to the restaurant business; he admitted that he had a lot to learn.

Late one afternoon, Maribeth came storming into the office and demanded, "Did you tell the chef not to roast those extra chickens?"

Bruckner was taken aback. "I most certainly did not."

"Well, he didn't roast them and we need them for tonight. When I asked him why he hadn't, he said that you told him not to bother. You didn't say anything to him?"

Bruckner replied, "No, I don't know what parties or affairs you have scheduled for today. We didn't discuss today's business this morning so I couldn't tell him anything. He did ask if I thought the chickens were for tonight or tomorrow night and I said I didn't know and that he would have to decide on his own. I guess I should have told him to check with you.

"I'm sorry if there was a mistake made."

Maribeth answered in a softer tone, "I'm sorry, too. I should have known that this would be a mix-up in communication. I will speak to the chef and make sure that he asks questions only of the person who gave him his instructions.

"I shouldn't have come in here without taking a deep breath. I'm on edge because I want this business to succeed. It should be able to. I don't want it to suffer the same fate as my father's business. This is one of the reasons I so want this restaurant to be a success.

"I owe you an apology. However, I need help. I'm trying to cover too many bases too fast and I'm fumbling the pigskin." She stopped for a second and began to laugh. "Now that's a completely mixed metaphor isn't it?"

"Maribeth, when are you going to have your list completed?"

"Soon, Bill. I have it almost all done in my mind. Actually, it is quite similar to the arrangement your father and I had. I just need to put it on paper." She was busy the rest of the week and Bill continued spending his time performing every job in the restaurant. He waited tables, washed dishes, cooked meals, bartended, scrubbed restrooms, and counted the day's receipts. He began to understand the complexity of running a large restaurant along with a busy bar.

Bruckner came to work a little early one Saturday and noticed Maribeth's car in its usual parking space. That was unusual because she didn't come to work as early as he did. She was already working extra long hours. She met him at his office door, dressed in a white chef's uniform and wearing a chef's hat. She carried a tray of cinnamon buns, pecan rolls, and a carafe of coffee.

"Good morning," she said, "I just love baking. I used to do the baking at our family restaurant. Whenever I feel either really good or really bad, I just have to bake up a storm. So, I did, and now we feast."

"Are we feasting happily or are we feasting sadly?"

"Definitely happily."

"In that case, I'll be only too glad to join you."

Maribeth took the tray into Bill's office and served both of them. They hungrily ate the sweet rolls and, after Maribeth licked a finger to clean some frosting off, she said, "Okay, I've been thinking this over and I have come up with a list of individual responsibilities for you and me. We need to work together to straighten this restaurant out and bring customers back. Right now, we are not a team. I know that we both keep long hours and we see each other all day long, but we are not really working together. We need to coordinate our activities and both need to know what the other is doing; and, to do that, we each will have to change the way we are presently working.

"Do you want to hear my suggestions for both of us?"

"Maribeth, I've been waiting for them."

"Well, for me, I will start coming in earlier to cover breakfasts and morning activities. However, I will delay any planning of schedules, meals, and food buying until you arrive in the early afternoon. Then, we will do it together so there will be no misunderstandings between us.

"You seem to be a quick learner like your father said you were and this ain't rocket science. If we work together we can get customers to come back and then begin to upgrade the facilities."

Bruckner said, "That takes care of your responsibilities. What are your suggestions for me?"

"I think that you ought to come to work in the early afternoon, oversee the dinner crowd as the maitre d', check out the nightly closing of the kitchen, the bar, and add up the daily receipts. This is almost exactly the way your father and I worked together."

Bruckner and Maribeth worked out the details and then he asked, "Have you thought about what you want as compensation for staying on at the Crossfire?"

"Yes, I would like to buy in as a partner, but I think that can wait until we get the business turned around. You have been perfectly honest with me and I trust your judgement completely. We can take care of that part of our agreement anytime you decide to."

Bruckner felt grateful for the compliment. He said, "I'll have our lawyer start working on drafting a contract. You have no idea how pleased I am that you're going to stay and become part of the business."

Maribeth hesitated for an instant before she spoke. "However, I do have one more suggestion that I really think is important and that you ought to consider."

Bruckner looked at her suspiciously and asked, "Ah, and what is this one suggestion that I ought to consider?"

"Well, don't get angry, but you do want this to be a family restaurant. That being the goal, you would look more impressive and friendly if you trimmed your wild truck driver's beard and pony tail and, instead, had a goatee or a Van Dyke."

He looked at her a second and burst into laughter. "You have to be in cahoots with my sister and my mother. From a business point of view, your suggestion is sensible. If we are trying to lure families, older generation customers, and middle class diners into our restaurant, they should not be greeted at the door by a hippy.

"When we start this new division of duties, I will be as smooth as a pane of glass."

The Monday that the new arrangement began, Maribeth got a phone call at noon. "Maribeth, this is Isabel. What have you done to my son? He came over here and I almost couldn't recognize him. He's beautiful; he's shaved and his hair is still long but groomed perfectly. He told me that was part of an agreement he had with you. You won't recognize him. I'm so grateful to you in so many ways."

Maribeth laughed at Mrs. Bruckner's comments; she had a pleasant conversation with her and then went back to work. When Bruckner did show up, Maribeth was glad that his mother had warned her. She would not have known this tall, handsome man, with a small Van Dyke, as the person she knew before he went into the barber shop. He seemed to enjoy the shocked looks he received when people noticed the changes.

For the next two months they each labored at their respective jobs. Maribeth worked with the chefs to update and change the menu; they cooked, altered, and sampled many foods in an attempt to make their meals tastier. She made the waitstaff aware that their treatment of the customer was vital in building good will. She instructed all of them to use a single routine in waiting on their tables, from bringing water without being asked, to serving rolls and butter before the meal arrived. She promised that good service would insure good tips and bring return customers into the restaurant.

Maribeth also started an intensive cleaning campaign on the physical facilities of the restaurant. She really wanted to remodel the interior but that would have to wait until business got better. Until then, she intended to scour the kitchen and brighten the dining room.

Sam Cutler's part-time hours were increased and he was redirected to ready the working area for painting. He scrubbed almost every inch of the kitchen floors, walls, ceilings, refrigerators, stoves, sinks; anything that caught Maribeth's glance was fair game for a bath. For a more efficient workspace, she ordered the kitchen painted a lighter color.

Bruckner put in equally long hours and he worked diligently on his assignments. He also handled the public affairs aspect of the business. Party arrangements, banquets, and business lunch commitments were funneled through him. He patrolled the restaurant and the bar during the busy hours to be sure that things were going smoothly and that there were no dissatisfied customers. His calm manner and pleasant personality soon gave the Crossfire a local appeal that the chain restaurants could not duplicate.

Closing the restaurant and the bar at the end of the day was a chore that he did not like, but it was part of his job, so he did it thoroughly. He made sure that the kitchen, dining room, bar, and restrooms were scrupulously cleaned. He knew the importance of cleanliness. That took a great deal of time and required constant attention. Counting the money and balancing the books was also time-consuming. These were the unglamorous parts of the job but they were necessary for the business to succeed. He spent as much time fussing over details he did not enjoy as those he did. He considered that part of his agreement with Maribeth.

Working together, Maribeth and Bruckner began to revive the restaurant. They spent hours each day talking, planning, and questioning each other. The privacy wrappers around their individual personalities began to melt; they became closer and they got to know one another. By the second month, they were friends; by the sixth month, they were in love; by the tenth month, they were in bed; and by the thirteenth month, they were newlyweds.

Their wedding took place at the Crossfire. The ceremony was a civil ceremony performed by the mayor of Milan. Maribeth selected each of these options herself. Even though she was born and raised as a Catholic, her first concern was how the church would view their up-coming union. Bill was not Catholic and Maribeth had long ago stopped attending church regularly. More important, she did not want to appear before a priest to undergo extensive discussions about her premarital relationship with Bill and her failed past religious responsibilities. The last thing in the world she wanted were lectures concerning her lifestyle; she didn't believe she had done anything wrong.

Maribeth wasn't sure what Bruckner would say about a Catholic wedding; he was completely nondenominational and he did not attend any church. Because his mother went to the Peoples Presbyterian Church each Sunday, Maribeth assumed that Bill's reluctance to go to church was based entirely on his heavy work schedule. When he proposed, he told her that whatever arrangements she decided on would be fine with him. Discussions about religion or religious rituals never came up; Maribeth didn't want to hear them and Bill was indifferent to talk about them.

To avoid any religious entanglements, Maribeth decided on a civil ceremony. After she thought about it, the idea of being married at her restaurant appealed to her. They could have a large reception, which would automatically advertise their business. All their choices proved to be good ones.

It was a joyous partnership that was to last the rest of their lives.

CHAPTER 3

Almost everyone was pleased when Maribeth Punkey and Bill Bruckner announced that they were going to get married. Bruckner's mother and sister couldn't have been more delighted. They had come to know and love Maribeth and they completely approved of how she changed Bruckner's life. He put his past behind him and was looking toward the future; he was happy and enthusiastic. Henry Tannenbaum was also pleased that Bill found a partner to share his life with. There is no finer testament to life than to embrace it wholeheartedly.

However, one person was not pleased. Sam Cutler was completely content with the living arrangements he had with Bruckner. Sharing apartment expenses and working at the Ford factory gave him a sense of belonging. Bill was his brother and his best friend; he relied on him for guidance. He didn't want any change to these arrangements.

Although it was Bruckner's father who hired Cutler to work part time at the Crossfire, Sam always got his directions from Maribeth. He liked Maribeth and he didn't mind working for her. She was a good boss and, if he did exactly as she asked, he never got into trouble. When Bruckner started working at the Crossfire, Cutler became apprehensive. He could see that his part-time boss and his best friend were becoming more than just fellow workers. He could also sense that seeing Maribeth as his boss was different from seeing Maribeth as his brother's wife. He was sure that a wife would disrupt their relationship. Bruckner would be less attentive to him, his problems, his needs. Once again, he began to be afraid that he would be on his own with no one to help him. He relied on his friends, especially Bruckner, to tell him what was best for Cutler.

Because Bill was working evenings, Sam began going to the Crossfire bar every night. Bruckner told the bartenders not to ask Sam for money, no matter what he ordered. Soon, Sam was both drinking and eating at the restaurant every night. His tab was given to Bruckner and was included with the day's receipts and transactions. Maribeth noticed Cutler's bills but said nothing; she figured this was Bill's restaurant and if he wanted to take care of a wartime buddy that was his business, certainly not hers.

When Bruckner told Cutler that he and Maribeth were going to be married, Cutler was not surprised and he was not happy. Sam began to think back to when he first reunited with Bruckner. He never again wanted to feel as useless and impotent as he did then. For him, liking his part-time boss was not as strong an emotion as the fear of losing his present life style. This was the main reason he was unhappy about the upcoming wedding: what would happen between the two of them after Bill got married?

He asked Bruckner which one of them was going to move out of the apartment? Either way, Sam knew his present living conditions were going to change. He felt a little better when he found that, if he wanted, he could keep living in the apartment because the newlyweds would rent their own home. Bruckner moved out of the apartment two weeks before the wedding and, much to Cutler's surprise, he was able to manage most of his normal living affairs by himself.

After Bruckner moved out, Cutler discovered that he was now free to do something he had never before thought of doing. He could bring women up to his apartment. He had always been too shy to make strong advances toward females. It never entered his mind until one of his dates suggested going to his apartment. Cutler enjoyed the rendezvous and began hinting that his apartment was available to each woman he met. He soon became the shyest lecher in Milan.

Another circumstance that helped him recover from not having Bruckner around began with a chance meeting with Henry Tannenbaum. They accidently met in the Milan Bakery one Sunday morning shortly after Bill's wedding and had coffee together. Tannenbaum invited Sam to join him fishing that afternoon. From that day on, Cutler sought Tannenbaum's advice as often as he did Bruckner's. In his soft spoken manner Tannenbaum discussed religion with Cutler, and he was not surprised to find that Cutler mirrored Bruckner's lack of faith. Without trying to convert Cutler, Tannenbaum threw his soft lasso of words around him and encouraged him to think for himself. Slowly, Cutler began to draw closer to becoming a believer; he listened mostly to keep Henry Tannenbaum as his good friend. Cutler started to attend the Immaculate Conception Church every Sunday with Tannenbaum. He didn't understand all the rituals but he did enjoy the company. Eventually, he joined the Catholic church and was baptized. His newfound religion didn't make him feel any closer to God but it did make him think that Tannenbaum liked him more.

Marriage is a fragile seedling that requires constant pruning as it matures or its fruit will wither. It begins in an aura of passion and emotion that nurtures the union until both partners satisfy their lustiness. From this point forward, each marriage becomes a delicate balance between the partner's personalities, their preferences, their desires, and their needs. It takes hard work and dedication to make marriage work. If both partners are mature, their chances for a happy marriage are good.

Although they had slept together and worked side by side before their wedding, neither Maribeth nor Bruckner realized what marriage really was like until after they married. The magnitude of committing to each other for the rest of their lives only became apparent after they wore each other's rings. It was a breathtaking revelation to wake up every morning and greet the partner they had each selected.

The Bruckner marriage was a marriage of give and take on both sides. Even though they worked together and saw more of each other than is the case in most marriages, the couple avoided getting on each other's nerves. They argued and they disagreed, sometimes intensely, but they never disparaged one another and they never lost their individual sense of humor.

The partners began by searching for the best way to approach each other when there were serious discussions. Bruckner started by saying, whenever Maribeth disagreed with him, "You should never have married a peasant." She would then counter with, "It's not so much a case of marrying a peasant as it is marrying so far beneath me."

Maribeth learned to ask Bill to do a single job by giving him a specific name for an individual task. "Would Tom the Trash Man take this bag to the garage?" or "Can Charlie the Chauffeur drive to the store?" Bruckner enjoyed this routine and used it himself. He would ask, "How would Helen the Housewife like to go the movies tonight?" Or, "Sally the Sandwich Maker forgot the mustard on my bologna."

The result was a marriage they both believed in and a life that was rich and satisfying. Bill and Maribeth couldn't have been happier.

Together, staying solely focused on their goal and working seven days a week, they rescued the Crossfire and made it into a successful restaurant. Within three years they had the entire building renovated inside and out. The interior was completely refurbished and rearranged and made brighter with new lighting; the exterior was landscaped with bushes and trees, the parking lot was realigned with a large, almost garish, sign proclaiming the entrance to the restaurant.

As a reward for their efforts, they decided to go away for a long weekend just by themselves. The Point Pelee National Park of Canada was not too far and it would be a quiet retreat. With that in mind, they made reservations at a bed and breakfast whose name they found in a travel brochure, the Iron Kettle. The first night, they dined in a fine restaurant in Leamington. Maribeth was quiet, almost non-responsive to conversation. Bruckner could tell something was on her mind.

"Sara the Silent, I could get more answers from a cigar store Indian. Where are you this evening?"

"I'm here, Honey. I'm not good at hiding things from you, am I? I've been trying to make plans and arrangements for both of us all day; I'm not having any luck. I need your help.

"Okay, this is what I'm talking about. I went to see my doctor this morning and he told me that I'm pregnant. I didn't know how to tell you that we are about to have our first child. How are we going to handle this?"

Bill grinned. "That's absolutely great," he shouted so loudly that several tables looked to see what the commotion was. He immediately became aware of their attention and he turned both palms up in an apologetic shrug.

He leaned over, grabbed his wife's hand and, much more quietly said, "I am so pleased for both of us and especially for you. It has taken a long time for this to happen."

Before dawn the next morning, they walked to the tip of Point Pelee and watched as both the birds and the day arose from their slumbers to display their beauties. The day was calm, Maribeth and Bill were serene. They held hands and thought of the child with whom they would be able to share this beauty and tranquility. That evening, Bruckner insisted they eat in the same restaurant where they dined the night before. They went to bed early. After all, they were in love and elated at the thought of having a child.

Bruckner was exhausted and fell asleep immediately. The next thing he remembered was Maribeth pushing on his shoulder and whispering, "Bill, are you asleep?"

"I was," he remarked groggily.

"Well, I haven't been. So wake up, we need to talk."

Bruckner rolled over on his back and reached over to pat Maribeth's thigh. He was sure that something was bothering her and he wanted to know what it was. "Can't you make an appointment?"

"I just did."

"Well, that's true, you just did, whether or not I like it. Okay, what are we talking about?"

There was a long pause before Maribeth said anything. Then, she asked quickly, "Do you believe in God?"

That question took Bruckner completely by surprise. He just lay there, trying to decide how to reply. He then asked his own question, "May I ask why, in the middle of the night, on our first real vacation, this subject has come up?"

"Simple answer. When our child is born, I want him or her to have some religious training. I want our child to go to church. I stopped going years ago but that doesn't mean that I've stopped believing. I will start going regularly again. Religion is important and I would like you to agree with me.

"You and I have never really had any religious discussions, although I think you may be against it. I fell away from the church so religion wasn't too significant for me. Now that I'm pregnant I'm having second thoughts. Don't you think our child should go to church?"

"Yes."

Maribeth was surprised at his answer. She could only ask, "What?"

"Yes, if you want our child to go to church, I agree."

Maribeth looked at her husband and said, "I don't understand. I guessed that you were against all religions. You don't go to church and you never talk about religion. You avoid any religious discussion and that's what led me to the question about whether or not you believe in God."

Bruckner didn't answer for so long that Maribeth asked, "Have you gone back to sleep?"

Bill sat up in bed and piled the pillows behind his back on the headboard. He leaned back. "No, I haven't fallen asleep. I'm trying to gather my thoughts so I can explain them to you. This explanation is going to take awhile, so make yourself comfortable.

"First, to answer your question, I do not believe in God, I am an atheist."

Maribeth was totally stunned by his declaration. She had never personally met anyone who openly professed to being an atheist. Now, the first person who admitted it was her husband. Adding to her complete confusion was the fact that her husband would allow their child to go to church. She said. "Let me get this straight. You don't believe in God?"

Bruckner answered, "I do not."

Maribeth didn't understand; there didn't seem to be any logic in her husband's attitude. "But, even if you don't believe in God, you will allow our children to go to the Catholic church with me?"

"Yes."

"I'm mixed up. That doesn't make sense to me. Doesn't one idea contradict the other?"

Bill answered her question. "Honey, Let me ask you a question. Do you think that a person who doesn't believe in God can still believe in peace and love?"

Maribeth faltered; she replied a few seconds later. "I've never thought about it before. I'd have to guess that it would be unusual but that it is possible."

"Let me ask you another question," Bruckner said. "What kind of person is your husband?"

"Bill, are you kidding me?"

"No, I'm serious. You want me to explain why I don't believe in God, which I will. However, you won't fully understand unless you know what I do believe. You probably still won't agree with me but you'll see that I'm a harmless kook who loves his wife.

"So, I ask, what kind of person do you think I am?"

Maribeth thought for a moment before replying. "I would use the word 'admirable' to describe you. You're very like your father, honest and blunt.

"I'm proud and pleased to be your wife. Now tell me why you became a member of the atheist party."

Bruckner laughed. At least Maribeth hadn't lost her sense of humor. "The simple answer is, I don't know how else anyone can explain what is happening in our lifetime. There is too much cruelty, too much hate, too much misery in this world. I cannot conceive of a God, capable of governing everyone's life, letting millions of people live in filth and pain. Innocent millions are slaughtered in war. Natural disasters kill tens of thousands of bystanders for no apparent reason. The idea of children dying of starvation absolutely sickens me.

"Until your God shows that he loves these simple people as much as you think he does, I don't consider that anyone, or anything, is in charge of this planet. Living seems to be nothing more than a crapshoot."

Maribeth was taken by surprise at the depth of her husband's convictions. "But, you aren't affected directly by what happens in the rest of the world. Why should you care?"

"Wife of my life, that's not the point. There are humans all over this planet. If the universe belongs to Him, let Him take care of all of them. The people of Africa, or Asia, or Europe, or where ever, should have as much chance at happiness as we have. Half the world is always light and half the world is always dark; that does not mean that His reign should be half heaven and half hell."

Maribeth let out a deep breath. "You are telling me that, even though you don't believe in God, you believe in love and peace; and because of that, our children can go to church with me?"

"Yes."

Maribeth could only say, "I'm still lost. Connect the dots for me."

Bruckner sighed as he patted her hand. "I didn't wake up one day and decide I was an atheist. I truly started out hoping that there was a God but I ended up sure that there wasn't. It was a long journey over a long time; however, that discussion will keep for another day.

"First, I'm not against the philosophies of any religion. The ones I'm familiar with, Protestant, Jewish, Catholic, all teach love and peace. But the way that people live today, there's not enough love and peace to solve our problems.

"I want our children, yours and mine, to have a positive upbringing. It is just as important for us, as parents, to teach them love as it is important for them to learn to love. In this world, teaching children positive values is far better than teaching them nothing. How can anyone think that teaching goodness, no matter which religion is doing the teaching, is wrong? After they are old enough, they can decide for themselves whether to remain with the church that taught them their values. If you want our children to be raised with love and peace, I absolutely vote YES.

"Now, once I tell you that I have no qualms about religious philosophies, I must tell you that I do have problems with the practice of every religion. Whatever the reasons, they don't follow their own philosophies. Christians of all denominations have been killing fellow Christians since Christianity was conceived, the same with the Muslims, and both of these religions have slaughtered the Jews, who are also fractured within their Judaism.

"Where is their peace and brotherly love outside their own religions? Have you seen how religions treat other religions? I like the philosophies of religions but their formalities make no sense to me."

Maribeth asked, "Aren't you hung up on small details by just concentrating on formalities?"

Bruckner grinned. "See, that's where the arguments start. No, I don't believe that I'm hung up on details. Every religion, because they propagate their own faith, downgrades their competitors. Religions don't really cooperate, they are in constant competition against each other.

"Listen, each religion claims that it is the only bus that goes to heaven and that no other religion will take you there. Think about that. Automatically, there is a back of the bus mentality in every religion in the world. Before you believe that is a minor detail, think of the consequences of that attitude.

"The Christians think that only through Jesus can you seek salvation. Christians are a minority in this world but they believe they are the route to salvation. So, what about a shepherd in Africa or a farmer in India who, because of geography, never heard about Jesus Christ? Even if they led honorable lives, are these non-Christians barred from heaven because they never got the word? Do they really deserve to be in the back of the Christian bus?

"I don't think so. And look at the rest of the people sitting in the second class seats of these religious buses. Catholics won't allow women to become priests. Protestants argue over gay and lesbian pastors. Jews condemn other Jews for not being Jewish enough. The second class seats way in the back really get crowded because of formalities and discrimination. Yet, if they truly followed their own philosophies, there should only be a first class section up front for everyone.

"Religious beliefs should flow from the pews to the altars to the heavens, not from the heavens to the altars to the pews. I think that a religion that flows backward, mostly from the heavens downward, is stagnant.

"I wonder what your God makes of all these rules and formalities and, as you call it, details?"

Bill sat back against his pillows. Maribeth leaned against him and snuggled. She rubbed her cheek against his chest. "You take this world seriously, don't you?"

Bruckner replied quietly, "Yes, I take the world very seriously because ruthless faith and ruthless patriotism are the two biggest testosterone factories in the universe. They both raise hatred and cause wars. I take them very seriously."

"Well, Darling Husband, I understand what you are saying and, to a degree, you do make sense. However, the difference between us is that I have faith and you don't. I do believe in God."

Bruckner chuckled. "You sound like our friend, Henry. He says, 'faith is the serum that prevents humanity from becoming animals.'

"I wish I could agree with both of you."

Despite their philosophical differences, they hugged, said goodnight, and fell asleep together.

The following morning was the last day of their vacation and they arrived early at Point Pelee; they walked to the beach holding hands. It was a foggy day with misty rain; there were hardly any other visitors or birds to greet them. They sat on a fallen log and drank coffee, not talking, each immersed in their individual thoughts. Finally, Bruckner asked, "Sally the Silent, you haven't said a word since we got in the car, what is going through your mind?"

"I have been thinking about you, Andrew the Atheist. I don't know why, but you took me completely by surprise last night. I don't think I have ever known a card carrying atheist before. Now I am married to one and I'm curious.

"You are intelligent. You are a good person, a wonderful husband, and you will be a marvelous father. I have no doubt about that. I'm glad that I took a vow to be faithful to you. I love you. But how come we never had this discussion before?"

Bruckner answered, "That's because most people look down on atheists as nut cakes. Many believers recoil when they meet an atheist. They won't persuade me to change my mind any more than I will persuade them to cross the line and join me. I just don't want to get into a discussion that leads to an argument and talking about religion usually does. Other people certainly have a right to their opinions the same as

I have a right to mine. I don't bother talking about my thoughts because there's no sense arguing over differences that can't be resolved.

"Being in the minority is a different feeling. Believers have churches to go to and brag about their religion. Atheists have no edifices to meet in and no one to congregate with. For the most part, we are loners in our thoughts and quiet about our feelings.

"I can't vouch for my fellow atheists. However, I can tell you that I believe in exactly the same virtues that religions supposedly do. As a citizen, I love my country, I pay my taxes, and I obey the law. As a human, I adore my wife, I try to be kind, and I'm dead set against injustice and prejudice.

"I am happy that we are going to have a child and I'm looking forward to being a father. This has been the best vacation I have ever had.

"And, despite her taste in husbands, I am deeply in love with my wife."

Their firstborn was a boy and they named him Milton, in honor of Bruckner's father. During the next three years, they had two more children, both girls, named in honor of their mothers. The first daughter was named Alicia, in honor of Maribeth's mother. Their second daughter was Isabel, for Bill's mother.

Their life together was pleasant and only small bramble bushes blocked their domestic path. These were easily trimmed to keep the trail open. As their children grew, Maribeth increasingly retreated from the business at the Crossfire. Bruckner took over Maribeth's responsibilities as well as his own.

She and Bill were adamant that nothing was as important as their family. They both wanted a mother's influence to surround their children. The idea of Maribeth working full time at the restaurant and only having visiting hours at home was never a consideration.

Equally important to Maribeth, was that Bill kept his promise. He not only allowed the children to go to church every Sunday, he went with them whenever he wasn't working at the restaurant. They made an attractive sight; a family of five in church and taking communion together.

Henry Tannenbaum soon noticed that Bruckner's family was coming to the church he had been attending for years. He also noticed that Bruckner was with them when he had the day off. Tannenbaum and Sam Cutler began to sit and talk with them before and after the service.

Seeing the whole family take Communion puzzled Tannenbaum; he was almost positive that Bruckner had never converted to Catholicism or been baptized. After the family began attending services regularly, during a private conversation between himself and Bruckner, he brought up the subject of taking Communion without being baptized. Bruckner responded that although it seemed hypocritical, he was more concerned with his children's upbringing than in following church rules and regulations. He took Communion so they wouldn't ask why he wasn't taking Communion. His children knew nothing about his feelings on religion. He deemed it important that they learn right from wrong even if he struggled with his own thoughts about religion. On that basis his friends and everyone else could judge him as they saw fit; he didn't give a damn.

Tannenbaum thought about that, agreed with him, and never brought up the subject again. Regardless of his Catholic background, Tannenbaum enjoyed the idea of Bruckner thumbing his nose at the establishment while trying to do the right thing in raising his children.

Tannenbaum and Bruckner became close friends. The relationship deepened when Tannenbaum, in his role as a counselor, once called Bruckner at the Crossfire to ask for any extra food he could give to a family that had nothing to eat. Bruckner had just brought his firstborn home from the hospital and the thought of a child going hungry bothered him. He responded without hesitation. From that first request,

Bruckner and Tannenbaum formed a quiet alliance. Tannenbaum, after alerting Bruckner, would show up with seniors, veterans, or an occasional teenager. Those he brought in were hungry. Tannenbaum was never turned down or questioned by Bruckner who simply believed in paying back to his community. Whenever Tannenbaum found someone hungry, he called for food; whenever Bruckner received a call, he fed the hungry.

To avoid anyone overhearing personal details of the people they helped, the two of them would walk outside the restaurant to talk. They both enjoyed this arrangement so much that these walks became a routine part of their lives. The exercise and the discussions were good for them; and, although their philosophies were different, opposites did attract. They found each other interesting. Rarely would a week go by without them walking around downtown Milan, talking and listening to each other. There was no set pattern. They would meet either downtown or at Wilson Park, stroll around, and discuss whatever was on their mind. Each was interested in the other's beliefs about religion, God and salvation.

One Saturday, early in the morning, Bruckner and Tannenbaum were walking in Wilson Park approaching a bench where a woman had just sat down. From a distance they could see that she was small and elderly. She opened a bag, took out a loaf of bread, and began pulling the loaf apart. She threw bits of the bread on the ground and immediately Canada geese began to gather around her bench. Dozens of squawking birds dropped from the sky to fight over the food. Bruckner and Tannenbaum took one look and decided to change their route. Neither wanted to be dive-bombed by those pesky birds. They laughed and walked away. After the same thing happened two or three more times on their Saturday morning walks, they avoided "the lady on the bench," as they referred to her.

One Saturday Tannenbaum dropped by the Crossfire to talk with Bruckner. They sat in his office and Tannenbaum said, "I'm a bit worried about Sam Cutler. Several times he has made appointments to see me and then has not shown up. He said he wanted to talk to me this morning but he never made it. Has he been here for work when he's supposed to?"

Bruckner answered, "Just like clockwork. I know that he left here late last night; it was after we closed. He had been drinking and he was with his latest girlfriend so I'm not surprised he didn't meet you this morning. Tojours l'amour! Maybe all night long. However, he comes to work on time and does his job. I talked to him a couple of nights ago and he seemed fine; he's not getting as much overtime as he had been at Ford, but he wasn't upset about it. He told me he couldn't spend much time talking to me because there was some lady at the bar that he was trying to meet.

"I think Sam Cutler is enjoying puberty."

Tannenbaum nodded. "You're probably right and I should have known better. Sam is a good guy but he spins around like a drinking straw in a river rapid. When he gets in trouble, he'll be around to see one of us. I'm sorry I bothered you."

Bruckner assured Tannenbaum that his visit was no bother. They chatted for a minute longer and, solely on a whim, Bruckner asked, "Henry, why don't you come over to my house tomorrow night for supper? It is a rare Sunday that I get a night off and Maribeth would enjoy showing off our family. We call it 'parading.'" Tannenbaum quickly accepted the invitation.

It was a pleasant Sunday evening. The three adults were relaxed and had playful conversations with the children, all of whom were in elementary school. Milton, the oldest, was the center of attention and he put on a good show; the other cast of young characters, Milton's two sisters, also helped to entertain Tannenbaum. When Bruckner and Maribeth went to bed, she told him that she had had a good time and that she had enjoyed Henry's visit.

The evening with Tannenbaum got Bruckner thinking. His mother had been a widow for so many years that she seemed passive about doing things for herself. Except for keeping track of her son, his wife, her daughter, and her grandchildren, she had few outside interests or a real life of her own; Bruckner wondered if she might be lonely. As for Tannenbaum, he had been a widower for a long time; he kept himself busy by helping other people but Bruckner wondered if he might also be lonely. Both his mother and Henry had known each other since high school, although they had not crossed paths in their adult years. Might they provide companionship for each other?

The next Sunday that Bruckner was not working, he invited both Tannenbaum and his mother over to his house. He asked Maribeth not to tell his mother that Tannenbaum would be eating with them. He didn't think his mother would object to Henry's presence but he didn't want to scare her away. He also didn't tell Tannenbaum that his mother would be there.

Both were surprised to see each other. At first, the atmosphere was a little cool. However, they relaxed at dinner and the two of them reminisced about old times and old acquaintances and became more cordial. When it was time to leave, both were at ease and comfortable. As she got into bed that evening, Maribeth kissed her husband and told him that he was lucky his plan had worked out as well as it did.

Bruckner, busy at work, put the evening behind him until he got a phone call from his sister about a month later. "Bill," she began, "did you know that Mother is seeing Henry Tannenbaum?"

He was taken aback, "What?"

Alice replied, "I said, Mother is seeing Henry Tannenbaum."

"How do you know that?"

"Because she told me herself. She said that you had them over for dinner awhile ago. Since then, they talked on the phone and now are going to the movies together."

"Holy Cow."

Alice laughed. "That's what I say. Mom sounds more animated than I've heard her in a long time. Good for both of them.

"And, good for you for bringing them together. Whatever gave you the idea of matching them up?"

"Alice, I don't know. I just wanted to see Mom happier than she is now. She deserves a chance for a good life."

Alice said, "You certainly have earned a pat on the back," and hung up.

For the next few weeks, news traveled back and forth. Alice would phone Maribeth who would call his mother who would call Alice who would then redial the chain. Bill was aware that the frequency of Cupid's communications was increasing, so he was not surprised when his mother eventually phoned him and asked him to come over to her house. When he arrived, his mother hugged him and they sat down at the kitchen table. Bruckner was pleased at her appearance. She was neatly dressed, freshly groomed, and looked relaxed. She started by asking, "Bill, has Henry said anything to you about us?"

"No, Mom, he has not mentioned a word to me about you."

"You do know something though, don't you?"

"I'd have to be deaf not to know something. I overhear most of the conversations among you ladies."

His mother laughed loudly. "Yes, I guess we have been chatting a lot lately. Then you do know that Henry and I have been talking about getting married?"

"Yes, and I couldn't be happier for both of you."

"Are you okay with my decision?"

"Mom, you've been a widow for too many years. If you have a chance to enjoy life, grab it. I'm more than okay with your decision, I'm absolutely pleased."

His mother hesitated. "Bill, do you think that your father would approve?"

"Mom, Dad was a very practical man. He loved you. I'm sure he would want you to continue loving and living.

"I also have no doubt that he would agree with me. Get married and look to the future."

His mother stood, walked over to her son and gave him a tight hug. There were tears in her eyes.

The next day Henry came to the restaurant to talk with Bill. "Isabel tells me that you two spoke yesterday."

"We did."

"Your conversation has cleared all her concerns. Your mother and I are planning to marry."

Bruckner immediately grinned from ear to ear as he slapped Tannenbaum on the back and then shook his hand. He couldn't contain his joy. He had never forgotten Tannenbaum's advice to him after he came back from Vietnam. He remembered word for word what Tannenbaum said, "There is nothing that will make the wine of life taste sweeter than someone with whom to share the cup." He always wondered why Tannenbaum had never remarried.

The two of them lingered a long time over coffee so Bruckner could hear all the details of their plans. He was so pleased for his friend and his mother. He knew that Maribeth and Alice would want to know Tannenbaum's perspective on every aspect of the upcoming wedding. Bruckner wanted the people he cared for to sip the honey tang of love that comes with marriage.

A few days later, Henry said, "You know, Bill, I haven't felt so alive in years. Sorrow destroys your life but it doesn't stop your clock. You're emotionally wounded and growing older and you don't even realize it. That's crazy thinking, isn't it?"

Then, before Bruckner could give him an answer, Tannenbaum continued. "My first wife Monica and I had so little time together and we were so in love. When your mother and I first got together recently, I began to wonder what Monica would have thought about my meeting a new love.

"Then I realized that this was really crazy thinking. Like snowflakes, no two loves are alike. Each love is a sacred potion, and each potion has its own ingredients and hidden flavors. That makes each love unique and distinct from every other love. I wasn't replacing Monica's love. After years of loneliness, I was starting a new love with Isabel. What do you think of that?"

Bruckner smiled at the pleasant thoughts that his friend was expressing. He replied, "I think that you are absolutely correct and I'm pleased that you and my mother are starting a new life together. The two of you will be good for each other and that's what is most important to me."

Tannenbaum sat for a second before he quietly began, "Perhaps I shouldn't tell you this but it is on my mind. I mean, this as no disrespect to you or your mother; I love both of you. My thoughts are foggy so I want to talk about them. It may help me."

Henry continued, "I'm different from you, philosophically. I believe in the afterlife, heaven and hell; you don't. At least, the last time we talked about afterlife you didn't believe in it and I don't think you've changed.

"Anyhow, what happens after I die and I enter into my life after death? How do I introduce my two wives to each other and what if they don't get along? What kind of living—wait, I can't use that word anymore—what kind of life-after-death arrangements will I find when I reach my final destination?

"You see, for the first time since you and I started talking about our beliefs, I'm a little confused about mine.

"I am beginning to appreciate your skepticism about humans and their afterlife."

Bill listened to his friend and thought to himself, "It gets even more complicated than that, Henry. What happens if the drunk who killed your wife repented and went to heaven? How would each of you handle the situation?"

Bruckner continued with his thoughts, "I don't know what I would do under those same circumstances." He did not express any of these thoughts aloud to Henry Tannenbaum. That left them both in the same situation; neither knew the answer to their questions.

Their uncertainties did not postpone the wedding of Isabel Bruckner and Henry Tannenbaum. They benefited from the arrangements that Maribeth and Bill had made for their wedding. Even though Isabel agreed to convert to Catholicism, they were wed outside the church. By avoiding a church service, no ghosts from either of their pasts were allowed to interfere with the celebration of the present. To begin a second life, with no past burdens, the ceremony took place at the Crossfire, a civil wedding performed, once again, by the mayor of Milan.

CHAPTER 4

From the moment their first child came home from the hospital until their third child left home, Maribeth and Bill Bruckner were good parents. Both as a mother and father team and as individual parents, they performed their roles gladly. They considered it their duty to raise well mannered, polite children who understood right from wrong. To fulfill these goals they spent much of their free time with their children. In the process of raising their family, they themselves relived part of their own youth.

Children need rules to live by. Establishing these rules is the responsibility of their parents. As they grow, children have to know what the boundaries are. Unless they clearly understand where their limits lie, they will never understand the consequences of breaking these rules.

It is also true that children have to rebel against family rules because they need room to expand their individual horizons. It is only by constantly butting against their borders that children learn right from wrong and how to tell the difference. It is in this gray area, between teaching the rules and disciplining those that break the rules, that parents need to excel. The results are children who know the rules, are delightful; children who do not, are monsters.

The Bruckner parents were consistent and quiet in their enforcement of the family rules. They had as few rules as possible and these were clearly defined. With this attitude, they had little trouble keeping their flock in line, focused, and moving forward. As a family, they went on picnics, trips, and vacations. They once cancelled a trip to Disney World because one of the children got sick and they didn't want to leave that child behind at Grandmother's house while they were in Florida. Wherever they went on vacation, the only rules imposed on the children were to be polite and not too raucous.

As a mother, Maribeth showed her children the feminine side of family life. Using the standards that were passed to her from her mother, she consciously instilled them in her offspring. She was always teaching lessons. Sometimes they were for her daughters only, sometimes they were for her son, and most of the time they were for all three children.

As a father, Bill showed his children the masculine side of family life. Using the standards that were passed to him from his father, he consciously taught them to his offspring. He was always teaching lessons. Sometimes they were for his son only, sometimes they were for his daughters, and most of the time they were for all three children.

More important than the lessons themselves was that the teachings of both parents be identical in moral truth and value. No lesson held any untruths, both parents taught from the same page. Their three children didn't realize until later on in life, what outstanding parents they had.

None of this careful upbringing was done in a sober environment—far from it. There was always noise and laughter coming from the Bruckner family. The children learned to play hard, study hard, work hard. It was a family unit led by parents who loved their children enough to want to raise them correctly, but who were wise enough not to surrender their roles as mother and father. Both Maribeth and Bill made it clear to the children that they were the parents and it was their rules that would be followed. Bruckner continually told his children, "A family is not a democracy." The children had the bit and bridle of family discipline in place before they knew how to protest.

When his youngest was still a toddler, Bruckner took a weekend off to rest and relax. That Friday evening, he turned on the television and got hung up watching a late night movie. It was a poorly conceived spy thriller with a stereotyped plot and stereotyped dialogue. There were many spies and each one was heroically dispatched on a secret mission somewhere around the world. Bruckner could predict everything that was going to happen long before it took place. He knew it was poor stuff to watch but he didn't have the strength to quit. He grumbled his way to bed late, knowing he had wasted his time.

The following morning he was making breakfast when, out of nowhere, he addressed everyone at the table. "How would you all like to go on a secret mission?" Maribeth looked at him quizzically while the children all agreed enthusiastically. His children had no idea of what a secret mission was. However, as long as it meant going somewhere and doing something, like all children, they were in favor of action.

With the family in the car, Bruckner was driving nowhere before he had an idea of where to go on his secret mission. He pulled into Lillie Park where the family spent a delightful hour strolling through the woods and watching squirrels and birds. After their walk, they went to an ice cream parlor. From then on, secret missions became part of family life. At least once a month the family would head somewhere with the children who never knew where they were going. At first, they visited local parks, but as the children grew, the secret missions took their developing interests into account. They went to places that would stir their imaginations: they attended movies, softball games at both Michigan and Eastern Michigan universities, Greenfield Village, and The Detroit Institute of Arts.

Going on secret missions became a family tradition. As they grew, they went on longer secret missions to the Upper Peninsula. The secret mission they talked about most was a three day trip to see the ships as they went through the locks at Sault Ste. Marie. They just couldn't break away from standing and staring as ship after ship entered or exited the locks after being raised or lowered twenty-one feet. It was hypnotic to watch the thousand foot long ore ships inch their way through the thirty-two foot wide canal. It was progress in slow motion.

Another family tradition began when their children started school. Maribeth and Bill made it a priority to listen to and talk with their children. They decided to make dinner a family event. By this time, Maribeth was a stay-at-home mom and Bruckner had enough staff to allow him to be home for the evening meal. Almost every evening the family would sit down and discuss whatever happened that day and any topic that was on anyone's mind. Opinions were listened to and problems were discussed. As innocent minds matured, the conversations became interesting. Whether the topic was washing your belly button, bullying, cheating on exams, sex, or using drugs, everyone had an opinion and every opinion was respected.

The price for being treated as adults was that the children had to follow adult rules. No one was allowed to interrupt the person who was speaking; everyone had to wait their turn to talk; swearing or personal insults were absolutely not allowed. From such family traditions, loving memories are stored and remembered.

Each of the Bruckner offspring grew from a child to an adult under the guidance of their parents and developed their own personalities and interests. Their parent's values were part of their make-up, along with their own independent ideas and thoughts. The next generation of Bruckners was ready to begin their lives.

Milton, the oldest, attended Washtenaw Community College and began a career as a chef. He had worked in the Crossfire kitchen when he was growing up and wanted to come back to the restaurant. However, his father insisted that he get a few year's experience working in other restaurants. Then, if he still wanted to return to the family business, he would be more than welcome. When he did return, he brought his own set of hard-earned skills and knowledge.

Alicia, two years younger than Milton, was a quiet, sweet person. Shy in public but fiery in private, she always wanted the world to be a happy place. She and her Aunt Alice were very close and it was almost automatic that she would follow the same path as her aunt. She went to the University of Michigan and became a lawyer. She also was a member of the American Civil Liberties Union and a determined advocate for women's rights.

Isabel was born the year after Alicia. Her mother said that she was born talking and never learned to stop; this was only a slight exaggeration. She was bright and chirpy and full of sunshine. She went through her childhood singing to the birds and flowers. Like her sister, she also went to the University of Michigan where she became a nurse. She moved to Ann Arbor and worked at the University of Michigan's C. S. Mott Children's Hospital.

When they were young and growing, Bill kept his promise to Maribeth that the children would go to church. He was better than his word; he went with his family on Sunday whenever he wasn't working. He would listen to their thoughts on religion and the church rituals without saying a word. He had promised Maribeth to bring them up in love and peace and let them choose their own paths in life. This he did, without ever telling them about his own thoughts and observations. Each of their children continued to attend church services, even after they finally discovered their father's beliefs about God and religion.

As his family began to leave the nest, Bruckner's attendance at church slipped, he stayed home most of the time. He would accompany Maribeth if she asked, but she rarely imposed on him. He had faithfully fulfilled his promise to her; he had put the job of raising his family before his own philosophy. She loved him all the more for that.

Of course, the Bruckners did not lose contact with their children after they left home. It was true that the frenetic noises of doors banging and kids rushing up and down the hall, calling to each other, were gone. There were now distances of miles separating all of them. Home intimacy was replaced with telephone calls and recorded voice messages. The parents were still available to their children but they had automatically been promoted to the rank of senior advisors.

When their nest was empty, the parents weren't sure they liked this quieter form of communicating. Then it dawned on them—for the first time in almost twenty-five years of marriage—they were alone. They were by themselves again and relieved of their parental responsibilities. After living with this new reality for a while, they were elated. They also realized that, sometime in the future their still unborn grandchildren would be visiting them. Maribeth and Bill decided to take advantage of this new freedom.

For years, Bruckner had worked extremely long hours at the Crossfire. He now found himself wanting more time to be with Maribeth. His restaurant, while important, was not nearly as important as enjoying his wife and family. He began working shorter hours and turned over more of the day-to-day operations of the restaurant to his son, Milton. It reminded him that his entry back into the business was much different from his son's transition. Competition from national restaurant chains was now more widespread. He was pleased with Milton's ability to handle the challenges of today's restaurant business.

Maribeth was also rethinking her values. She no longer had to cook, clean, and keep house for a whole family. She had more free time than ever before and she wanted to spend it with her husband. They had finished their job of raising the children, now they could now get back to enjoying each other and their grandchildren. They could make plans for themselves, with only little thought of business or family.

They began to talk about what they had once thought of doing—going to Mexico and seeing the pink flamingos. They arranged a journey to tour the Yucatan Peninsula, visit Cancun, see Chichen Itza and several other Mayan sites, and ending up in Merida. From there, they visited the Celestun Biosphere Reserve where they saw hundreds of different bird species and thousands of pink flamingos. They were overwhelmed by the sight of so many flamingos taking flight at the same time. The beauty of the old city of Merida enchanted them. They enjoyed themselves but soon realized that two-week trips out of the country were not for them. Although their bodies were in Mexico, their thoughts and hearts had not come with them. Those had never left Michigan; they found themselves calling home to check on their family and friends.

They decided they would both be happier with shorter, two-, three-, or four-day trips. As they drove home from their first short trip, they were feeling a little guilty and apprehensive; they were concerned that problems may have arisen while they were having fun and enjoying themselves. They relaxed when they found that their family, their friends, their neighbors, and their business had survived their three-day absence. They made further trips to Chicago, Toronto, Traverse City and the Upper Peninsula without any fears that the earth would stop revolving before they returned. Maribeth and Bill enjoyed each other, which meant that they enjoyed life.

They soon adjusted to this new, more relaxed, middle-aged life. One Sunday afternoon, Maribeth and Bill went to Gallup Park for a walk along the Huron River. It was colder, rainier, and windier than expected and they cut their walk short. As he drove the car into their driveway, he saw Sam Cutler sitting on the front porch steps; he was huddled in a poncho against the rain. Bruckner was puzzled because he knew that

Sam had a key to their front door. He rolled the car window down. "Sam, why aren't you inside? You have a key."

"I figured if I stayed outside you wouldn't have to worry that I would take anything from the inside."

Maribeth was quick to reply, "Sam, that's ridiculous. Why would we think that?"

Bruckner said, "Honey, get out and let him in the house. He looks miserable. I'll park the car." Maribeth got out, ducked through the rain, and ran into the house. She made coffee and sandwiches. There was not much talking until Cutler finished eating. When the three of them were warm and comfortable, Bruckner started the conversation by asking, "Sam, what the hell were you doing sitting out in the rain?"

Sam replied, "I needed to talk to you. I'm sorry if I'm a bother to you and Maribeth. I guess I'm not thinking straight. I got notified Friday that I was laid off at Ford and I'm worried sick."

Bruckner asked, "You were caught in that layoff? An entire shift was let go. It will be months before they'll be recalled. That's a shame."

"For me, it's terrible. I'm out of a job and my part time job won't cover my expenses. I don't know what to do. I was hoping you could give me some ideas."

"Sam, you don't have anything to worry about. If worst comes to worst, you can always eat your meals with Maribeth and me or eat at the Crossfire. I'll talk to Milton about that. You should have enough money to keep your apartment until you're called back to work."

Then, in an attempt to put some humor into the discussion, Bruckner added, "Although you may have to cut down on the number of ladies you escort into your apartment."

Cutler replied quite seriously, "Bill, I've already done that. I'm getting old. That's one of the reasons I was so worried about being laid off."

Bruckner looked sharply at Cutler; he hadn't thought about age. Sam was correct, he was getting old. His hair was graying, he was getting stoop shouldered and he had a paunch.

"He is getting old, and aren't we all?" Bruckner thought. "I should not be yanking his chain about age, because I'm in the same category."

By the time Sam Cutler left, Maribeth and Bruckner had calmed his fears. The rest of the afternoon Bruckner hardly said a word. At dinner, he only replied when Maribeth spoke to him; otherwise he had nothing to say. He did not watch television; instead, he wandered around the house not settling down to do anything. He was ill at ease all evening.

As they got into bed, Maribeth said, "Bill, I'm not going to let you go to sleep until you tell me what is bothering you." Bruckner sighed and gave his wife a kiss on the cheek. "Ah, Maribeth, Sam made me sad this afternoon. After he said that he was getting old I really looked at him for the first time in years. He is getting old and so are we. However, it's not just that we're all getting old. It's that he is so dependent upon people to make his decisions for him. He is like a lost puppy, he needs someone to feed him and scratch his ears."

Bruckner paused to gather his thoughts, then he started speaking. "Then I thought about both of us for a long time and I felt worse. The randomness of life bothers me."

"What do you mean by that?"

"Well, no human has any idea when he is brought into this world or when he leaves. All I know for sure is that I was born and that I will die and I have nothing to do with either of these events.

"I also know that you are the major reason I love life. However, what if you had been born at a different time and in another country? What would our lives have been like?

"I felt sad, and I still feel sad. I began to ask myself—where did our time go? How much time do we have left? Will anyone younger even remember that we came before they did?"

He stopped talking. They both lay quietly for a while before Maribeth snuggled against Bruckner. "My Dear Husband. What deep thoughts. No wonder you haven't talked much. Of course we'll be remembered. Our children and their children will be proof that we did live and that we are remembered. You and I are a link in the chain of humanity.

"See, that's where my faith in God helps me. I'm sure we will meet in heaven after we leave this earth. I have no doubts about that."

"And I will be with you?"

"Why not? You are one of the kindest, most loving men in the world. That is why I let you choose me."

Bill replied, "That may, or may not, be true. But that's not enough according to you Christians. You also have to believe in Jesus Christ.

"That prohibits millions of good people in other parts of the world who never heard of Christ from entering your Pearly Gates. I'm not sure that is fair or right that only one religion gets to guard the gates to God's Domain. Doesn't that show a bias if God puts one faith in charge of all the other faiths?"

Maribeth sighed. She didn't agree with her husband but there was some logic in his statements. She knew that he was never one to go along to get along with the crowd; he was an individual who drew his own conclusions. She decided his attitude toward religion was part of his rebellious nature; he definitely did his own thinking. She answered, "When you put it that way, I'm not sure that is fair or right either. Why the devil do you spend so much time thinking of these things? It's easier to have faith and not ask questions."

"You're right, Maribeth. It is easier to accept faith and believe without examining religion too deeply. I can't because I don't understand why all these faiths that believe in one God can't let mankind enjoy a peaceful life. Why do they have to think that their religion is the only true avenue to heaven, valhalla, jannah, or whatever their particular afterlife is called?

"I can't figure out why love and peace harden into warfare. Why is there so much hate in this beautiful planet of ours? Anyhow, now that we've settled absolutely nothing, there are many more important matters we can begin to consider"

They held each other close, and decided that making love was a lot more fun than trying to pierce the barrier of the beyond.

CHAPTER 5

When John Calvin Collins first came to Milan he insisted that everyone call him "Preacher John." He wanted to make the point that he was a Christian evangelical minister who was seeking a new flock. He looked the part. He was in his late thirties, just over six feet tall and he always wore a gray suit, a maroon clergy shirt with a white tab collar, and black shoes. His face was thin and his features were plain, except for large eyes, which seemed able to separate truth from fiction. His voice was his most positive feature; it was deep, lyrical, almost hypnotic. Unfortunately, the appearance was better than the product. John Calvin Collins became a minister because it was the easiest way for him to earn a living. It took him many years to discover his chosen profession.

John Calvin was the last of seven children—three brothers and three sisters preceded him. His father abandoned the family before John reached his first birthday and his mother struggled to keep the family together. He wore nothing but hand-me-downs, usually first passed through six children, regardless of gender. At the different schools they attended, the Collins kids were the butts of mean jokes and nasty comments. John grew up with an inherent dislike and wariness of everybody and everything.

When John turned sixteen, he ran away from home and never looked back. At no time did he ever think of getting in touch with any member of his family; he wanted to avoid his past. He spent years working menial jobs at bowling alleys, restaurants, warehouses, and hospitals. As far as the community was concerned, he was invisible. As far as he was concerned, the community would have to pay for this status; he wanted revenge for the way he had been treated.

To that end, he did the same thing that many invisible people do, he broke the laws. He tried shoplifting, purse snatching, breaking and entering, even automobile theft. Fortunately for him, he was never caught so he was never charged. However, he was arrested for vagrancy and panhandling a few times. It was while he was in jail for these minor offenses that John Calvin began to see his future. He noticed that any inmate who could quote scripture was able to gather an audience. Even if it was a complete misquote, or an ignorant lie, his fellow jail mates would listen. He also was aware that negative emotions helped bond people together. Preacher John soon realized that a minor chord of hate and fear mixed into the music of love and peace would always get the audience dancing faster.

He began to think of his own possibilities, and the more he thought, the more convinced he became that he would make a good preacher. He began to read the Bible; he discovered that not only could he quote verse and chapter far more accurately than most lay preachers, but also his voice seemed to calm any doubts about his authenticity. One evening, in a Bible study group, he overcame his fears and began speaking. He quoted a Bible passage, elaborated on it, and made his point. To his amazement, his audience listened and agreed with him.

It was then that John Collins decided to become a minister. He spent much of his free time in libraries, studying religion and reviewing each of his fledgling preaching performances. He looked up various Bible colleges and institutes in library catalogues and built a resume that falsely stated that he had studied at the Prairie Bible Institute in Canada.

John Collins was ready to step full time into the world of religion. His first ministry took place in a small store he rented and remodeled in Minneapolis. His ministry lasted just over two years. He did well as a preacher but was undone because of a rapacious carnal appetite that he refused to control; he absolutely craved sex—a lot of sex. The money to pay for his excesses came, without their knowledge, from his flock. This first ministry ended unexpectedly when several of his parishioners finally insisted on inspecting the church's finances. He knew they would discover that his expenses bore no reflection on what was budgeted. He retired from his preaching career in the middle of the night. He moved to Florida, and for several months, he hid himself to study both the good and the bad details of his first ministry.

Collins had learned several things. One was to cover his private actions better. Moreover, he decided that if he had acknowledged his errors and pleaded repentance, he would have been forgiven for his sins. This was a ploy he would use repeatedly in his next ministries. Confession became good for both his soul and his checkbook.

His second ministry in Indianapolis lasted almost six years. It would have lasted longer had he and a judge's wife not been found naked in the bushes at midnight. He was aware that, with an angry judge against him, his acknowledging the errors of his ways would not be enough to save his reputation. Again, he retired after sunset and left the state of Indiana.

John Collins was thoroughly enjoying the dangers of his sexual adventures associated with his ministries and was eager to begin his third ministry. He chose Milan, Michigan, because he saw an advertisement in a real estate magazine about a large, furnished, white house for rent on the edge of town. He decided that a small city might be a better place for his ministry than a large metropolitan area. He rented the house and moved in. And this is how a religious smog descended upon Milan, Michigan.

Preacher John spent his first few days driving around his new town, familiarizing himself with its layout. He drove to every church in the city, parked his car, and attended each of their services. Like every wise businessman, he measured his competitors. He visited the public library, City Hall, and drove by all the downtown businesses and restaurants. He finished his tour by exiting and returning to Milan from all the main roads that led to the downtown area. He was, as he thought to himself, "Ready to go to war for Jesus; 'Onward, Christian Soldiers.'"

A few days later, Bruckner was standing in the Crossfire dining room after lunch when a tall man approached him; he was wearing a maroon clerical shirt and a gray suit. "Mr. Bruckner?" he asked as he raised his right hand to his shoulder as if taking an oath of office. "The Lord bless you and keep you. I want to speak with the management of this fine restaurant. You are the owner?"

"Actually, I am a co-owner with my wife. And you are?"

"My name is John Calvin Collins, although I prefer to be called Preacher John. I am starting a new ministry in Milan and I wanted to talk to you. My church is named The Evangelical Church of Christ Glorified. Here is my card."

Bruckner took the business card offered him. He read it and then asked, "Affiliated with?"

The reply was a little louder and sharper than Bruckner expected. "God and Jesus Christ together. No other religious affiliation is needed to find individual salvation."

Bruckner thought, "I guess not." Aloud, he said, "Preacher John, let's sit down and have a cup of coffee. Then, you can tell me what you want to talk about."

After they were settled, Preacher John said, "Mr. Bruckner, I expect my ministry will have a small staff and a large number of parishioners. I was wondering if the Crossfire had any policy regarding discounts to nonprofit groups?"

"Are you married, Preacher John? Do you have a family?"

"Unfortunately, the Lord has yet to bless me with a wife and a family. I am not married and I have no family."

"Let me tell you about the Crossfire and Milan," Bruckner continued. "This is a small city that is very close knit. The Crossfire continually supports community events. We give money and food to the Boy Scouts, Girl Scouts, and other nonprofit organizations. We support Milan.

"Now, whenever a new minister or pastor comes in, we offer that person and his entire family a free meal as our way of welcoming the newcomer. After their free meal, as a matter of community spirit, we offer the clergy a fifteen percent discount whenever they dine with us. That goes for every denomination and affiliation. Does that answer your question?"

"It explains your policy but I was hoping for a better discount for myself. I'm planning on building a large ministry. I will be glad to suggest that they patronize your restaurant. In return, I was hoping you would offer me free food and drink for my endorsement. You would stand to benefit financially from such a recommendation."

Bruckner was taken by surprise and he was angry. He had never heard of a business arrangement like this. Carefully controlling his temper and speech, he answered. "Preacher John, I think the largest church in our city is the Catholic church; they are a big parish. However, their priest is not given any special treatment.

"I'm not going to be put in a position of giving different preferences to different leaders of religious groups, especially individual discounts based on their size. That would not only be hard to keep track of, it would be bad for my business.

"I'm sorry, but there will be no special discounts; you will still be personally eligible for a fifteen percent discount on your own meal."

Collins looked at Bruckner thinking, "This guy is going be a tough nut to do business with. I'll have to be careful handling him." Aloud, he said, "Mr. Bruckner, Jesus and I are going to have to pray hard to get you to open your heart to your fellow human beings.

"I pray that we will someday be successful." With that, Preacher John left.

Bruckner sat at the table for a few minutes staring at Preacher John's business card. He thought, "The Evangelical Church of Christ Glorified my foot. That sounded to me more like a scam than a church."

That evening, he and Maribeth went to his mother's house for dinner. Isabel and Maribeth spent most of their time talking about family and bringing each other up-to-date on their activities. He and Henry had little chance for a private discussion. After dinner, the four of them were sitting in the living room when Bruckner remembered the business card in his shirt pocket. He took it out and handed it to Tannenbaum without saying anything. Henry read it aloud, "The Evangelical Church of Christ Glorified, what does that mean?"

Bruckner replied, "Trouble, I think." Then he explained in detail his visit from Preacher John. He finished by saying, "We weren't together very long. My personal impression is that he has a different attitude than our other religious leaders. He appears to be much more of a ringmaster than a reverend. I hope I'm wrong."

"We will see," Tannenbaum said as he handed Preacher John's business card back to Bruckner. Bruckner filed the card away when he got to his office the next day.

Time passed, the business card stayed in the file and Preacher John faded from Bruckner's memory. He heard rumors about the preacher and his church but he wasn't the slightest bit interested in religion so he didn't pay much attention to what was happening at The Evangelical Church of Christ Glorified. This same passage of time changed the family dynamics for both Bruckner and Tannenbaum. Henry Tannenbaum's marriage to Isabel Bruckner reshaped both of their lifestyles. The couple cut back on their social responsibilities to spend more time with each other. After they were married a year, they decided to be snowbirds, spending time in Florida during the cold Michigan winters.

Bill and Maribeth, were grandparents now and Bruckner spent less time at work. Both Bruckner and Tannenbaum grew apart from Sam Cutler. They were available, but they didn't look him up as often as they had in the past. Neither of them noticed that Sam was also drifting away; they assumed that his life was routine, without stress or worry.

Sam Cutler was aware that he was seeing less of his friends, but it didn't bother him. By this time, he was sure that he could run his own life. He earned his own living, had his own apartment, had his own social life. He wasn't faced with making decisions so he wasn't aware that he still needed someone to tell him what to do. He did not realize that he was still vulnerable. If a problem ever did arrive, he would stand frozen, on the ledge, waiting for someone to tell him when it was time to "Jump!"

One day, in late fall, Sam showed up at Bruckner's office. He walked in. "Hi, Bill. Haven't seen you in a while."

Bruckner was surprised, pleased to see him. "Well, look what the cat dragged in. It's been what, two months, since you came in for a free drink?"

"No. I can't go that long without a beer, so let's say a month and a half. I just thought I'd drop by and say hello. How's Maribeth and the family?"

"Very well, thank you. How are things at your bachelor pad?"

They chatted about half an hour and then Sam said, "Listen, I have a question to ask you. Six or seven guys from the Ford plant are going to go hunting next month. They rented a camp just north of Grayling and I'm going with them. Would you be interested in coming along? I know you won't hunt anything but you might like to get out in the open. We would be together; you could do the cooking and I would help clean up."

The initial thought appealed to Bruckner. He asked, "What are the dates we would go?"

"Well, we want to be there right at the start of the hunting season, November 15 until maybe November 19. Would you come along and be our cook?"

Bruckner reached for his appointment book. He looked at the schedule and shook his head. "Sam, the week of the fifteenth Maribeth and I have several medical and dental appointments we can't miss. I don't want to reschedule them so I guess I'll have to decline your invitation. I'm sorry, we haven't been together in a long time."

Cutler was also disappointed. He looked forward to spending time with his best friend and it just wasn't going to happen. However, that didn't stop him from going with his new friends. It was different from what he expected but he did have a good time. He didn't do any hunting; instead, he drank, smoked pot, and listened to his friends talk about a minister who called himself Preacher John.

The following October, Bill and Milton were sitting and discussing business in his office, when Sam entered the Crossfire and joined them. They both greeted him, and Bruckner asked, "Sam, where have you been? I haven't seen you around in months. Did you fall off the face of the earth?"

"Well, I come by once and they told me you and Maribeth was off on a trip somewhere and I ain't been back since. I've been real busy. You didn't call me so I didn't call you. The reason I came by now is to find out if you could come hunting with me like I asked you last year?"

Bruckner had completely forgotten about last year's invitation. However, he was free to go this year, if he wished. He was trying to decide when Cutler said in a wistful tone, "Bill, I need to get away and talk to you. I was hoping you'd say, 'yes' so we could get together." Bruckner was almost sure that something was bothering Sam. He felt that obligated him to help his friend. He said, "Okay, a-hunting we will go."

They discussed what arrangements were necessary and decided to go to the camp a day early to look over the facilities; with no hunters around, they would be together without any interruption. On the drive up North, the talk flowed easily. They spent the majority of their time reminiscing about Nam and their lives since then. They wiped the rust off their friendship and began to re-polish it.

The next day, their relationship changed. Sam was withdrawn and didn't talk much. They cleaned the cooking area and walked in the woods but Cutler's vocal cords seemed to be frozen; Bruckner couldn't get him to talk.

The hunters arrived and they were no longer by themselves. The pattern for the next five days was established: Bruckner cooked, Cutler cleaned up.

It turned out to be a miserable trip for Bruckner. The hunters assumed he was in camp for their convenience and rarely talked to him. He was not a hunter like they were and most of them had no reluctance in giving him orders. What bothered him more than their attitudes was their conversations; they were not worth listening to. When they were sober, they talked about hunting and sex while smoking pot; when they were drunk, they talked about sex and hunting while smoking pot. Occasionally, they talked about Preacher John. Most of them liked him, some did not.

None of that would have bothered Bruckner if Cutler hadn't changed his demeanor. He began to drink heavily with the hunters. Something was really bothering Cutler. That was the only reason Bruckner didn't just leave; he knew he had to help his friend.

On the morning of the third day, after the hunters had left for their blinds, they were alone. Bruckner asked Sam, "How did you meet Preacher John?"

"How did you know that I know him?"

"Come on, Sam. You don't have to be Sherlock Holmes to see that all of you know him."

Sam took a swig of whiskey from the bottle he carried. "Yup, I know him and that's what I wanted to talk to you about. I think my conscience is bothering me."

"How?"

Cutler took another swig from his bottle. "Well, when I'm alone and I talk with Preacher John he makes good sense to me and he makes me feel good. But, then, when he's in my apartment and I don't know what's going on, I don't feel so good."

Bruckner looked at Cutler and felt a chill. There was something missing in the conversation. "Sam, you'd better start at the beginning. This isn't making sense. How did you meet him? What's 'going on' in your apartment?"

"Well, after Henry married your mother and your kids left home, both of you stopped going to church every Sunday. Henry and Isabel started traveling and you sort of drifted away. After awhile, I stopped going to the Catholic Church.

"I was never sure of all that mumbo jumbo that went on every Sunday anyhow. How could a virgin have a baby? That kind of stuff is too deep for me and I don't care about it. I mostly went to church because Henry was good to me and he wanted me to believe in God. I tried real hard but I don't think I ever did.

"These guys in camp now are the same ones that were here last year. They're the salt of the earth, aren't they?

"Anyhow, a couple of them used to see me in church and they asked why I wasn't going anymore. When I told them my thoughts they started arguing with me. One of them started talking about Preacher John. They have opinions about everything. These guys are real deep thinkers. One of them told me he would tell Preacher John about my thoughts on religion."

"I didn't pay any attention to him. Then, one day after I got home from work, there's a knock on my door and I open it and I see Preacher John standing there. He gives me a blessing and says he wants to talk to me about my soul. He comes in and walks around my apartment and notices the spare bedroom, your old one. I remember he said, 'This would be a perfect hideaway.'

"Then he says to me, 'I understand that you are an atheist.'"

"Oh my God, Bill, you and I fought in Nam. How could he think such a thing about us? I tell him absolutely not. And then he starts to tell me about how his mission in life is to bring the love of Christ to everyone in the world that will listen. Honest to God, it sounds marvelous. I'm not sure why everyone can't have Christ's love, but those who have it are fortunate and will go to heaven. After three or four meetings with him, I'm baptized in the Evangelical Church of Christ Glorified.

"After I'm baptized, Preacher John tells me he wants me to tithe; but I don't have much money. So, instead of money, he wants me to tithe ten percent of my time fixing up his house and the church he just rented. I can do that, so I agree.

"That's when he says that there is one more condition. I ask what the other condition is and he tells me that, as a man of the cloth, he is under constant pressure. He needs a secret place to let off steam. My place would be a perfect hideaway for him and it would in no way interfere with what I do. He would use the spare bedroom occasionally and not bother me at all.

"That sounded reasonable coming from a preacher, so I said, "Okay." This is where I think my conscience is bothering me. He may be a man of the cloth who needs to let off steam but he has more steam than a parish teakettle. Sometimes, when he and a woman are in there, I think I hear crying. Once, two women came out with him. I don't want to know what's going on but, whatever it is, I'm pretty sure that it's not right." When Sam stopped speaking, he took an even bigger swig from his bottle.

Bruckner was shocked. He hadn't expected to hear anything like this. He stood up and walked around aimlessly.

Cutler asked, "Bill, you're not mad at me are you?"

"Why should I be mad, Sam?"

"Well, every time I have a big mess on my hands I seem to wind up on your doorstep."

Bruckner walked over to where Cutler was seated and put his hand on his friend's shoulder. "Bro, we were on each other's doorstep in Nam, weren't we?

"We go from there. Let me think a little."

Bill continued questioning Sam about Preacher John and his use of this hideaway. Sam told him that Preacher John only used his apartment on Thursdays. He usually arrived about dusk and shortly after, a woman would come to the apartment and join him. Maybe an hour and a half later, the woman would leave and Preacher John would go home. He only used the bedroom and the bathroom. He kept several suits in the bedroom closet. Sam never went into that bedroom, but he could see the clothes hanging in the closet from the bedroom door. He didn't know if the dresser held any clothes.

Bruckner also learned something that disturbed him even more than finding out about Preacher John's hideaway. Preacher John was supplying Sam with as much liquor and marijuana as he wanted. Sam also mentioned that Preacher John had given him vague promises of a better "candy." Bruckner was afraid for Sam. He had no idea how to help him because Sam always responded to the last person who whispered in his ear.

Bruckner tried to counsel Sam. He wanted Sam to break his relationship with Preacher John and Sam said that he'd think about it. However, Bruckner realized that when Preacher John talked to him, Sam would again change his mind. Bruckner felt helpless; there was nothing he could think of that would break Sam's reliance on Preacher John.

He returned home in a savage frame of mind. That night, as he and

Maribeth lay in bed, he held her close and told her about Sam and how frightened he was for him. Thinking their separate thoughts, both were confused and unhappy with what they believed Sam Cutler's future might be.

CHAPTER 6

Both Maribeth and Bruckner spent a miserable night. Thoughts about Sam Cutler's possible future bothered them. They would doze, have nightmares, and lie awake wrestling with terrible options. When they were awake, they thrashed in bed or paced around the house. They put their thoughts in coffins of horror and kept visitation hours all through the night.

Trying to change their moods by thinking happy thoughts didn't help; in the morning, both were tired, unhappy, and cranky. Their outlooks were heavy and unpleasant. Because of their individual relationships with Cutler, their minds wandered down entirely seperate paths.

Maribeth knew Sam first as an employee and then as a friend. Her impression of Cutler as an employee was that he was always conscientious in trying to follow her orders. He also tried to do whatever she asked him to do and she felt almost guilty asking him to correct his work. It was only after she found out that he was raised as an orphan and was a Vietnam combat veteran that she understood why he was so eager to please her.

From then on, her feelings, Christian and human, changed her attitude toward him. She believed that Sam Cutler was short changed by life; he was deprived of his share of the harvest of happiness that each person expects. He was not a strong-willed individual and had no family and very few friends to fall back on. That bothered her because it showed exactly how vulnerable he was. As a result, Maribeth was not sharp with him the few times he failed to do what she wanted.

That evening after hours of worrying about Sam, she realized her concerns wouldn't change a thing; what would be would be. Because of that, Maribeth sought relief by changing her focus.

She forced her mind to go from Sam Cutler to her favorite subjects—her husband and her marriage. On these subjects, her thoughts flowed naturally, like water in a pebbled stream. Thinking of them brought her a little peace of mind.

When they first married, Maribeth and Bill were trying to bring their restaurant back to profitability. They labored long, hard hours, working their way together through all the restaurant's problems; almost no time was spent on anything other than the business of reviving the business. Concentrating on their immediate challenges, neither of them got around to talking about anything else. She did get to know her husband as a warm, caring person; however, they never discussed anything but business. She had no idea about his attitude toward anything except work.

It was only after Maribeth was pregnant with their first child that she thought about returning to her Catholic roots and going back to church. She was pleased that Bruckner agreed to let their children go to church but she was shocked when he told her he was an atheist. She had been raised in a Polish family in a Polish community where the Catholic churches were the community lighthouses. Hamtramck considered atheists as dandelions on God's green lawn.

Maribeth was puzzled by Bill's attitude. The idea of a tolerant atheist was something she had never given any thought at all. Since their initial conversation in Point Pelee, Bruckner avoided discussing religion. She would tell him what her plans were for their children and he would agree without argument. But this did not satisfy her; she wanted to know more about why he didn't believe in God.

After starting a conversation with him a few times and not making much headway, Maribeth opted for a different approach; she decided to talk to her mother-in-law. She and Isabel had formed a strong bond when they first met. Isabel reminded Maribeth of her own mother. Not in appearance, as Maribeth's mother had been hefty, like an old-fashioned peasant woman, but in the same way they thought about life; work hard, be happy, and do what you think is right. Even before she fell in love with Isabel's son, Maribeth thought of Isabel as her second mother.

When Maribeth started working at the Crossfire, Isabel was surprised by her business sense and her intelligence; she brought a spirit of hope back to a restaurant that needed help. And, after Maribeth and Bill got together, Isabel saw how Maribeth's presence gentled her son. She grew to love her daughter-in-law. Now that she herself was remarried and had become a grandmother many times over, Isabel felt that her life was complete.

Isabel and Maribeth met often to discuss and plan every detail, from birth through college, of Maribeth's first child. It was during one of these sessions, while they were having coffee, that Maribeth said to her, "Isabel, I don't understand Bill. He admits to being an atheist, yet, he's given permission for any children we have to go to any church that I choose. He doesn't appear to be the slightest bit interested in talking about religions and their different rituals. Knowing him, he has opinions but he avoids discussing them with me. Has he always been this way?"

Isabel laughed. "Oh, he has opinions all right, but he's like his father; two subjects they never talked about were their religion and their politics. Bill believes that talking about them causes arguments because of the personal emotions associated with both of those topics.

"Henry told me that when Bill first came home from Vietnam, they talked around the subject for months before Bill got around to actually discussing religion with Henry. Once they started, they talked about it constantly; they still do."

"Does Henry say anything about their discussions?"

"All he says is that he believes that my son is one of the most intelligent atheists he has ever met."

Maribeth sat up quickly. "That's a good a description of my husband—an intelligent atheist. I didn't even know that he was an atheist until we went to Point Pelee for a weekend."

Isabel looked puzzled. "You didn't know before then?"

"I was taken by surprise; I don't think I had ever met an atheist before. Bill and I had never discussed religion and, for me, atheists were like aliens from a foreign planet. Bill is no alien and he is absolutely normal in all respects."

"He is. He just doesn't believe in God."

"Isabel, this is what surprises me the most. He is an atheist but he has standards that are as good as those of any religious person. In my younger days, if our parish priest ever heard that I was exposed to an atheist, he would have told me to read my Bible and bathe every day so that I wouldn't get infected."

Then Maribeth asked, "Does it bother you that Bill is an atheist?"

Isabel sighed before replying. "As his mother, I'm not at all pleased. I wish he believed in God. He is a good person and I hope that someday he will change his outlook. I pray for him. He cares about people but, in my opinion, he is missing the Holy Spirit."

"Do you think he will get to heaven?"

"That's an interesting question. I go back and forth on the answer. I have decided that he probably will. God loves everyone, even those who make dumb mistakes. My son is certainly not malicious and he's done much good for his community and the people he loves and works with. Isn't that really what God asks from each of us? I can see God pointing his finger at Bill for not showing more faith. However, his works and his life entitle him to a spot in heaven."

Maribeth said quietly, "I hope you are right. He certainly doesn't begin to fit my description of an atheist. Do you think that he will ever discuss his atheism with me?"

Isabel patted her daughter-in-law's hand. "My dear, I'm sure he will. He loves you too much not to tell you anything you want to know. Just be patient and Bill will come to you."

Maribeth thought about that conversation over the next few days. In the past, she considered atheism as a disease and she never thought about what atheists were like as people. To discover that her husband was one surprised her. Her observations were that nothing had changed, her husband acted the same way he had before he announced that he was an atheist. She stopped worrying about him. Her life was as comfortable as a pair of old slippers. If she was sleeping with the enemy, then, so be it. She admired and loved the enemy.

A few months later, Maribeth and Bill snuggled in bed before they went to sleep. Out of the blue, Bill casually said, "Did you know that when I was a boy, I sang in the choir at my mother's church?"

"No, I did not know that. What happened?"

"My voice changed."

Maribeth playfully slapped him. "That's not what I mean and you know it. What changed you from Charlie the Choir Boy to Anthony the Atheist?"

Bruckner rubbed his shoulder in mock agony. "I know that's not what you meant.

"Okay, let me explain. Going to church as a youngster I was taught that religion was based on peace and love. I believed that is the way it should be. Just think how much better our world would be right now if peace and love prevailed over hate and war. However, that ain't the way it is; religions seem to be based more on their formal rules and rituals than on their ideals of peace and love.

"As I grew up, I was totally disappointed with what I found out about religions. I discovered that each religion believes in one God but, their own one God is different from all the other "one Gods" of the other religions. Worse, you can't get to God unless you follow the religion of that particular God. "This doesn't make sense to me. If there is one God, why isn't peace and love available to everyone the same way oxygen is available for everybody to breathe? Look at all the fighting, hating, and bloodshed there is in the world today in the name of formal religions."

Maribeth lay quietly for a while before she said, "That's a damn grim assessment of religion. How come you feel that way but you will allow our children to be brought up in the Catholic faith?"

"Because that's only my personal feeling. There is absolutely nothing wrong with teaching a child peace and love. What other chance does humanity have? After they are grown they can make their own decisions about religion. The only people I have any problems with are those who absolutely insist that their religion is the only true religion. I don't know how they figure they are the chosen few and I'd like to know who did the choosing? I have no argument with anyone who believes in God and allows others to make their own choices; and it's true that religion helps people in times of stress. There are periods in everyone's life when they need help."

Maribeth asked, "What about you? What do you do when you need help?"

"As an atheist, I have no mechanism to fall back on when things go bad. I have to count on the love of my family and my friends. I'm totally dependent on compassion and love. That's the price I pay for my beliefs.

"Believe me, it's harder to be an atheist than it is to believe in God. Religion does give its believers a routine that helps reduce the pain inflicted by personal loss. When my father died, I had to rely on the solace of people who loved both my father and me. Believe me, I have searched my soul looking for answers to the mystery of death. I still am groping for an understanding."

Her husband paused before adding, "I would be a hypocrite if I told you that I found any answers by believing in God."

Maribeth asked, "So, you have no faith that there is a God?"

"No faith at all. I see too much misery to believe there is a loving force in charge of this cockeyed world. There were twenty-eight million people killed during World War II, hundreds of thousands of Japanese were blown to dust by atomic bombs, tsunamis wiped out tens of thousands of people whose only mistake was to be born in the wrong place. The list is endless and the torments just continue to pile up.

"I don't care about the race, the color or the creed of any of those innocents. What good comes of their catastrophes? If there is a God, or even Gods, who love peace and happiness, why can't they show us the way instead of having hidden paths? There may be a pattern to the life on our planet but it is not apparent to me. I see no orderly progression controlled by an authority higher than we human beings. Why can't we all just get along no matter what our race, creed, or culture?"

Maribeth recalled Bill's thoughts, word for word, for years after they were spoken. They reassured her that her husband, despite his wrong thoughts on religion and God, was a man filled with love. Is there any better type of human? Maribeth didn't think so. Even though she didn't agree with him, she could not say that he didn't make sense. What did matter was that her husband was an honorable man and one of God's creatures.

She was proud and happy to be his wife.

These wholesome memories helped Maribeth offset the disturbing ideas she had while thinking of Sam Cutler falling under the influence of Preacher John. They helped ease her into a few periods of calm during the night.

Bruckner had no such relief to help him. He was worried about Sam Cutler. He also felt guilty that he hadn't checked on Cutler when he didn't hear from him. He knew how weak Cutler was and how strong Preacher John was. It would be no contest; Preacher John would use

Cutler until he didn't need him anymore and then, like a saliva soaked toothpick, he would throw Cutler away. The only question in Bill's mind was whether or not he could do anything to help Sam; he wanted to prevent anything bad from happening. He thought of many schemes and scenarios but none of them seemed to be practical enough to work. Bruckner finally decided that he needed to discuss Sam's problems with his closest friends. With that, he spent a fitful night trying to get some rest.

He arose early the next morning, made a pot of coffee, poured himself a cup, and went out on the porch. He was overwhelmed by how beautiful and quiet the day was. The sun rose over the trees, the birds begin their morning chirping, and he felt miserable. Bruckner knew he was obligated to try to help his brother, Sam Cutler.

In a few minutes Maribeth, clad in a bathrobe and carrying her own cup of coffee, came out on the porch to join him. She kissed him on the top of the head. "I'll bet you had one hell of a bad night."

He squeezed her hand and nodded. "Yes, as I'm sure you did, too."

They sat together drinking their coffee, not saying a word. After the sun was completely over the horizon, Bruckner turned to Maribeth and asked, "What time is it?"

She glanced at a clock, visible in the living room. "It's almost 8:30."

"Good." He reached for the phone.

"Who are you calling?" Maribeth asked.

Bill held up a finger asking for silence. When the phone was answered on the other end, he inquired, "Henry, did I wake you up?"

He heard Henry's reply and continued, "I'm glad I didn't. Listen, the reason I'm calling so early is because Maribeth and I need to talk with you and mother as soon as we can. It's about Sam Cutler. He's in trouble, and the mess he's in explains why we've had such a hard time getting in touch with him."

There was a pause while Bill listened, then continued, "Yes, I just found out what happened during my hunting trip with him. It's not good. We have problems facing us and I really must talk with you and mother.

"How soon can you two get here?" he asked. "Good. Will you stop at the bakery and pick up some doughnuts? Maribeth likes lemon cream filled and I like plain. Thanks, we'll be waiting."

When Tannenbaum and Isabel arrived, the four of them briefly chatted about normal activities while they had their coffee and doughnuts. Then Bruckner told them, in detail, about his hunting trip with Sam Cutler and what Sam had revealed to him. By the end of the discussion all four were disgusted with Preacher John and very concerned about Sam Cutler.

They talked about what could be done to help Sam, but no conclusion was reached; they weren't sure what to do. The best they could come up with was that Bruckner and Tannenbaum would try to speak privately with Sam and get him to leave Preacher John. In the meantime,Tannenbaum and Bruckner decided to attend one of Preacher John's services to see just how he performed in public.

Preacher John was furious when he found out that Bill Bruckner and Sam Cutler had been together for five days at a hunter's camp during the hunting season. He knew the complete history between Cutler and Bruckner because Cutler crowed, like a rooster at dawn, about his past; he bragged about his friendship with Bruckner. Sam Cutler was a non-stop radio broadcast describing, in detail, how they met each other in Vietnam and stayed friends all these years. Preacher John was sure that Cutler told Bruckner about the relationship between the two of them. This bothered Preacher John because his hideaway, and his gymnastics within his hideaway, were his special reward for bringing Jesus to his flock.

He had found an expensive pimp in Ann Arbor who delivered girls to him and he did not want this delightful service interrupted. Preacher John's hideaway was his most treasured stroke of good luck. Only he and Sam Cutler knew it existed, and he thought he kept Cutler isolated enough to keep it a secret. Supplying Cutler with all the liquor and marijuana he could use was Preacher John's way of keeping him quiet.

Preacher John assumed that Cutler told Bruckner about his secret and that did not please him. He would go to any length to conceal his hideaway diversions. He needed to know what Cutler and Bruckner had talked about at camp. In an attempt to find out what had been, he questioned those hunters who were members of his church. They couldn't give him much information because none of the hunters heard any of the discussions between Bruckner and Cutler. That reassured him to some degree; at least information about his hideaway was not public. However, he needed Cutler to keep his mouth shut. Preacher John would have to do something more drastic to keep him quiet. He didn't want anyone finding out about his secret. He would protect it at any cost. He had worked too long and too hard to give up his sweet treat.

The truth was that Preacher John himself was surprised at the success he was having with this third ministry—The Evangelical Church of Christ Glorified. Before he started this latest ministry, he reviewed every mistake he made in the first two ministries and then worked out a system to camouflage them. His bookkeeping became more inventive, and his sexual cravings, even though they were becoming larger, became more secretive. His new approaches to protect his secrets only hid his appetites, they certainly did not diminish them.

He also decided to display his strengths more openly. He knew that even though he could quote scripture, he was not a religious scholar. However, his marvelous speaking voice, along with his personal charm and his charismatic manner, soothed peoples' fears and anxieties. His sermons were his strong point. He concentrated on making them even more personal for his parishioners.

Preacher John taught himself to better deliver his sermons than he had in the past. Fear was still his main motivator but he no longer blatantly pronounced it; instead, he subtly implied it. He divided his sermons into four parts. The first part he thought of as, "The Benediction." When he started speaking he would bless everybody that came to see and hear him. He used individual names and specific reasons why he thought they were blessed. He wanted everyone to feel good about themselves, the world around them, and, specifically, the person blessing them, namely Preacher John.

The second part of his sermon he called, "The Damnation." His subject would either be individual sins from the Bible or social sins from society. He was not reluctant in his warnings about any of the seven deadly sins, religions that didn't believe in Jesus, non-English speaking minorities, gay and lesbian rights, or whatever else was on his mind as he began his sermon. This is where Preacher John wanted to improve the most because he wanted to singe his flock but not cremate them. He needed them warm for the third part of his sermon.

This part he referred to as "The Call." He would tell his congregation how he, Preacher John, had been inflicted by the same sin he just described. He would then tell them how Jesus Christ had saved him and that this path was open to anyone who would accept Him into their lives. He elaborated on how Jesus blocked off the path of damnation and opened the road to salvation. This was where Preacher John was at his best. He was moving, eloquent, and sincere.

His parishioners would be fired up, ready and eager for the fourth part of the sermon, "The Redemption." Preacher John would invite anyone who wanted to change their lifestyle to come forward and receive the Blessings of Our Lord and Saviour Jesus Christ. And they did. There would be a surge of people who truly felt a need to repent and start a better life. That they would also fill the coffers of The Evangelical Church of Christ Glorified was incidental to them, but not to Preacher John.

His ministry succeeded. He took over a small, abandoned church on

Stoney Creek Road and everything was going smoothly until Sam Cutler and Bill Bruckner went on the deer hunting trip.

Preacher John decided to make sure that his personal rewards for helping others to see their sins would not be interrupted. With this in mind, he called his pimp and spent a long time talking with him. Afterward, he hung the phone up, smiling to himself over the insurance policy he had just selected. Absolutely no one was going to interfere with his ministry.

After the morning meeting when they discussed Cutler's problems, Maribeth and Isabel did not see or speak to each other the rest of that week. They were both busy running their individual routines. They did meet the following Friday, the day that their bridge club normally gathered to play cards. The 1:15 Club, as they called themselves, was made up of ladies who loved bridge and were excellent players. They were cutthroat competitors during the game and staunch friends afterward. The other two regular partners, Jane Squires and Matilda Preston, were in their late sixties. Both of them had been teachers in the public school system for forty years and they knew almost everything about almost everyone in Milan. They met every Friday afternoon at 1:15 and they played and talked until close to 5:00 P.M. The ladies were more dedicated to their Friday bridge playing than they were to their Sunday church going. As individuals, they would occasionally skip church; as a group, they never missed a deck shuffling. Only unusual personal difficulties ever interrupted their Friday get togethers.

Friday was their first opportunity to talk; Maribeth and Isabel immediately began to express their feelings about Cutler and Preacher John over coffee. Their conversation instantly caught the attention of the others who had heard nothing about the relationship between Sam and Preacher John. Maribeth and Isabel found themselves explaining the entire situation to Jane and Matilda. This delayed the start of the bridge game and that alone was a rarity. After each hand, Maribeth and Isabel continued answering more questions and giving more specifics on the backgrounds of Preacher John and Sam Cutler.

Matilda didn't say much until they were almost finished playing. As they were ready to tally up the score, she asked, "Aren't we ladies going to try to help this unfortunate person?"

The three other women looked at her. Matilda added, "Isabel, you said that Bill and Henry are going to attend one of Preacher John's services and talk to Cutler. That's good because I don't want to have anything to do with that Preacher John. At the same time, we should be doing something to try to help Sam Cutler."

Jane looked at her quizzically and asked, "Well, what would that be?"

"I don't know yet but I think we should do something for this poor man. He's a veteran who is stuck in the middle. We just can't let him twist in the wind. We have to do something out of conscience's sake.

"Maribeth, didn't you say that Preacher John is on the prowl most every Thursday?"

"Yes, Cutler said that he arrives about dusk and he leaves sometime after dark."

Matilda replied, "Well, that's all we know so far. That's probably a good place to start."

Jane shook her head from side to side. "Start what?"

"Why, to start to collect information, that's what."

Jane asked another question, "What information do we collect and what do we do with it if we collect it? I can't see anyone at this table who is either a Sam Spade or a Miss Marple."

Matilda sighed, "Jane, you're getting snippy. As an ex-teacher you should know that sometimes you don't realize the value of information until you finish collecting it.

"I suggest we watch and see if we can figure out Preacher John's patterns of coming and going to learn everything we can about him and the ladies he associates with. That certainly is better than doing nothing while this hypocrite runs amok. I absolutely resent bad people taking advantage of good people and I want to do something about that."

All four women joined in with suggestions of what they might do. After a lively discussion, sometimes with more than one person talking at the same time, a consensus was reached. When each of them finished expressing their ideas, Isabel made the final summation. "Here's what we're going to do. We have been talking about going out to eat, as a group, for quite awhile. So, next Thursday, we will; we will meet at the Milan Grill just before dark. We'll see if we're able to learn anything about Preacher John by just watching. That's all we will do, just watch.

"Does everyone agree with that?"

There was no dissent or disagreement from any of the others. The members of the 1:15 Club were looking forward to playing detective.

The next Thursday, four very nervous ladies appeared at the Milan Grill an hour before the dinner crowd straggled in. They selected a table that looked out on Main Street. The Milan bakery and the front entrance to Cutler's apartment on the second floor were clearly visible. They sat down and suspiciously eyed the few customers already there. Each of the four ladies was sure that everyone sitting at the bar knew what they were up to. They sat quietly, fidgeting with their purses and sizing up every newcomer who came through the door. Each of them was as close to exploding as a kernel of corn in a hot kettle. When the waitress brought menus, they sat in complete silence.

After a few minutes of pointless small talk, they admitted that they were earlier than they needed to be and they decided to have a drink. They told the waitress they would order food later and, in the meantime, to please bring four large Margaritas. Sipping their drinks was relaxing and they soon ordered another round. By the time they finished the second Margaritas, they began to enjoy their newfound private investigation profession. Jane took a stenographer's pad out of her huge pocket book and announced she was ready to write down any information or description given her. Matilda told her to "Hush," and to put that thing back in her purse.

As the restaurant filled for dinner and their table became less and less conspicuous, the ladies became increasingly comfortable. They ordered their food and ate slowly. While they were eating, Jane suddenly dropped her fork and repeatedly pointed her finger at the window. Across the street they saw Preacher John slowly walking down Main Street, heading toward the Milan bakery. When he reached the front entrance to the second floor apartments, he quickly stepped inside. Within a minute, a light was turned on in the window of Sam Cutler's apartment.

The ladies were so pleased with their vigilance that they failed to notice, a few minutes later, a black car stopped in front of the bakery and a young woman getting out of it. The car drove away. It was only after the young woman stepped into the entranceway to the apartments that they realized they had missed an important piece of their puzzle. They finished their meal, payed individually, tipped frugally, and went home.

The next day, their usual 1:15 Club bridge date, the four private investigators reviewed their performance as they played cards. They decided that, for a first-time surveillance, it wasn't a bad effort. However, they must do better if they were going to collect anything significant.

And they did do better. Over the next few months they began to figure out Preacher John's patterns. They found where he parked his car on Main Street to walk to Cutler's apartment, and what time he left the apartment to return to his vehicle. They discovered that Preacher John was punctual and he always arrived about five minutes before 6:00 PM for his assignation. A black car would pull up about ten minutes after he arrived at the apartment and a young woman would leave the car and go up to the apartment. Some time later, the black car would return, the same woman would leave the building and get into the car. Preacher John would leave shortly after the black car drove away. They even began to recognize the two or three women who serviced Preacher John.

When they were sure of this pattern, Matilda played what she called, her "ace in the hole." She had a nephew, Arny Matusak, whom she dearly loved; he was a reporter for *The Ann Arbor News*. He was tall enough to be a basketball player and thin enough to be a knitting needle; he had a shock of red hair, ears that stuck out, and a grin that wouldn't wash off. She wouldn't admit it, but he was her favorite relative. She had previously contacted him about writing a story on Preacher John, a minister who had an illicit love nest. At the time, he said that the story may be worth pursuing but he would need a lot more information about what was going on, including the background of these ladies who visited Preacher John. With some of the tryst facts now available, Matilda again contacted him and he came to Milan to meet with her and her sister detectives. After listening to them, he told them that he still needed to know more before he could even approach his editor to write an article about Preacher John. However, he did offer to help them gather more background information because it might lead to an exclusive story. He figured that not only would it help his favorite aunt, he could also be advancing his own career.

With a telescopic lens, he shot pictures of Preacher John, the women he met, the license plate of the car, and the driver. He traced the owner of the car to a man who owned an escort service; the man had a long criminal record.

Armed with a story outline, Arny Matusak went to see his editor to ask permission to write an article about Preacher John. After listening and asking many questions, his editor told him there was merit to the story but that there was more innuendo than there was fact. *The Ann Arbor News* could face a lawsuit if they published an article based solely on the information that Arny had presented to him. However, his editor told him to continue digging and not be discouraged; there could be a juicy story if Arny could get solid details.

When Arny broke the news that his editor wouldn't allow him to pursue the story, the ladies of the 1:15 Club were bitterly disappointed. They felt that the work they had done and their newly acquired skills added up to nothing. They hadn't accomplished their goal to help Sam Cutler. They thought that this was the end of their adventure. It was over.

When Matusak left the ladies of the 1:15 Club, Matilda privately thanked her nephew for his help, even if his editor wouldn't let him continue. He surprised her by giving her a hug and a single red rose. She was pleased and touched by his thoughtfulness.

Although the 1:15 Club didn't accomplish what it set out to do, they did set a pattern to continue meeting at the Milan Grill because they enjoyed each others' company. Every Thursday became "girl's night," and it became as important as their Friday bridge game. They eventually were successful; the new dinner meeting of the 1:15 Club was instrumental in finally bringing Preacher John to justice.

While the 1:15 Club was organizing itself into a detective agency, Tannenbaum and Bruckner went ahead with their plan to talk to Sam Cutler. At first, they waited. They hoped that he would come into the Crossfire as a customer and then they would be able to talk with him. After he arrived home from the hunting trip, Cutler disappeared. They were not able get in touch with him. It wasn't because they didn't try. After he didn't show up at the Crossfire, they called Sam at his apartment; when no one answered, they left messages on his answering machine. No calls were returned. Because the machine did allow them to leave messages, Tannenbaum and Bruckner concluded that someone must be listening to their recorded messages and deleting them. Otherwise, the machine would be full and could not accept any new messages.

Their next attempt to reach Cutler was to go to his apartment and leave a note, asking him to call them. This also brought no response. They canvassed the bars where he usually could be found. They couldn't find him. It was as if Sam had walked into a fog bank and then separated into wisps of smoke. After weeks of trying, they decided to carry out their original plan; they would attend a service at the Evangelical Church of Christ Glorified. They would be able to watch Preacher John conduct his service and, possibly, they could make direct contact with Sam and talk to him.

One Sunday morning, Bruckner and Tannenbaum drove to Preacher John's church. It was a plain, one-story building set back from the road with a large asphalt parking lot in front. It was originally built for a restaurant but several businesses had opened and closed before Preacher John found it empty and available for his ministry. Tannenbaum and Bruckner arrived early because they wanted to see everything that went on. There were very few parked cars when they arrived so they sat in their vehicle and waited for more people to show up. They noticed that the majority of the people who came to the church were young couples with small children.

When the parking lot was about half full, they got out of their car and entered the church. They were met by an usher who said, "Good Morning, and peace be with you, Brothers." Bruckner was behind Tannenbaum and could not see the man who greeted them. When he was able to see the greeter he was surprised to recognize one of the hunters who had been at camp with him and Cutler. Bruckner couldn't remember his name but he did recall that he was one of the more pleasant hunters.

The usher remembered his name. "Good Morning, Mr. Bruckner. I'm Elijah Thomas; we met during this last deer hunting season. You and Sam Cutler cooked for us.

"I'm glad you are here for our morning service."

Bruckner, hearing Cutler's name, decided that he had been given an opportunity to find out about his friend. He replied, "Oh, yes, I remember you at the camp. Sam asked me to help him do the cooking and I couldn't refuse. We have known each other for many, many years.

"Will he be at today's service?"

Thomas answered, "Oh, yes. He is Preacher John's right hand man. He lives at the church here and is responsible for its upkeep and maintenance. He works real close with Preacher John."

Bruckner was quick to pick up on what Thomas had said. He thought, "He lives here? No wonder we couldn't reach him at his apartment. Did he ever get the phone calls and messages we left?" Aloud, he asked, "How long has he been living at the church?"

"Let me see. He moved in shortly after we got back from hunting, so that would be what, over half a year ago? That's as close as I can get." With that, Thomas left Bruckner and Tannenbaum to resume his ushering duties.

They sat and watched as the church filled and the service began. When the Processional entered, they turned in their seats to watch Preacher John come down the central aisle. He wore an alb with a green sash around his waist. Behind him, in a red robe, was Sam Cutler. Bruckner studied Cutler and was puzzled at his appearance. Cutler's face looked puffy and Bruckner thought that maybe his hands were trembling. Bruckner closely watched only Sam Cutler and Preacher John throughout the entire service.

The service was plain. There was the Call to Worship, the Call to Confession, the Gospel and New Testament Lessons, and the Sermon. It was the sermon that brought the congregation to life. Preacher John had spent years developing his techniques for giving sermons and he was very good at it. He walked slowly down the aisles as he spoke, sometimes putting his hand on the shoulder of an individual parishioner. That brought him closer to his flock. His baritone speech was pleasant to hear and he projected it without raising his voice or shouting. He made it a point to place his hand on Bruckner's shoulder, patting it a few times, squeezing it lightly. He wanted to let Bruckner know that he, Preacher John, was aware that he was in attendance at his church. He announced the subject of his sermon and then slowly wove his audience into his web. As he captured them, his tempo and tone picked up and, midway through his homily, voices began to respond to his words with "Hallelujah," or "Right on Brother."

The exhilaration continued and Preacher John became more passionate. He expressed his guilt, his love of Jesus, and he began to exhort his flock to show their love. The reaction was more verbal responses and the clapping of hands. At the end, when he talked about donating and tithing, his parishioners were at a fever pitch. Dollars appeared where dimes had been planned. Preacher John's sermons had cleansed souls and emptied wallets.

Bruckner and Tannenbaum knew they had witnessed an amazing performance. They shook their heads and each put a twenty dollar bill in the collection plate. The service ended, they walked up the aisle and saw Preacher John standing at the back of the church. He was greeting his parishioners as they left. When they finally reached Preacher John, he put out his right hand to shake their hands. He said, "Peace be with you my brothers. I'm happy to see you at our Evangelical Church of Christ Glorified. Perhaps you will consider becoming members."

Bruckner replied only with the word, "Perhaps."

Preacher John waited a second before he began again, "You probably would like to talk with my assistant, Brother Cutler. Right now, he's doing important work for the church, he's counting the offering we received this morning. However, if you want to wait in my office over there," as he pointed to a door with his name on it, "when he is finished, you can talk to him privately."

Without saying anything, Bruckner and Tannenbaum walked into Preacher John's office. Within ten minutes, Sam Cutler opened the door and slowly shuffled into the room. He had removed his red robe and he was wearing a white tee shirt and blue jeans. He stood in front of Bruckner and Tannenbaum waiting for them to speak. Cutler's hesitancy in greeting his two oldest friends did not bode well.

Bruckner studied Cutler. He was a little thinner than he remembered and his face was definitely puffy. What bothered Bruckner was that Cutler had a nervous tic on the left side of his face. "Sam, where have you been the last couple of weeks? Henry and I have been trying to find you. How are you doing?"

"I'm doing okay; I moved here a while back. Preacher John needs me at the church, to keep it up. It's a lot of work making sure this place is neat and clean. I guess I moved so fast that I didn't have a chance to call you."

Bruckner replied, "We were concerned when we didn't hear from you. The last time you and I talked, you were having doubts about Preacher John."

Cutler waved his hand and said, "Aw, Bill, that's all been settled. There's nothing to be concerned about. Preacher John and I talked things over and we resolved all our problems. We're both on the path to salvation and he's supplying me with everything I need."

Tannenbaum was alarmed at what Cutler said; he immediately wanted to know what Preacher John was "supplying." He asked, "Sam, what are you getting from Preacher John?"

"Why, the love of Jesus Christ.

"He admitted that he had been screwing around when we talked and he told me to pray with him and he would give it up. And he has. He's no longer a sinner and my helping him has been part of his change.

"So, I was happy to leave my apartment and live at the church. I keep it clean and neat so that Preacher John can carry on with his work."

Bruckner asked, "What's going to happen to the apartment?"

"Preacher John isn't sure. He may use it as a downtown office or he may let it go."

Tannenbaum was skeptical. "Are you sure that he didn't move you to this church to get you out of the apartment? With you gone, no one will know what he's doing. He now has a meeting place for his own private affairs. He could still be having his hot sex parties there and they would be completely secret."

For the first time, Sam Cutler showed emotion in his voice. He sounded angry as he answered, "What a terrible thing to say, Henry. Listen, he confessed to me that in the past he had screwed as many women as he could get to fuck him. He admitted that he was a sinner and that he was going to repent. He and I prayed to Jesus for forgiveness and we both felt the Holy Spirit. Preacher John is a man of the cloth and he should be respected."

Tannenbaum and Bruckner looked at each other. That was the moment that they realized there was no way that they were going to lure Cutler away from Preacher John. Whatever his hold on Cutler, it was stronger than their past friendships. Cutler belonged to Preacher John because he was there to influence Sam Cutler every day. He had the inside track. Tannenbaum and Bruckner were both on the outside.

The three of them chatted about nothing for a few more minutes before Bruckner and Tannenbaum left the room. They walked past a smirking Preacher John and returned to their car. The pain, the frustration, the uselessness of the situation hit them hard as they drove home.

Tannenbaum asked Bruckner, "Is he on drugs?"

"Yes, and I'll bet that bastard purposely got him hooked. Now he has Sam living at the church. He doesn't have to worry about Sam's conscience and he has control of Sam's apartment. He has his own private whorehouse whenever his dipstick gets dry."

Tannenbaum asked, "You are mad, aren't you?"

"Goddam right I am. I am furious. Henry, Sam and I have been friends since we were teenagers in the army That was over forty years ago. We lived through Nam together. All Sam ever wanted was to please people. He would do anything to make you like him.

"He's been taken advantage of by someone who doesn't give a damn about him. I have lost my little brother. Yes, I'm very upset. Aren't you?"

Tannenbaum didn't answer right away. Then he said, "Yes, I'm angry, too. You've known Sam for many years longer than I have. You're absolutely right about him. All he has ever wanted was to have people like him. He was a Catholic for me and an atheist for you and a flunky for Preacher John. He wasn't being hypocritical, he just wanted to accommodate the people he was with.

"Preacher John has to be sick. Why else would he introduce Sam to drugs? That bastard gives you atheists a good name."

Bruckner snorted, "You may be right but that's no consolation to me. I hate that son of a bitch." They both choked up emotionally, closed up vocally, and were wrapped in negativity all the way home.

CHAPTER 7

Preacher John was happy, he was elated, he was terribly proud of himself. His plan had worked. Sam Cutler was going to stay with him and do his bidding. His hideaway and his luscious extra parish activities were in no danger. He was safe.

He initially had some concerns when Tannenbaum and Bruckner met with Cutler in his office. He wasn't sure whether or not Cutler's old friends would be able to persuade him to leave and go with them. He stared at the door to his office until it opened and Sam's friends came out. The grim looks on their faces pleased him immediately. He watched as they left the building and got into their car. Preacher John was convinced that he had won.

He went striding into his office where Cutler was quietly sitting in a chair. Preacher John innocently asked, "Sam, did you have a good visit with your friends?"

"Oh yeah, we've known each other for years. They're the best friends I've ever had."

"What did they want to see you about?"

"Nothing really. They hadn't talked to me in awhile. They didn't know that I moved here. They just wanted to know how I was doing. They're real friends. I just wish they would join your church."

Preacher John replied, "So do I."

Then, Preacher John sat for a second and gloated over the idea that he had beaten them. Cutler was staying with him and he had complete control of his hideaway. He was so pleased that he unlocked a drawer, for which only he had a key, and picked out several small packets. "Sam, you certainly have been working extra hard. You deserve a reward for your efforts. Here's some extra 'candy' for you."

Sam eagerly reached for the cocaine packets. His life seemed to be focused on the handouts that were provided to him. "Thank you, Preacher John," was all he could say. He left immediately to immerse himself inside a drug induced Utopia. Nothing mattered to him more than booze and drugs. His life was disappearing into a drug filled fantasy world.

After Cutler left with his reward, Preacher John sat at his desk congratulating himself on his success. He had risen from a nobody to a somebody to whom people payed attention. He had a life that most people could never achieve and he had earned respect. Life was good and his rewards were richly deserved. Preacher John was truly satisfied with himself.

However, like every other man-made heaven, Preacher John's bliss didn't last. It began to change shape and, as it did, it developed a leak. Reality seeped in, slowly at first, and then in torrents. Preacher John found himself manning the pumps of perjury in his attempt to keep his hideaway sex parlor afloat and secret.

His troubles unknowingly began when, some months before, he had cold bloodily decided to introduce Sam Cutler to drugs. He reasoned that if Sam, a meek and timid person, became dependent on him, he would be even more subservient. That would keep Cutler from revealing Preacher John's secrets. Preacher John never considered the morality of ruining someone's life. His only concern was the enjoyment of his illicit pleasures.

It was easy enough for Preacher John to get Cutler hooked. At first, he had Sam smoke some crack cocaine that he bought from his pimp. Once Cutler became addicted, he switched to packets. For Preacher John, it was a painless procedure and it made Sam Cutler dependent upon him.

Only after Cutler was addicted did it dawn on him that if Cutler didn't live in his apartment, he would not know anything about Preacher John's evening trysts. Once he thought about this, it became his goal; he would move Cutler out and take complete control of the apartment. Preacher John had a small flat built in the cellar of his church. He flattered Cutler by telling him he was very necessary in keeping up the church maintenance and he persuaded Cutler to move into the new basement apartment. Preacher John ended up in control of both Cutler and Cutler's old apartment.

The only thing wrong with Preacher John's plan was that it didn't work. He hadn't taken into account that other people also act in their own interests, and that conflicts exist even between allies. He was surprised when his simple goals became difficult to reach because of the reactions of the very people necessary for the success of his plan.

His first surprise was Cutler's reaction to his addiction. It was easy for Preacher John to introduce Cutler to drugs but he hadn't considered the consequences. Cutler was more dependent upon him as his supplier of course, but as his addiction grew his craving for snorting coke now consumed him. In the beginning, when the effects of the drug and liquor wore off, Cutler was irritable. When Cutler became more obsessed with the need for cocaine, irritability was replaced with anger and veiled threats aimed at Preacher John. Preacher John understood that the easiest way to deal with the cocaine monster he created was to feed it; he let Cutler have as much coke as he wanted. Preacher John also believed that frugality was an important virtue and supplying drugs was proving to be an expensive proposition. He realized he had a situation that he needed to fix.

His second surprise was the attitude of his pimp. Preacher John had turned to him for drugs because he knew that he supplied them, as well as call girls. He originally thought that his pimp would be a convenient source for both, something like one-stop shopping. This would keep him from dealing with a host of sleazy characters. Preacher John overlooked the fact that his pimp was one of the worst of these characters.

At first, Sam didn't need too many fixes; however, as Cutler's addiction grew, Preacher John had to buy increasingly more cocaine. His pimp raised the price of the drug almost every time he made a purchase. Fortunately, there was not a corresponding increase in the price of his girls. Preacher John decided that his pimp was blackmailing him. He was convinced that the pimp's other drug customers were not forced to pay such high prices. He also thought that, if he wasn't a man of the cloth, his pimp wouldn't dare to charge him so much. The idea of a pimp fleecing a priest rankled him. Preacher John believed that his pimp was not treating him honestly. He didn't like dishonesty. This became a situation that he had to resolve.

Preacher John also worried that this pimp had the capability of blackmailing him. He didn't like the thought of such an unsavory person being in a position to extort him. He vowed to resolve this trouble before it got worse. Preacher John would find another drug dealer, one that didn't know what his profession was. He first went to a thrift shop and bought two pairs of secondhand blue jeans and several shirts and sweaters. Wearing these nondescript clothes he began to loiter around the bars in Ann Arbor, listening to private conversations and trying to find the names of other drug dealers. He was looking for a dealer that he could buy from without revealing any details of his personal life. Privacy and trust were essential for Preacher John. He watched several drug dealers in action, but he didn't feel comfortable approaching them.

He finally found a dealer he thought he could buy from in a small bar in nearby Ypsilanti. His business name was Benny the Bear, a large black man who looked more like a professional football player than a drug dealer. He stood six feet six and must have weighed over three hundred pounds, and not much of that weight was excess. He was clean shaven, from the top of his head to beneath his chin. Preacher John assumed that Benny the Bear's business name was because of his size. Benny was quiet with a sense of humor; Preacher John thought that this was a drug dealer with whom he could do business.

After watching Benny conduct business, Preacher John approached him and discovered that his prices were lower than those of his pimp. He bought one or two fixes from Benny and monitored Cutler closely to see how he reacted to his new source. No matter the source, the effect of the drugs on Cutler was the same.

Preacher John felt as if he had busted a cartel. He bought a week's supply of coke and thought he got a bargain. He was sure that he was not only a smart businessman but that he was getting a handle on his problems.

The morning after his large buy, Preacher John had his usual meeting with Cutler. He told Cutler what needed to be done that day, then gave Cutler a few extra packets as a bonus for finding a cheaper source of drugs. Cutler was pleased and grateful that his boss thought so highly of him.

Preacher John left his church to make calls on several parishioners. He came back just after noon, walked toward his office and noticed Cutler sitting in a pew at the front of the church. He walked down the aisle to talk with him. When he drew abreast of Cutler, he was shocked at his condition. Cutler had dried blood under one of his nostrils and his shirt was stained with blood. He was hunched over and trembling. He looked up at Preacher John and said, "I don't feel so good."

Preacher John sat down by Cutler and asked, "How long have you been feeling like this?"

"I don't know. I have a headache and I have a pain over here." He pointed to his chest. "What should I do Preacher John?"

"Sam, go downstairs and lie down for awhile. That should make you feel better."

After Cutler left, Preacher John went into his office and looked in his personal phone book; he pulled out a slip of paper on which was written three phone numbers. He dialed one of the numbers; it was answered on the fifth ring.

"Hello."

Preacher John asked, "Who am I talking with?"

The answer came in a gravelly voice that he recognized immediately; it was Benny the Bear. "You are talking with the person who owns this cellphone. What can I do for you?"

Preacher John was taken aback. Evidently, Benny didn't want to identify himself over the phone. Maybe he thought the police were listening. He decided to be just as cautious as Benny; he asked, "Do you know who this is?"

"Yeh, I recognize your voice. I saw you last night. What can I do for ya?"

Preacher John hesitated before replying; he wasn't sure how much detail to go into, especially if the conversation was bugged. He wanted to be vague but still convey his message. "This morning a friend of mine tried some of my stuff and now he isn't feeling well."

There was silence on the line; it lasted so long that Preacher John asked, "Hello, did you hear me?"

The answer came from the same voice in the same volume but the tone was much different. What little pleasantness there had been was gone, replaced by hardness and anger. Preacher John suddenly understood why his new supplier was called Benny the Bear. He said, "What the fuck makes you think this is the emergency room?"

Flustered by Benny's response, he replied, "I'm sorry. I'm not accusing you of anything. I just wanted to find out if anyone else mentioned that they were having problems."

The reply was a little less angry but still not pleasant. "This ain't a hospital and I ain't a doctor and I don't have a medical bulletin board. Nobody else has called in sick. Listen, if you have a friend who is not feeling good, take him to the hospital. Don't call me." With that, Benny abruptly hung up.

Preacher John had not expected to be cut short with such hostility. After he thought about it, he could see why Benny the Bear got upset. His product was being questioned by a new customer and this could be a touchy problem between the two of them. A dissatisfied customer could always turn his dealer into the police. He should have driven to Ypsilanti and talked to Benny face-to-face. Now, it was too late; he would have to talk with Benny after the Bear cooled down.

Later that afternoon, Preacher John went downstairs to see how Cutler was doing. He tapped on the door to Cutler's and got no response. He rapped harder. Finally, he heard Cutler say, in a weak voice, "Come in."

He found the apartment in a mess, as if it had been ransacked. Two kitchen chairs were overturned, the sofa pillows were thrown on the floor, and a table lamp was knocked over. Cutler was slumped in an arm chair still wearing his bloody shirt. He was spread eagled in the overstuffed chair with his legs straight in front of him. He looked miserable and he was trembling. The left side of his face was in a constant twitch. What alarmed Preacher John was the drug scene pictured in the flat. In front of Cutler was a coffee table with a large facial mirror. There was a small line, about an inch of white powder on the mirror, and on the floor, just under the table, was a short plastic drinking straw.

Preacher John's first thought was, "Shit. If an ambulance comes here, and they see this, the cops will get involved. I've got to get this mess completely cleaned up." He was angry with Cutler. He curtly said,

"I thought I told you to lie down. Why didn't you do as I said instead of snorting another fix?"

Cutler pleaded, "Preacher John, please don't be mad at me. I did try to lay down but everything is going wrong. I ache and I'm sweating and I got scared. I thought another fix would help but I feel so funny. I've never felt like this before. I'm scared."

Preacher John relented, a little. "Well, let's see if we can get you feeling better." He looked around to see how he could straighten out the room to hide the telltale signs of drug use. It wouldn't take too long if he could get Cutler out of the way.

He thought for a second and then said, "Sam, I think the first thing we should do is move you out of here so we can get your place cleaned up."

Cutler pleaded, "Preacher John, I don't want to leave my little apartment. I like it here and I really don't feel good. Wouldn't it be okay for me to stay?"

"Sam, You won't be gone for long. I have a youth group coming into the church soon and they'll be noisy and disturb you. You need to rest. If you move back into your old apartment for a day or two it will be quiet and you can recover without any disturbance. It's really in your best interest."

Cutler was in no condition to argue or protest; he meekly accepted Preacher John's decision. It was almost dark when Cutler was driven to the back of the Main street apartment by Preacher John. He supported Cutler as he climbed the back stairs to the second floor. Preacher John got him undressed and into bed. Then, he asked, "Sam, you don't have any more of the 'candy' I gave you this morning with you, do you?"

Sam lied when he answered, "Oh no, Preacher John."

"Good. Until you're feeling better, you better lay off it. I'll call you first thing in the morning to see how you're feeling and if you need anything. Right now, get yourself a good night's sleep."

Preacher John waited until Cutler was settled and then he left to clean up the apartment at the church. He really didn't have a youth group meeting; he wanted private access to the church apartment. Any trace of drugs had to be hidden so that he could not be implicated in any way. It took two hours of hard work to straighten up the furniture, dispose of incriminating items and wash everything that might have been touched. When Preacher John finished, the apartment was clean enough to rent. He drove the trash to a public dumpster and threw out four plastic bags. As he drove home, he believed that he had masked all traces of drugs in Cutler's church apartment. Preacher John was free and clear of any responsibiity.

The next morning he called Cutler at the Main Street apartment. The phone rang but Cutler did not answer. Preacher John figured that he was in a deep sleep. He tried half an hour later and with the same result; Cutler did not answer the phone. He began to get edgy; he didn't like the idea that Cutler was not picking up the phone. Something could be wrong. After another failed attempt to get a response, Preacher John just sat there, deciding what next to do. He would contact someone he could trust to go to the apartment and check on Cutler. He remembered that Elijah Thomas knew Sam Cutler and that he had been at camp the time Bruckner had cooked. Thomas worked as an auto mechanic, close to the apartment. He would be the perfect person to help Preacher John find out what was going on.

He dialed the number for Schultz Motors and asked to speak to Elijah Thomas. When he had Thomas on the line, he said, "Brother Elijah, this is Preacher John. How are you this fine morning?"

"Preacher John? Why I'm fine, sir. This is a surprise. What can I do for you?"

"Brother Elijah, I'm having a little problem and I need your help. Brother Sam decided to sleep at his old apartment last night because he wasn't feeling well and he wanted to be by himself. I tried to check on him this morning and he isn't answering his phone. You're the closest parishioner to him, only a few blocks away. Could you drop by and see how Brother Sam is doing?"

There was a pause before Thomas replied, "Preacher John, I can do that but it will be awhile before I can leave. I'm working on a car for a lady who has to pick up her kids. I'll check on Sam as soon as I finish repairing her vehicle.

"But how will I get into the apartment if I have to?"

"Easy enough. As you face the door, run your hand over the top of the door jamb. There is a spare key that we keep there. It is on the left side.

"When you talk to Brother Sam, please tell him to contact me immediately. I am concerned about his well being."

The morning passed and Preacher John kept busy with his normal routine. He talked on the phone with his parishioners and wrote one or two letters. He also tried calling Cutler several times without getting any response. The phone usually never rang more than twice before Cutler answered. The longer Preacher John didn't hear from Brother Elijah the more concerned he became. He thought of again calling Brother Elijah but decided against it; he didn't want anyone to know he was getting worried.

It was early afternoon when he got the call he had silently been telling his phone to receive. He answered the ring immediately, expecting Brother Elijah to speak. The line was silent.

He said loudly, "Hello." Still no response.

He almost lost control. Again, and louder, he said, "Hello!"

Brother Elijah stuttered, "H-h-he's d-d-dead!"

"What?"

Brother Elijah screamed, "H-HE'S DEAD, Oh God, Preacher John, Sam Cutler is dead, dead, dead."

"Damn it, are you sure?"

"Yes, I'm sure. He's sitting in front of me not breathing or moving."

Preacher John understood what Brother Elijah was saying, but he didn't want to believe it. He asked, "When did you get there?"

"Just a few minutes ago. It took longer to fix the customer's car than I expected."

"Then what?"

"Well, there was no answer when I rapped on the door so I took the key from where you told me and I walked in. Sam was sitting in a chair and I said, 'Hello.' He didn't answer so I came in front of him and I saw that he was dead. I've never seen a dead man before. He looks so different than when he was alive. What am I supposed to do?"

"Have you called the police?"

"No."

Preacher John quickly said, "Don't touch anything else. Hang up and call the police immediately. They'll take it from there and tell you what to do." He hung up his own phone. He was angry at Cutler for disobeying what he had been told to do, which was to get better. Instead, he had died. Preacher John immediately knew that Sam Cutler's passing would complicate his life.

Brother Elijah did what Preacher John told him; he hung up the phone and then dialed 911. He was nervous though, because he had never seen a corpse before, never mind one sitting in a chair. That fact, and his concern that he might be implicated in Cutler's death, made Brother Elijah skittish. He was extremely jittery when he talked to the emergency dispatcher who was only interested in determining what assets, police, ambulance or fire, were needed. At the same time, Brother Elijah kept telling the dispatcher that he was a completely innocent bystander who was only doing a favor for his minister. As a result of Brother Elijah's insisting that he had not committed a crime, the dispatcher warned the Milan police of a possible homicide.

Brother Elijah became aware of his mixup when he heard a siren screeching down Main Street and brakes squealing to a halt at the front entrance of the apartment. He looked out the window and saw the flashing lights of a police car. He became even more nervous and felt he was being dragged deeper into something that had nothing to do with him. He decided to meet the police at the door and proclaim his innocence. When he met the officer at the apartment door he felt relieved. He didn't even need to read the name tag to know who Bill Jawleski was. Brother Elijah had worked on his car almost all afternoon the day before. He was happy to find someone who knew him and would believe his story. He started to talk but Jawleski held his palm up, walked into the apartment, and studied the scene.

The officer looked at Cutler's body, which was propped in a chair with a broken cocaine packet and a straw on the table in front of him. Finally, he asked, "Mister Thomas, are you the person who found the body?"

"Yes."

"How did you get into this apartment?"

"Preacher John told me that there was a key located over the door."

"Did you touch anything else in the apartment beside the phone?"

"No."

"You're pretty sure about that?"

"Yes, I came over to check on Mr. Cutler because Preacher John asked me to and I got scared when I found him like that. I didn't touch a thing, I just wanted to get out of here."

"Mr. Thomas, I'm going to call for assistance. With all the drug items lying around, this should be labeled a suspicious homicide. I'll have to ask you to come with me."

"You don't think I had anything to do with this, do you?"

"No Sir, but there are other people who will want to talk with you. My job is to protect the possible crime scene and keep you secure. So, if you will hand me the key, I will lock up and we'll go down to my squad car."

The next few hours were confusing for Elijah Thomas. He sat in the front seat beside officer Jawleski, while Jawleski made and received, numerous radio calls. Personnel from different agencies and jurisdictions came and went without paying much attention to Brother Elijah. Finally, after listening to one of the static filled messages, Jawleski turned to Thomas. "That message was for us. We are going to drive to the police station and you can talk to the officer who will be in charge of this investigation. After that, it looks like you will be free to go."

When they arrived, Brother Elijah was asked if he needed to use the rest room and then he was escorted to a small office and given a cup of coffee. As he was drinking it, Bill Jawleski and another uniformed officer walked in; the second officer's name badge read "Nolan Nalley" and he had a small silver bar on each shoulder. Jawleski pointed to the other officer. "Mr. Thomas, this is Lieutenant Nolan Nalley. He will be the lead officer in this investigation."

Thomas saw a bald man of medium height in his late forties. His crisply pleated uniform fit his slim build. He looked as if he tolerated no nonsense and Brother Elijah immediately thought that he was in for a grilling. However, Nalley's voice was friendly. He smiled and said, "Mr. Thomas, I need to ask you a few questions. Once we do that, you can be on your way. Is that all right?"

Thomas immediately answered, "I didn't do anything but what Preacher John asked me to. I had nothing to do with Cutler's death."

"We know that, Mr. Thomas. You are not a suspect. We're trying to put together a timeline of events and your help would be gratefully appreciated."

Some of Thomas's fears subsided. He watched as Nalley set up a recording machine and talked into it for a few minutes. After announcing the formalities of the interview, the time, and who was present at the interview, Nalley asked Thomas, "Did you know the deceased, Sam Cutler?"

"Yes, he and I are members of the Evangelical Church of Christ Glorified. I also went on one or two hunting trips with him. This morning, our minister asked me to go to Mr. Cutler's apartment and check on him."

"Had you ever been there before?"

"No."

"Why did Preacher John ask you to check on Cutler?"

"I don't know. Preacher John told me he was busy and that I was close to the apartment. He told me that Mr. Cutler was not feeling well and was not answering his phone. So, I did what Preacher John asked me to do. He told me that the key was over the door and it was. When I entered the apartment after knocking, I found Mr. Cutler sitting in the chair."

"What did you do next."

"I called Preacher John."

"Why didn't you call the police?"

"I don't know. Preacher John was the one who sent me to check on Mr. Cutler so he was the one I called."

"And what did Preacher John tell you to do?"

"He told me to call the police, which I did immediately."

"Did you touch anything except the telephone while you were in Cutler's apartment?"

"No."

"You are sure that you didn't touch anything else?"

"Yeah, I think so. I was scared and just wanted to get out."

Nalley sat quietly for a moment and then spoke some final words into the microphone and shut off the machine. Then he looked at Thomas as he spoke, "Mr. Thomas, I thank you for your cooperation. Even though the investigation has just started, there are several things I can share with you.

"First, even without an autopsy, the cause of death appears to be a drug overdose. You aren't aware of this but, prior to this incident, there have been three deaths and a lot of near deaths due to bad drugs. In the last six months, Washtenaw County has been flooded with doctored drugs. The cocaine used by the victims in the other cases was contaminated with poison. It looks like this is the same thing but we won't be sure until we get both the coroner's and the lab's reports.

"In the meantime, the only thing we will need from you is that you read the transcript of our interview, make any corrections, and sign it. We can arrange the time and place for you to review the transcript at your convenience. Other than that, you are free to go."

Elijah Thomas lost no time in taking advantage of Lieutenant Nalley's offer. He stood up and quickly walked out of the police station. The fresh air had never smelled so good.

CHAPTER 8

Death is the obverse side of the coin of life. When the coin is flipped, life ceases and death marks the end of all physical activities. That cruel rule is true for every organism on our planet. There is no animal or plant immune from this cycle. There are no exceptions. The A to Z list, from aardvarks to zebras, includes everything that lives. All humans—kings, popes, or presidents will meet the same fate as beggars, commoners, and crooks. Death is the final state on this earth and it awaits us all.

Long ago, humans unilaterally decided that they were the most intelligent of all species and that they could understand everything they witnessed. They pondered over death even before they developed written records. After centuries of observation and study, we now have doctors who can measure death, scientists who can define death, and poets who can write about death.

Yet, on an individual basis, we don't come to terms with it. Death is dreaded, and for good reason. We can't control it and we have no say about it. The worst fear of all is that we don't know what happens to us after we die.

Each new child born arrives with no past memories; its future lies completely ahead. Children are at the beginning of the life cycle while death is far away at the other end. Death is not considered because the child is too busy learning to live. It is only as the child reaches old age that he or she realizes that life is a fleeting, fragile condition and it does not last forever.

Most humans come to terms with the fact that they are mortal and that the coin flip is inevitable. And, because humans do not really know as much as they think they know, they have questions for which there are no answers. Is there a God in charge of the universe? Is there life after death? Does the body have a soul? Is there a heaven and a hell?

These are daunting questions that each person wrestles with and resolves individually. Because no one has the definitive answer, there is no right or wrong. Whatever a person chooses to believe regarding an afterlife must be respected. Because the truth of what happens is unknown, each person selects how to face his or her own demise.

Along with coming to terms with the philosophical theory of death, is the highly charged problem of human emotions. To have someone you love disappear from your life is devastating. How do the living handle their feelings when a loved one passes? When death goes from a theoretical discussion to a heart wrenching reality, it forever scars the hearts and souls of the survivors. The pain is as brutal as a branding iron. Humans never forget those they loved and the loss changes them. After the passing of someone dear, some survivors shrivel under the intense emotions of loss and never recover their equilibrium. The majority of survivors slowly regain their balance and become more beautiful by passing their love on to other people in their lives.

This happens because humans realize that they need to give and receive love, respect, and admiration every bit as much as they need food, air, and shelter. Life would be hollow if there were no positive feelings to ease the wear and tear of life. Good feelings make good humans, bad feelings make bad humans.

The death of Sam Cutler affected the four people who had been closest to him. Isabel Tannenbaum, Bruckner's mother, had met him when he had first arrived in Milan. She was not as close to Sam as her son was but Sam Cutler had been a visitor in her home many times. She had cooked for him and fed him and talked with him for hours. She had heard about his life and deeply wished he had been happier. Now he was gone and he hadn't much joy in this world. This was sad. She could only hope he would get his reward in the next world.

Maribeth Bruckner knew Cutler first as an employee and then as a friend. She had always thought of Sam as a meek person who wanted everybody to like him. He would do whatever his friends asked him to do. All he ever wanted was to be accepted. Maribeth believed that that was no way to live. She felt sorry for him. When she heard of his death, she cried at how empty of happiness his life had been.

Henry Tannenbaum took Sam Cutler's death hard. For many years he tried to guide Cutler to believe more in himself and enjoy life. He had failed, and Cutler had lived a second-class existence without tasting the real richness of life. Now he was dead and all earthly pleasures were past him. Hopefully, a merciful God would grant him what he didn't receive while he was alive.

Tannenbaum was angry that Cutler had died because of drugs. Worse, he was furious that Preacher John was involved in Cutler's drug habit. He wasn't exactly sure how Preacher John was involved, but he was certain that he was. Tannenbaum, because of his religion, was usually calm and forgiving. Now he was almost rabid in his hatred of Preacher John.

Bill Bruckner was Sam Cutler's closest friend and he was the person who hurt and grieved the most. They had known each other for almost forty-five years. They had gone through combat together, they had protected each other, and Bruckner had stood beside Cutler almost all those years. Even though they had grown apart after Cutler met Preacher John, Bruckner was always ready to help Sam. He considered Sam as his brother. The idea that he had failed bothered Bruckner. He felt he should have tried harder to rescue Sam from Preacher John. Bruckner missed Sam and he felt guilty. He was so angry at Preacher John that his temper rose just hearing the name of the person who was responsible for Sam's death.

The four of them were the only friends Cutler had and they were all diminished by his death. At death, love curdles to grief and the sourness of the grief is a measure of the love.

The only other person that Cutler was close to, Preacher John, did not feel any of the sadness that wracked Sam's friends. He was too busy making sure that he wasn't linked in any way to Cutler's death. He sat in his office, reviewing the events of Cutler's last days over and over. He would make up a scenario of what happened and then build an explanation or an alibi for what he, Preacher John, did or didn't do. Like Pontius Pilate, he washed his hands of any responsibility for the death of Sam Cutler. In fact, he was more than a little annoyed that Cutler had died and put him in such a compromising position.

Oddly enough, the first person among the friends and acquaintances of Sam Cutler to learn of his death was Matilda Preston. Her nephew, Arny Matusak, called her late on the same day that Cutler's body was discovered. When she answered her phone, Arny asked, "Aunt Matilda, how are you?"

She replied, "Fine, Arny, and how are you doing?"

"Very well, thank you. Listen, the reason I'm calling is because I have a question for you. Do you remember that you asked me to work with you when you were trying to help Sam Cutler?"

"Yes, of course I do. Why?"

"Well, he was found dead in his apartment early this afternoon."

Matilda gasped. This was totally unexpected news. The surveillance her bridge club had established on that apartment was almost a lark. The 1:15 Club enjoyed themselves doing something that was so out of character for them. However, this was entirely different. The thought of death disturbed her; the image that it was someone she knew was even more upsetting. All she could do was ask, "What happened?"

"I don't know yet. My editor has assigned me the story because we had a conversation about this apartment before Cutler died. I'm just gathering the details myself. Would it be possible to drop by your house this evening and talk with you about the stakeout we made on that apartment? I should know a lot more about what's going on when I get there."

They made their arrangements and when Arny Matusak arrived, he found Matilda, Maribeth, and Isabel waiting for him. His aunt explained that the fourth member of the bridge club, Jane Squires, was out of town or she would also be present. He helped himself to a cup of coffee and settled into a straight chair in the living room. He faced the three women and slowly began, "I know that you three knew about Sam Cutler and that you are shocked by his death. I am truly sorry.

"Let me tell you what I know about his passing. This is only preliminary because an autopsy will be performed to establish the exact cause of death. Right now, the authorities are looking at a cocaine overdose as the probable cause of death."

Maribeth spoke up immediately, "Is there any chance of foul play?"

"Why would you suggest that, Mrs. Bruckner?"

"Because we are almost positive that Sam Cutler was introduced to cocaine by Preacher John. There are many things we don't know but we are sure that Preacher John is somehow involved."

Matusak didn't reply for a while, then he chose his words carefully. "You ladies recently got together to try to help Sam Cutler; I was part of that attempt. At that time, Preacher John and Cutler were somehow tangled together. Since then, something happened and now Cutler is dead. Preacher John may, or may not, be involved. This will become evident as the investigation goes forward.

"However, let me give you some background the investigation is facing and how I'm involved. Over the last few months there is almost an epidemic of bad coke being distributed locally. Somewhere along the line, the unadulterated drug is being diluted with cheaper, lethal, fillers. The result is at least a dozen poisonings and three deaths in Washtenaw County. Local and federal agencies are trying to find the source of this bad coke. Sam Cutler's death could be the fourth death in the series.

"I know all this because I have been writing articles about the victims, both those who have died and those who have survived. When my editor got news of the 911 call about Sam Cutler, he remembered that name and called me. My opinion is that Sam's death looks like a continuation of the bad drug scene."

Isabel replied, "Arny, you may be correct. I didn't know anything about these other drug related problems. However, I do know that Sam's death is disturbing to us. We would hope for an honest, open investigation."

"Oh, you'll get that, Mrs. Tannenbaum. I have known the Milan investigating officer, Nolan Nalley, for years. He was our neighbor and his oldest son and I grew up together; Mr. Nalley was our Boy Scout Troop Leader. He's honest, hard working. Even my editor, who is tough to please, thinks he's a good cop. If anyone can get to the bottom of Sam Cutler's death, it will be Lieutenant Nalley.

"But, I'm not here to investigate Cutler's death right now. That will come later. I'm here to gather material about his life. I want to know him as a person, how he lived his life and how his friends saw him. A person just died and his life should be celebrated. That is my present assignment."

Isabel replied almost instantly, "That's a noble thought and I will be happy to talk with you but you will probably get a more accurate idea of who Sam Cutler was by talking with my son and my husband. They were his closest friends for years and can tell you both the good and the bad about him."

"Thank you for that information, Mrs. Tannenbaum, and I will follow through by talking with both of them. However, I would be interested in hearing your thoughts about Sam Cutler; women usually have different impressions about an individual than men do. I would like to know your impressions of him." For the next few hours Matusak was busy listening and taking notes about Sam Cutler's life.

Lieutenant Nalley sat staring at the folder lying in the middle of his desk. He was not hypnotized by it, he was annoyed at it. The folder was labeled "CUTLER" and contained all the information gathered since Cutler's death three weeks earlier. It included pictures taken at the apartment at the time of death and all the statements from the people who had been interviewed. What was missing from the folder was the medical examiner's report. It had not yet been issued and it was that report that was causing Nalley's annoyance.

Less than a week after Cutler's death, the other investigating agencies, primarily the Washtenaw County Sheriff's Office and the Drug Enforcement Administration, concluded that Sam Cutler died in the same manner as the other users of the contaminated cocaine. This transferred his death from a suspicious cause investigation to a search for the sellers of the poisonous drug. The other law enforcement agencies were not as interested in the details concerning Cutler's death; they needed to stop the person, or persons, from killing more victims.

Nalley had a different perspective on the circumstances of Cutler's death. He agreed with his contemporaries that Cutler's death was probably attributed to an overdose of bad drugs, but for Nalley, there were other considerations. Sam Cutler was a Milan resident who had died within the city of Milan and under suspicious circumstances. He needed to investigate to be sure that no other crimes were hidden within these suspicious circumstances. There were loose ends to be resolved and it was his responsibility to examine all the details surrounding the death.

That type of investigation was within the boundaries of Nalley's responsibilities as a police officer.

Duty and responsibility were traits he was taught early in life. His father was a cop and he had raised his family with tough love and a sense of honor. Nalley's Irish Catholic background gave him a strong sense of right and wrong. He and his two brothers never had any other goal than to be cops. Nalley enjoyed bringing order and sense out of chaos.

When he was first hired by the Milan Police Department, Nalley bought a house in Milan and never left the area. He was happy raising his family in a small city and he enjoyed his job. Nalley disagreed with the idea that people need drugs to shield them from life and he didn't particularly like the users he met. However, he strongly believed in the rule of law and that he was obligated to protect everyone. He could not pick and choose his cases based on personal choice.

Nalley had examined the apartment where Cutler's body was discovered. Although he did notice a few oddities, nothing made him think that anyone other than Sam Cutler himself had administered the fatal overdose.

His first interview was with the man who discovered the body, Elijah Thomas. He quickly recognized that Thomas was someone who had been caught in the wrong place at the wrong time.

Nalley's next interview was with Preacher John. He selected him because Preacher John was the last person to see Cutler alive and he had two suits and some clothes in one of the two bedrooms. Preacher John answered all his questions but the answers were curt and he offered no additional information. He told Nalley that he used the apartment as a second office and that he had driven Cutler to the apartment at Cutler's request. He couldn't explain why Cutler wanted to go back to the apartment, especially since he had moved out months before. He had tried to talk Cutler into staying at the church but Cutler wouldn't listen to him; Cutler insisted on being alone at his old apartment. At the end of their interview, Nalley felt that Preacher John was reluctant to talk but he didn't think that he was hiding anything.

However, when Nalley finished interviewing Henry Tannenbaum and Bill Bruckner separately, he realized that Preacher John had withheld crucial information. Nalley knew both men personally and was sure that their sworn statements were true. He interviewed the older of the two, Tannenbaum, first and was taken aback at the anger Tannenbaum displayed as he outright blamed Preacher John for Cutler's death. Tannenbaum showed Nalley the pictures that Matusak took of Preacher John's pimp, his car, and his girls. Nalley recognized the pimp immediately but he had no idea that Preacher John was in the habit of soliciting prostitutes. Using the apartment for his sexual pleasures helped explain his reserved attitude and his relationship with Sam Cutler. Bill Bruckner's interview was similar in its angry tone and accusations against Preacher John. He also blamed Preacher John for Cutler's death and confirmed the validity of the photographs Tannenbaum gave to Nalley. The lieutenant reread all the interviews, restudied the photographs, and decided that, before he did anything else, he needed to find out more about why the pictures were taken. He called Arny Matusak and they set up a date for him to come over to Nalley's home for dinner.

Matusak arrived early; he had a small bouquet of flowers for Nalley's wife, Glenda. He hadn't seen or spoken to her in a long time and felt a little guilty. She took the flowers and hugged him; he had been in and out of her house many times as he was growing up. The three of them happily shared their memories and recollections of the past over dinner. When they finished eating, Nalley invited Matusak into his den.

Once settled, after Glenda left them with coffee and dessert, the mood changed. Nalley asked Matusak how he had become involved in taking pictures of a known pimp and his girls. Matusak explained that his aunt, who was a member of a bridge club that included the wives of Bill Bruckner and Henry Tannenbaum, had asked him to document the comings and goings of Preacher John. When they explained to him what they were trying to do—to help Sam Cutler—he took the pictures for the bridge club. He really didn't think the club ladies could help Sam Cutler but he decided to work with them. He was fond of his aunt and the bridge club was trying to do something good for someone who needed help. No laws had been broken and there was no intent on doing anything malicious. They finished talking and Matusak asked Nalley to let him know the results of the investigation as soon as he could. Nalley promised he would.

After the discussion with Matusak, Nalley decided that he needed to have another interview with Preacher John. He had to find out if Preacher John was more deeply involved with Sam Cutler's death than he led Nalley to believe. Nalley called Preacher John and set up a meeting. The location would be in his office inside the police station; Lieutenant Nalley wanted all the advantages to be on his side.

When Preacher John sat down for the interview, Nalley said to him, "In your bedroom in the apartment, along with your suits and underwear, there was a drawer that held quite a few pairs of women's panties. Are you aware of that drawer?"

Preacher John looked straight at Nalley. "Absolutely not. Sam must have been living a secret second life. I know nothing about what you just told me."

Nalley handed him pictures of his pimp and two of his prostitutes. "Have you ever met this man or these women?"

Preacher John took the pictures, glanced at them, and shook his head. "No."

Lieutenant Nalley replied in a low forceful tone, "Preacher John, be careful. I can pick this guy up and interrogate him. He has a long criminal record and he is a known pimp. He owes you no loyalty. To save himself, once he sees these photographs, he will sing like an opera star and tell us all about you and his girls. I'm not trying to trick you, I'm only interested in getting all the facts concerning Sam Cutler's death. So, I ask you again if you have ever met this man?"

Preacher John stared at his adversary for a long time. The pictures completely surprised him. He knew he was trapped, and he had to figure out how to minimize the damage. When he answered, he was defensive and his voice had an unpleasant tone. "Lieutenant Nalley, you are a practicing Catholic. As such, you must be aware that many of your priests have carnal desires. When they fulfill their desires and their parish becomes aware of these human transgressions, there is compassion and forgiveness extended to the wayward priest.

"I am only human and, in the past, I have transgressed. However, I am under a doctor's care and having treatment. My past problems have nothing to do with Sam Cutler's death and they really don't require any further investigation.

"How else can I help you?"

Nalley was not pleased with Preacher John's answer. It was not Preacher John's responsibility to determine what was relevant and what was not. That was Nalley's job. It was Lieutenant Nalley's case, not Preacher John's. In addition, he didn't like the excuse that his use of prostitutes was similar to the wrongdoings of Catholic priests. For Nalley, uncovering a human weakness in a religious leader was a sad obligation. However, Preacher John's rationalizing his own faults by comparing them to others was inexcusable. He was justifying his errors, not taking responsibility for his sins. That attitude did not sit well with Nalley.

"Listen, if your hiring of prostitutes has nothing to do with my investigation, then it goes no further. I'm not your conscience. My job is to examine the death of Sam Cutler. I'm trying to determine how he died. That's all.

"Did you know that he was using drugs?"

Preacher John appeared to relax. "No, I didn't, but I'll admit that he was acting different for the last few months."

"How was he 'acting different?'"

"Well, mood swings, for example. He would be very talkative and lively one minute and two minutes later he would be absolutely quiet and would not say a word. He would disappear to his downstair apartment for hours without telling anybody where he was. I don't know how a user acts but he certainly was different the last few months.

"I told you this the last time you talked with me."

"Yes, you did tell me that he was acting different. I'm still trying to figure out where he got his drugs. There is an epidemic of bad drugs and people are dying. Our whole team is working to find the source of this deadly coke."

Preacher John felt himself panicking. If Nalley interrogated his pimp he would find that it was Preacher John who supplied Cutler his coke. He had to stop that from happening. He took a deep breath to make the tone of his voice more relaxed as he asked, "What can I do to help you?"

"Can you remember anything Cutler did or said that might lead us to his source of supply?"

Preacher John knew that this is where he had to be extremely careful. He was asked this question before and he denied knowing anything. Now he had to give information that would divert attention from himself and his involvement. He was sure that Benny the Bear had no idea who he was or how he earned his living. He had to steer Nalley away from his pimp and over to Benny. He replied, "No. I know that he made several phone calls from my office. Cutler would cut the conversation off as soon as I walked in. He would say, 'I'll call you back,' or 'I've got to go now.'"

Preacher John stopped for a second, as if he was searching his memory. "Wait. There was one time he was talking about someone. It was a strange, strange name. I can't remember."

Nalley sat patiently. "Think of something. For example, what was

Cutler wearing or where were you coming from when you entered your office. Sometimes associating your thoughts with other events helps you remember specific details."

Preacher John finally replied, "Well, as I remember, he had on a Michigan, 'GO BLUE' tee shirt. He was on the phone with his back to the door. When I entered he turned around to face me and said, 'Benny the Bear, I got to go.' I think that's the name he spoke, but that's a crazy name. That can't be right, can it?"

Nalley looked at Preacher John. "It could be a person of interest. It's possible that there's a new drug dealer using that name. We need to find who is pushing this poison. It certainly deserves checking into.

"Why didn't you volunteer this same information the first time you were interrogated?"

Preacher John waved his left arm in the air. "I should have, and I apologize. However, I didn't lie to you; I was just trying to protect my reputation. I wasn't aware of this epidemic of death that you are fighting.

"Now that you know that I have personal problems and that I'm under treatment, I can be completely honest and above board with you. I feel so much better telling you everything I know."

Nalley looked at Preacher John and wondered how much more of the truth he was holding back. He wasn't sure he would ever find out, but he'd been given a new lead to pursue. He said, "If you think of anything else, no matter how small or insignificant you think it is, please let me know."

With that, the interview was over. Preacher John was free to go.

A few weeks later Lieutenant Nalley called Arny Matusak and invited him to come to his office. Nalley closed his door so the two of them could talk without being overheard. "Okay," he said, "the report on

Sam Cutler's death will be released tomorrow. I'll talk to you on the record for your reporting, and off the record for you and your friends. You can quote me as an unnamed source for your reporting but you cannot write one word of what I tell you off the record. If you agree, I'll begin."

After hearing Nalley's offer, Matusak took a pen and a small notebook out of his pocket and waited. "I understand completely and I agree to only write about what you say is on the record."

Lieutenant Nalley relaxed, sipped some coffee. "You and your friends are not going to like the official report on Cutler's death. The medical examiner's report came back a few days ago and he gave the official cause of death as a self-inflicted overdose of cocaine laced with, among other things, traces of arsenic. Because the ingredients are identical to the other poisonings, the investigation has been officially closed."

He sat back in his chair and waited for Matusak's reaction, which was almost instantaneous. Matusak sputtered, "You mean that no charges will be brought against Preacher John?"

"What kind of charges do you think are possible?"

"I don't really know, but his fingerprints seem to be all over Cutler's death."

Nalley nodded in agreement. "You may be right, but there is no proof of any wrongdoing by anyone. Sam Cutler had no known enemies; he was alone in his old apartment and he was found with contaminated drugs in his body. The drug paraphernalia he used had his fingerprints all over them. There is no evidence that anyone visited him from the time that Preacher John dropped him off until Thomas found him. Considering the fact that he took the drug himself, there is no other conclusion that the medical examiner could reach.

"You have heard my opinion on the record statement. Now let me talk off the record.

"During my last talk with Preacher John, he gave me a name that could have been Cutler's drug dealer. I gave that name to the detectives who are trying to find the source of the poisoned coke. They went undercover and found that Benny the Bear is the dealer that cut the poison into the coke to make a larger profit. He was finally caught, courtesy of Preacher John.

"These same detectives had decided, long before the medical examiner's report, that Cutler's death was due to an overdose. So, they really weren't interested in following up to see if Preacher John was implicated. And, after they nabbed the bad guy because of the tip, they weren't interested in pursuing the relationship between Sam Cutler and Preacher John anymore.

"I have strongly urged the Prosecuting Attorney's Office to continue to examine Preacher John's role in the death of Sam Cutler. They have refused. There is not enough substantive evidence to continue an investigation. They also said that pursuing further inquiries without better evidence could bring defamation of character charges against the agency making the inquiries.

"While I agree with you that Preacher John probably had something to do with Cutler's death, there is no way to prove anything. I think he withheld information about Cutler's dealer until he was caught using that apartment as his own personal whorehouse. I don't think he has told the entire truth but he is innocent until proven guilty. That is his right and that is where the matter now stands.

"I'm sorry, Arny, there is nothing more I can do."

Matusak tapped his pen on his teeth for a few moments while he put his thoughts in order. He closed his notebook. "Well, I have enough material to write several stories about the life and death of Samuel Cutler. Nothing you told me, off the record, will appear in any of my stories.

"Just out of curiosity though, Mr. Nalley, did you ever know Sam Cutler personally?" Whenever Matusak addressed Nalley directly he always called him "Mr." He had grown up calling him Mr. Nalley long before he became aware that his troop leader was also a policeman.

Nalley answered the question, "I knew of him but I wasn't friendly with him. He was a quiet guy. He helped me in setting up a couple of Scout Jamborees at Wilson Park. You might remember him from there."

Matusak replied, "As a matter of fact, now that you mention it, I vaguely remember talking to him once or twice at those jamborees. I joined the Boy Scouts when I was fourteen and that's when I met him. That was what, fifteen years ago? It's odd. I didn't know him when he was alive but now that he's dead, I know all about him. That's because I've met the people whose lives he touched. I hope my story will give him the remembrance he deserves. All he ever wanted was to be accepted. That's a sorry epitaph.

"Mr. Nalley, I truly appreciate your help.

"Now, I have to tell his friends, including my aunt, what the medical examiner's report says and the reasons behind it. Sam's friends are not going to think that justice has been served in this case."

Matusak was correct. He was able to gather Bill Bruckner, Henry Tannenbaum, and the four members of the 1:15 Club together that evening at Bruckner's home. He brought them copies of the report. After much discussion and disappointment, they agreed that regardless of their feelings, the case was closed.

Tannenbaum said, "The medical examiner based his conclusions on the facts he had and the results of the autopsy. Obviously, he knew nothing about Preacher John and his influence on Sam Cutler. Poor Sam, he'll have to receive his justice and due reward in heaven."

Slowly and sadly Bruckner said, "I hope you're right, Henry. Sam certainly deserved a better life than he received. The law paid no attention to any of the circumstances behind his death. I'm not sure that it could.

"I can only honor my friend the best way I can, by remembering how kind and simple he was. Sam never understod that there were people who would take advantage of him. He was done in by one such son of a bitch. A sad ending for such a decent guy.

Justice was not done. That evening, his friends felt that the world seemed sad and whopper jawed.

CHAPTER 9

When Lieutenant Nalley showed Preacher John the pictures of his pimp and the prostitutes in front of the apartment on Main Street, Preacher John panicked. Until he looked at these pictures, he was sure that the only person who knew anything about these trysts was Sam Cutler, and he had never told Cutler who supplied him his prostitutes. Someone else must have been spying on him for a long time.

This bothered Preacher John. Questions flooded through his mind. How could the pictures have been taken without him being aware of it? Who else knew what he used the Main Street apartment for? Was it more than one person? How long had he been spied on?

He immediately realized that he had to stop the authorities from questioning his pimp. If they did, the police would find that his pimp had, in the past, supplied Preacher John with coke. Once they knew that, they would figure out that he fed the coke to Cutler. Preacher John could not let that happen. His entire lifestyle and his livelihood were in jeopardy.

He needed to change his story and do it without losing his credibility. He had to keep the drug connection between him and his pimp from being investigated. The pictures of the prostitutes already had tarnished his reputation. If Nalley didn't connect him to Cutler's death, he couldn't say anything about his private life. If he did, Preacher John could claim police harassment. Preacher John had to think quickly. He decided to give Nalley the name of the dealer who sold him the poisoned drug. Benny the Bear became his sacrificial lamb.

When he left the police station following his latest interrogation, Preacher John wasn't sure what would happen. He had implicated Benny the Bear. He left it at that. Although Preacher John knew that Lieutenant Nalley was contemptuous of him, it didn't bother him in the slightest. He didn't care what Nalley thought. As long as they couldn't charge him with any criminal activity, he was safe.

Until the results of the investigation were made public, Preacher John was a dormant volcano, prepared to explode on the inside while appearing calm on the outside. He immediately decided that the people who had spied on him were Tannenbaum and Bruckner. What bothered him was that he couldn't understand how they had done it. He went over his trysts, again and again, to recall any incident that stood out as different. He couldn't remember anything out of the ordinary. He was at a complete loss to explain how someone was able to take those pictures. He finally decided that Tannenbaum and Bruckner must have hired private investigators to spy on him.

Preacher John also worried about what he should say if he were called in for another interrogation. He continually made up a list of questions and answers for every "what if" situation that came to his thought.

When Preacher John read of the arrest of Benny the Bear on charges of drug dealing and several counts of manslaughter in the Ann Arbor News, he felt like a new man. The Lord had forgiven him for his past transgressions and he was reborn, free to make the world a better place.

After Arny Matusak's articles about the tragic life and death of Samuel Cutler were published, he used them as texts for his sermons. The attendance at his church, along with the donations, increased dramatically.

He used his newfound love of himself to vow to change his ways. He would obey all Ten Commandments and confound his enemies with his purity. Part of his pledge was based on the fact that he could not figure out who discovered his secret life or how they did it. So, with high resolves for the future and barely a look over his shoulder at the past, Preacher John began a new phase of his life.

Unfortunately, his resolve was softer than butter in the summer sun. His predatory nature and his uncontrollable lust made him horny within a few months of his vow of chastity. Again, he began craving sex. However, he would not repeat his past ways; he would stay away from pimps and prostitutes. He started to look more carefully at the females in his ministry. There are always women who are dissatisfied with their lives or who misinterpret church doctrine; it was not hard to seduce these ladies in the name of religion. Preacher John studied some of the middle-aged women in his congregation and began to make subtle advances to one or two of them. He was grateful that he had kept his occupancy of Cutler's apartment. It was the perfect location for his new conquests; he just had to make better arrangements. He would still come in the entrance on Main Street early Thursday evenings; however, his seduced victim would come in from the parking lot behind the building and enter through the back entrance. Because these women were under Preacher John's spell and not professional hookers, their arrivals were rarely on time. Depending on their personal lives, they most often were late. The use of two entrances would make it difficult for his enemies to connect him to any of his paramours, especially if he changed partners frequently.

This was Preacher John's reasoning. With this new approach in mind, Preacher John began, again, to feed on his flock.

Although there was no reason for meeting now that Sam Cutler was dead and buried, the 1:15 Club continued to meet on Thursday evenings. Their original purpose was replaced by the enjoyment of having a ladies' night out with no meal to prepare. Unlike their Friday time, which was dedicated to spirited competition, their Thursdays were spent talking about their families and their lives. Thursday night was almost all talk, Friday afternoon was almost all business.

The ladies met at the Milan Grill by force of habit. They did eat at other area restaurants, including the Crossfire, when the spirit of adventure moved them or they had discount coupons. They enjoyed their newfound wave of independence. These middle-aged and senior caterpillars began to blossom into social butterflies.

Early one fall Thursday evening, when the air was so heavy with fog that the streetlights didn't seem bright enough to illuminate the roads, Jane Squires was late for the get together at the Milan Grill. The club hadn't met there the last two weeks and Jane was on her way to another restaurant when she remembered where she was supposed to be. She knew she was late and hurried to catch up with her friends. Before she entered the restaurant, she glanced across the street at the Milan Bakery. What caught her eye was the light in the bedroom of Cutler's apartment suddenly lighting up in the fog. This was a surprise because she had assumed the apartment was empty.

Jane caught her friends up on her personal news and got back into the gossip line to await her turn. It wasn't until the group was almost ready to leave when Jane suddenly remembered seeing the light in the apartment. "Does anyone know who rented Sam Cutler's apartment? I saw the bedroom light come on as I came in here."

Isabel Tannenbaum replied, "I don't know anything about the apartment. Maybe Henry knows. I'll ask him. I'm sure someone will rent it, it's in a convenient location. Does anyone else know anything about it?" The other women shook their heads. Maribeth answered, "Bill might know. I'll check with him."

Both Isabel and Maribeth forgot to ask their husbands. The incident was forgotten and might have stayed buried except that, as Maribeth was walking to the Milan Grill a few weeks later, she noticed Preacher John entering the apartment building. She slowed her pace and looked up at the apartment window. The bedroom light came on. She was surprised and puzzled; this was similar to Jane's experience.

As Maribeth and the other three ladies were sipping their pre-dinner Margaritas, she described what she had just noticed and it immediately caused a stir. The weekly family updates and the local gossip snippets were put aside, replaced with guesses about what Preacher John was doing. The four of them agreed that he most likely was still using the apartment as a bordello, but they weren't sure. They were angry that he was up to his old tricks and using the same apartment that he had taken from Sam Cutler. After much discussion, they designed a new plan of action.

The first decision was unanimously and enthusiastically accepted. They would return to the detective business. The thought of snooping again made them excited; they felt like Jessica Fletcher in "Murder She Wrote."

Their second decision was the result of their first decision. They decided not to say a word about their suspicions until they were sure that they had absolute proof. As far as they were concerned, Preacher John was implicated in the death of Cutler but had escaped without punishment or censure. That he was not held accountable bothered them; it also made them wary. This time, they would not accuse him of anything unless they had solid proof of his misdeeds.

The four detectives wanted to capture Preacher John in flagrante delicto but they knew they never would. They did catch him in suspicious circumstances but were not able to prove anything. They tracked his arrival on Thursday evenings at approximately the same time, his entry into his apartment, and his departure about two hours later. However, they never saw any women enter the building. They were positive that he was up to his old habits but were without any proof.

It was easy for Jane Squires and Matilda Preston to keep a secret; they were both longtime widows and had no close relatives. For Maribeth Bruckner and Isabel Tannenbaum, it was a little more difficult. Neither of them ever hid information from their husbands. And, since both of their spouses were angry at Preacher John, any mention of impropriety would set their partners off. Both Maribeth and Isabel were disciplined and intelligent enough to understand that they shouldn't say a word until they were sure of their facts. However, they were not able to prove anything. Within a few weeks, Maribeth decided she had to turn to her husband for help.

She was frustrated. She wanted justice for Sam Cutler and she wanted Preacher John's activities stopped. Because she and her detective cohorts were getting nowhere, she decided to break her promise and ask her husband for advice. Maribeth was not at all happy with going back on her word but she needed direction.

One Thursday evening, following another fruitless surveillance, Maribeth lay in bed and said, "I have a question for my Model Husband." This was how Maribeth alerted Bruckner that a serious discussion was coming; she used the tag, "Model Husband," before she began the particular subject. The phrase "Model Husband" started when she needed his help or when she wanted him to do something he would prefer not to do. She would begin her request by saying, "A 'Model Husband' would be willing to…" and then continue. She was aware that the tag got his attention and she used it whenever she needed help.

Bruckner was amused by her ploy and when he heard the words "Model Husband" he knew that Maribeth wanted a serious discussion. His reply let her know he was ready to help: "What question is my 'Thursday Wife,' going to ask this 'Model Husband' of hers?" His tag for Maribeth came when one time, after agreeing on something, Maribeth completely changed her mind the next day. To cover his confusion over her apparent contrariness, he began to call her his "Monday Wife," his "Tuesday Wife," or whatever day he was talking with her. Maribeth had no problem being addressed as her husband's, "Wife of the Day." She enjoyed twitting Bill. Occasionally, she would change her opinion just to hear him complain.

Now that she had Bruckner's attention, Maribeth explained that she and the 1:15 Club believed that Preacher John was again using Cutler's former apartment as a sex crib, but they hadn't been able to discover how he was doing it. She ended her explanation by saying, "We believe he is up to his old tricks but we don't know how he's getting the women into the apartment or who they are. I'm sure that son of a bitch is doing something bad and I want to put a stop to it."

Bruckner listened to his wife without saying a word. He wanted justice for Cutler even more than she did but he also wanted to be sure of his facts. He thought about what Maribeth had told him before he said, "Seeing him enter that apartment at the same time when he used prostitutes looks suspicious. However, it doesn't prove he is back to his old habits. I'll admit that It doesn't look kosher but you need more proof than just your suspicions."

Maribeth volunteered more information. "Well, we checked and found that he has a maid service come in and clean that apartment every Friday morning. He started that recently and that's exactly what he did when the apartment was his private whorehouse."

Bruckner was surprised and pleased that Maribeth had some indirect evidence to support her suppositions. "Now, my 'Thursday Wife,' we might be getting somewhere. How did you and your detective agency find out about his maid service?"

"That's easy. When Sam was alive and we first started checking on Preacher John, Matilda Preston happened to be walking by the apartment building's back door. She always parks her car on Wabash Street behind the back of the apartments and then walks around the corner to Main Street. This particular time, she saw a small car with a maid service logo on its doors parked near the back entrance. Two young Latino ladies got out and Matilda walked up to them and started a conversation because she was thinking of hiring a cleaning service. She spoke with them a few more times and developed a casual relationship; the ladies were friendly and glad to answer her questions. When we weren't sure whether or not Preacher John was up to his old tricks, Matilda went back and talked to these same ladies. She found they were scheduled to clean Preacher John's apartment every Friday; that confirmed our suspicions. But, we don't know how he is getting his women into the apartment."

Bruckner reached over and mussed his wife's hair. He laughed and said, "I think you do know; you're just not paying attention. Preacher John has changed his routine slightly. What door did you say the maid service used?"

Maribeth sat up. "Oh my God! The back door! The back door! Of course! We knew the answer all the time and we didn't even realize it. Oh, Honey, you are a so smart 'Model Husband.' I'm so happy I asked you. I love you."

They celebrated their collaboration by making love.

That next Thursday, Arny Matusak was in position to take pictures of the women who entered the back door around the time Preacher John went through the front. In a few weeks he had photographs of two women who arrived on alternate Thursdays. When Matusak showed the pictures to the 1:15 Club, the retired teachers Matilda and Jane were stunned. Both women were daughters of students they had taught.

Maribeth brought her troubles to Bruckner. She was almost in tears as she finished her tale. He put his arm around her shoulder and spoke softly, "Maribeth, I understand why you feel so bad but I don't know if there is anything you can do. This is consensual sex between adults. Even if the women are married and the man is an unmarried minister, it is consensual. They can't be arrested for having sex in a private place.

"Besides, I'm not sure that blowing the whistle on that bastard wouldn't do more harm than good. A lot of people will get hurt and I'm not sure Preacher John will ever be punished. It's something you will have to think about carefully."

It was an agonizing time for the 1:15 Club detectives. They didn't want to hurt anyone but they wanted to end Preacher John's practice of seducing members of his own church. The longer they waited, the more upset they were. Fortunately, their problem was solved in a dramatic and completely unexpected way.

One Sunday morning, just as Preacher John faced his congregation to start the morning service, there were two loud interruptions. First, a motorcycle was heard speeding across the parking lot followed by a crashing sound. A cyclist had performed a high speed wheelie and smashed down the front door of the church. Next, another motorcycle roar, another wheelie, and the door into the sanctuary was splintered apart. A motorcycle drove through the entrance. The noise of doors being ripped off their hinges happened so rapidly that everyone froze in their seats and all heads turned in disbelief to watch what was happening.

With everyone looking, Motorcycle Man halted his motorcycle at the back of the sanctuary and throttled the engine. All eyes followed him and he was a fearsome sight. He was a huge, barrel chested man dressed in black on a black motorcycle. He wore black boots, black leather pants, and a black leather jacket with a large white skull and crossbones on both the front and the back. His stomach bulged against his jacket, adding to his forbidding image. His helmet was also black, his head and face hidden from view.

As Motorcycle Man sat on his Harley Davidson, no one moved, no one spoke. Everyone watched and listened. He revved the engine from full throttle to idle several times to make sure his audience was paying attention. The noise was deafening when the engine roared in the sanctuary at full throttle. Then he lifted the visor of his helmet to reveal two eyes, a nose, and a beard that hid all other features.

Motorcycle Man shut off the engine, raised his right arm and pointed a finger at Preacher John. He spoke slowly and loudly. "Preacher John, you son of a bitch, you have violated the Ten Commandments. You bastard, you have coveted my wife and have been fucking her every Tuesday night for months. I'm going to kick you in the balls and beat the living shit out of you."

He straddle-walked his motorcycle down the narrow middle aisle. Everyone watched him, the only noise was the clicking of his boot heels on the wooden floor. As he neared the front of the church, a boy of about eight stepped into the aisle to get a better view of what was happening. Because the child was blocking his forward progress, Motorcycle Man stopped and swung his right foot over the saddle. Because he still wore his helmet, his vision was partially blocked and his boot heel hit the back of one of the pews. The momentum knocked him off balance and he fell to the floor, knocking over his bike. Motorcycle Man shouted, "Goddamn it." The spell was immediately snapped.

Five or six male church members rushed to where Motorcycle Man was trying to get up. Some were ready to help him stand; some were ready to keep him down. The result was crazy—complete pandemonium—a lot of noise, shoving, and shouting. It was resolved in a few minutes. Motorcycle Man's arms were pinned by husky parishioners on each side of him.

When the thrashing and swearing stopped, no one was sure what to do. They looked to the altar and, for the first time, they noticed that

Preacher John had fled. His robe was lying outside on the lawn and his car was gone. He was never seen again in Milan, Michigan.

Rumors began to fly like snowflakes in a blizzard. By Tuesday, the name of Motorcycle Man's wife was known and Preacher John was, truthfully or not, linked with other wives' and widows' names. Preacher John suddenly became an outcast. It was not until two weeks later, when a member of the Evangelical Church of Christ Glorified, a Certified Public Accountant, examined the church financial reports. Preacher John had disappeared, along with almost $150,000. Those who had believed in Preacher John were suddenly barren, bitter, and furious.

Maribeth and her detective agency followed the details closely. They were glad to be rid of Preacher John but agonized over the pain he inflicted on so many people. They spent hours on the phone talking with each other as rumors and facts surfaced and faded. It was only when they heard that Preacher John had absconded with so much money that they threw up their hands in disgust and began to lose interest in him. They started to focus on what was ahead and not what was behind. Their attitude was that he arrived, he hurt those who trusted him, and now he was gone. Let life continue to flow and let normal living return.

One morning, when Maribeth and Bill were almost ready to get out of bed, Maribeth said, "Honey, a couple of days ago we talked about getting a new refrigerator and stove and I decided against it. Do you remember?"

He looked at her and smiled. "You are going to give me a headache. I remember my 'Tuesday Wife' saying that we really didn't need new appliances. Now, my 'Friday Wife' is going to say that we do. Which side of the question will my 'Saturday Wife' be on? Why can't any of my daily wives agree with each other?"

"Hah. A 'Model Husband' would have known that Sears is having such a big sale on appliances that it makes sense to get rid of our old ones. A 'Model Husband' would know that common sense and love would show him how to deal with whichever wife shows up on whatever day. A 'Model Husband' would know how to handle any situation and he would be fortunate to have so many wives to deal with."

After a few more minutes of banter, they quickly agreed to buy new appliances. Maribeth was silent, then she asked, "Bill, what will happen to him?"

Bruckner lay there looking at Maribeth for quite awhile. He knew she was referring to Preacher John and he was aware that the tone of their conversation had changed. He finally answered. "I often wonder that myself. Sometimes, I think he'll get caught and sometimes I think he will never be brought to justice. Either way, he was lucky he wasn't beaten to a pulp. Just think of what might have happened if Motorcycle Man ambushed him in an alley instead of confronting him in his church. He escaped this time and he's probably in hiding, planning to resume his way of life in the future.

"However, he'll have problems. Preacher John is a predator and he always will be. His success depends on his deception. However, he's not as young and magnetic as he was when he began his ministry. He's still appealing but his skills are declining as he ages. He'll have to work harder than ever to make himself seem a credible minister.

"His second problem is notoriety. He will have to call attention to himself to succeed but, if he attracts too much attention, someone from his past could recognize him. That will always be on his mind. Preacher John will always be toe dancing on a razor blade.

"My guess is that one of his victims, either male or female, will turn against him. Revenge is a powerful motive, it can turn friends into fanatics. History has never been kind to predators and Preacher John has hurt many innocent people who trusted him. He could easily become his own victim. But, I don't think we'll ever know what happens to that bastard. He will hide for a time and we may never hear of him again. I hate him and I say good riddance."

Maribeth snuggled against Bill. "He's a terrible person, a scavenger. I hate to think how many more people he will hurt. He's the only person I have ever heard you say you hated."

When Bruckner finally answered, it was in a low voice. "I guess you're right. I hate him for all the misery he caused. Especially because his only purpose in life is his own satisfaction. That's not right and it's not fair.

"My best friend is dead and Preacher John had something to do with it. I hate him for all the injustice he's caused and all those he has made miserable. I will try to forget him but I will never be able to forgive him."

He returned his wife's snuggles and, soon, all thoughts of Preacher John were forgotten.

The final discussion concerning Preacher John took place a few weeks later when Bill and Henry were on a walk by the Saline River. Henry began. "Bill, it surprises me that no one talks about Preacher John's disappearance anymore. Once the fact that he absconded with so much money became public, his defenders have stopped making the case that he 'really was only human.'

"The funny thing is that the bridge club ladies tried to find out what he was doing every Thursday night but the scandal broke because he was screwing around with the women in his parish on Tuesday nights. It raises the question, were there other nights when he was using that apartment for his sex activities?

"Lord, he was a piece of work. I told you once that he gave you atheists a good name. He really did."

Bruckner smiled. "Listen Henry, I'm not sure I'm honored by such a comparison. Even atheists have scruples. Preacher John is bad news whether or not you believe in God. Preacher John is behind us and what we have left is the chaos he caused. You, I, and everyone will eventually get over this bad dose of life. I think I've learned to treasure love and family even more after seeing so much greed and gluttony. That's necessary for all people, whether believers or nonbelievers.

"Would you agree?"

Henry chuckled. "I'd even go so far as to say, 'Amen' to that."

CHAPTER 10

Time is a river that rises in eternity and flows to Infinity. It is mysterious, broad, and deep, Time transports every living organism in the universe on their individual journeys. One of the spaceships that conveys and nurtures these travelers for billions of years is a small speck of a planet known as Earth.

Earth is the name selected for this planet by a species who inhabit this tiny sphere in the solar system. This individual species tries to understand how the universe began; where it is now in its life cycle; and what will happen to it. This species calls itself *Homo sapiens* and is the most intelligent and the most inquisitive of all Earth's animals.

Homo sapiens have evolved from brutes who grunted and pointed as their first means of communication to a species that can express individual thoughts and ideas by speaking, reading, and writing. Homo sapiens are the only genus who can think in rational terms and express abstract feelings so powerfully that they can reason with their contemporaries to change opinions. They have gone from huddling around a campfire in animal skins, avoiding frostbite, to sitting in an air-conditioned room with a cold drink, avoiding melt down.

This unique capability, logic, has allowed Homo sapiens to survive on Earth wherever their ancestors settled. They adapted to every type of climate and geographical condition in which they found themselves. As a result, there are Homo sapiens of every color, culture, and language throughout our Earth. There are so many diverse branches of Homo sapiens that individual races have trouble communicating with their fellow humans. (The words *Homo sapiens* are derived from Latin and mean "wise man." Human is the name accepted by Homo sapiens to denote our present-day species.)

It has taken the particular solar system, of which our Earth is a part, billions of years to evolve into its present form. It has taken humans only tens of thousands of years to learn how to reason and to partially understand what took place before we evolved into our present condition. From savages to savants, we humans gained enough understanding to recognize that our species moves on a different time scale than the planet we inhabit. Our individual life span is a flashbulb at midnight compared to Earth's long winter eve.

This makes gaining knowledge hard. Each generation must grow and mature before it can begin the learning process and contribute to the understanding of the universe. Moreover, every human realizes, sometime during their life span, that the individual journey on the river of Time is short. Each generation learns that they live for only a short span of time. During their life, they have no idea when the journey will end. They also know that their final destination lies well beyond their knowledge.

This has bred an inherent fear of time in humans. They know Earth is billions of years old, while individuals are fortunate to live to the age of one hundred years. For centuries, humans could not reconcile themselves to understand that the world they lived in was vibrant and evolved long before their presence. It was difficult to compare a brief human life cycle of a superior species with the agelessness time of Earth.

The fear of time usually doesn't appear until later in life. Young people are not conscious of the passing of time; it is only when they begin to wonder how much more time they have that they realize what a valuable commodity they possess. As they age, they understand that they are mortal and their life will end. Because human life falls far short of eternity and humans cannot define the how and why of time, man begins to develop many theories and propositions in an attempt to explain the universe.

They do know this much. When man first began the struggle to survive and evolve, their natural surroundings were a basic part of their lives. The beauties of the primal sunrises and sunsets brought them happiness and joy. The black skies of night, dotted by uncountable numbers of twinkling stars, awed them. Life threatening weather and storms made them fearful. They lived so close to these deep emotions that nature became their first religion. It was the primal attempt of humans to rationalize what they couldn't explain. Rituals, rules, and ostentatious religious rites came much later, when philosophical beliefs replaced nature.

Humans quickly learned that weather changed from one season to the next. They also taught themselves to catalog time incrementally to keep track of its passage. Although time flows endlessly, humans measure its passage by breaking it into years, months, weeks, hours, minutes, and seconds. This brings order to the chaos of our uncertainty; for example, we can track the age of Earth and examine how its weather cycles effected its development.

However, the trek from cave to computer was not always a straight path. The trail to knowledge has been long and torturous with many detours and dead ends. Misunderstood facts and roused emotions hid progress like fog hides a countryside. A straying from the path of understanding occurred when humans once believed that the earth was completely flat. Another detour, due completely to emotion, involved Galileo Galilei who was put under house arrest by the church for believing that the earth revolved around the sun.

As a species, humans are still puzzled today by the uncertainties of who they are, where they are, and what lies ahead for them.

As individuals, we are thrust into and taken out of this world entirely by chance; we have no say in the matter. We are pawns in a system that we think we know but we really do not fully understand. We have taught ourselves mathematics and physics and we have reconstructed much of our past, but we know nothing about our future. The best we can do is make assumptions about what happens after life ceases.

We humans really do not know as much as we think we know. The more we learn the more we realize that we have limits. The finite cannot overtake the infinite. That may be a good thing.

In addition to being unsure of the answers concerning our origin, there is a fault into which all humans stumble. Each person knows that time is the quiet metronome that governs life. In times of happiness, we think it speeds up; in times of stress, we think it slows down; in reality, the beat is constant. Each of us travels the river of time at the same speed. Our emotions are the reason we think there's a change of velocity in our lives.

This does confuse humans and, as they age, their memories about past events change. Facts can fade and time lines get jumbled. We continue with our lives but we are subject to making errors based on our faulty recollections.

This is what happened with Bill Bruckner's prediction for Preacher John. "I don't think we'll ever know what happens to that bastard. He will hide for a while and we will probably never hear of him again." Bruckner was sure that Preacher John would be clever enough to escape detection. However, he forgot that Preacher John was a sex-driven egomaniac. Such a person cannot control his actions and will repeat his past activities. Eventually, Preacher John would come full circle and repeat his mistakes.

Many years later, by a quirk of fate, Maribeth and Bill finally did find out what happened to Preacher John.

When their son Milton was a child, he met a boy in his fourth grade class and they became lifelong friends. Coleridge Hawkins and Milton Bruckner were almost inseparable through elementary school, middle school, high school, and then Washtenaw Community College. They were with each other almost daily until the Hawkins family moved from Milan. Over time, the friends went their separate ways. Coleridge went to business school, graduated with a Masters degree in business and moved to Spokane, Washington. Coleridge lost touch with everyone in Milan, except Milton. When Milton married, Coleridge returned to Milan to be best man at Milton's wedding. He arrived a week earlier than the ceremony to renew his friendship and catch up on what was happening in his former hometown. At the time of Milton's wedding, Coleridge was still single.

Twelve years after Preacher John fled Milan Coleridge Hawkins phoned Milton to say he was finally getting married and he wanted Milton to be his best man. Milton arranged with his mother and father to manage the restaurant and his two children; Milton and his wife, Dorothy, flew to Spokane.

The two couples spent their first day getting to know each other. Milton and Dorothy were introduced to Coleridge's fiancee, Claudette. It didn't take long to plow the field of friendship and soon, they were at ease with each other. Milton and Coleridge chatted about the past, bringing their personal lives up-to-date. They shared decades of memories; their childhood adventures were resurrected and laughed over. Eventually, the past was behind them, and their recent lives became the topic of their conversations.

One evening, as they were relaxing on Coleridge's veranda, looking at the night sky and drinking martinis, Coleridge casually asked his guests, "Does the name Joshua Best ring a bell with either of you?"

Both Dorothy and Milton shook their heads. After a pause, Coleridge said, "I wasn't sure that it would. Well, let me ask you this, how about the name Preacher John? Does that ring a bell?"

That name, so far in their past, spoken in such a pleasant atmosphere, stunned the Bruckners. Milton finally replied. "Is there a connection?"

Coleridge replied, "Yes, they are both the same person. Preacher John changed his name to Joshua Best when he came to Spokane."

Dorothy asked, "How do you know that?"

"Joshua Best, or Preacher John, told me himself. I was his business advisor."

Dorothy shook her head. "He brings up such ugly memories from the past. Do you know anything about Preacher John's history?"

"More than I want to. As I said, he consulted me about his business dealings. He was not a nice person; in fact, he was a sick person. However, he needed my advice. He first hired me for his business dealings and, later on, he consulted me when he drew up his will. Before he passed, I spent a lot of time with him; he wanted to talk."

Milton said, "You seemed to have quite a connection with him."

"Maybe toward the end of his life I did, but not at first. Many years ago he called to ask me if I knew about real estate and business sales. He said he had come to Spokane about six months earlier and that he had read about me in our local newspaper, the *Spokesman*. At the time, I had helped a nonprofit charity reorganize to avoid unnecessary taxes and Preacher John was hoping to hire me.

"We met, he introduced himself as Joshua Best and said that he was buying a local business and wanted me to review the finances of the contract. That was the beginning. Over the next few years he expanded the business, added a few stores, and bought a lot of real estate. He brought all his financial questions to me and would occasionally talk about his past. He told me that he was a retired minister, that he was burned out, and was starting a new career. That is how I learned about his past as Preacher John."

Coleridge stopped speaking and checked to see if anyone, besides himself, wanted another martini. With drinks and nibbles refreshed, he returned to his story. "The business Preacher John bought was a non-profit thrift shop. You know, the kind that takes donated clothes and furniture and sells them; the profits then go to charity. With hard work and his personalty, Preacher John turned the shop into a thriving success. He soon opened several of these thrift shops and bought some prime business buildings. He seemed to have a knack for making money. I didn't suspect there was anything wrong with either him or the business until much later.

"Many business lunches and dinners with Joshua Best led me to believe that he was a person who would skirt the rules, if he could get away with it. Still, he followed most of my recommendations and I saw nothing illegal. His business appeared to be on the up-and-up, although I did suspect that he wasn't telling me everything. My first clue that there was more to the story than I knew was the time he came into my office after he was beaten up. Preacher John was a mess; he was bruised all over and had a black eye that was almost swollen shut. I asked him what happened and all he would say was that he wanted to sue the bastard who attacked him.

"I asked him if he called the police and he said 'No.' I asked him if he had seen a doctor and, again, he said 'No.' I told him he should get in touch with the police immediately; he said he wouldn't do that. The best I could do was get him to have some photographs taken and see his personal physician. Those were stopgap measures but they got him moving. I wondered why he had been assaulted. I couldn't understand why he didn't want the police involved in arresting the person who beat him. After a day or two, I completely forgot about the episode, as I was overloaded with filing tax returns for my big clients.

"Joshua Best came storming into my office a few months later to ask for my advice. He handed me a letter to read. Unless he paid ten thousand dollars within a week, his name would be released to the newspapers for engaging in sex and impregnating an underage teen. It was so repulsive to me, the differences in their ages, that I felt sick.

"Best asked me, 'What should I do?' and my immediate thought was, 'Cut the goddamn thing off.' However, that wouldn't have helped anything. Instead, I asked if the letter was true? He said that he didn't know the age of the girl. At that point, I got out a pad of paper. I knew that I would have to take detailed notes. It turned out to be a lengthy interview. Once Joshua Best started to talk, I could hardly shut him up. He told me all about his personal life in Spokane; it was seamy and steamy. After this disclosure he told me about his prior life in Milan as Preacher John. I have to tell you that, when we ended our discussion, I went home and took a hot shower. I felt filthy, unclean, as if I had been naked and pelted with fresh pig shit.

"My first question to Best was about his prior beating. Was it related to this blackmail letter? After trying to dodge the answer, he finally told me that it was. He enjoyed having sex and he was always on the lookout for women who would do what he wanted. He was also willing to pay for sex when no volunteers were available. That's how he got connected with the pimp who had him beaten. The pimp said he reneged on their agreed price and Best said he hadn't. The pimp called an enforcer to show Best what happens to a client who doesn't pay the agreed price. Since the beating, he had paid without argument because he wanted sex. He was sure that the pimp felt he was an easy mark and upped the ante with the blackmail threat.

"I told Best not to do anything until I got back to him, not to contact the pimp and definitely not give him any money. I needed to make some inquiries and find out more about the blackmailer. What I discovered was that Best was dealing with a bad man and that Best was very, very lucky.

"After talking to friends who were in law enforcement, I found that the man attempting to blackmail Best had a long rap sheet of violent crimes. He didn't specialize in pimping, he had tried his hand at car theft, breaking and entering, and assault and battery. By chance, the pimp was arrested two days after he mailed the letter to Best. He tried to rob a bank and completely botched the job. He fled the scene and, after a chase and a gunfight in which an officer was wounded, he was caught. Best's blackmailer seemed inept at his illegal activities and this worked in Best's favor. The blackmailer would go to jail, which meant he was in no position to threaten Best.

"In the meantime, I called my father, who no longer lived in Milan, but knew almost everyone there. He checked on Preacher John and his Milan ministry. Milton, you probably know more about those details than I do, but I did learn of his sordid past. I wanted as little to do with my client, Joshua Best, as possible.

"After the blackmail scare, I lost track of Best and I was glad of that. About two years ago he came into my office just as I was going home. At first, I didn't recognize him; he was standing with the help of crutches under each arm. He was only a little more than half as tall as he used to be and he needed the crutches to steady himself. His face was gaunt and he spoke with a hoarse whisper. He asked, 'Don't you recognize me, Coleridge Hawkins? I recognize you.'

"I was stunned. It was Best. He told me he had syphilis and that he didn't have much longer to live. This was why he came to my office. He needed help arranging his finances. I wanted to tell him to find another CPA because I didn't want anything to do with him, but I couldn't. He was pathetic. So, I not only took care of his financial needs, I helped him until he passed. He died two months after his will was written.

"In the end, he tried to do some good. He thought that, if his money helped one child have a decent life, maybe some of his lesser sins would be forgiven. He left almost a million dollars to two orphanages.

"That's the sad end for a man who was rotten to the core. He may have done some good, but he also did much harm."

The evening ended on that melancholy note. Early the next morning, Milton called his parents and he repeated the story of Joshua Best for almost two hours. He went over every detail at least twice because his parents wanted to hear, verify, and understand all the details. When Milton finally hung up, he took a deep breath to clear his lungs and his memory; he had done his duty. He had closed the book on the story of Preacher John; it was something his parents always wanted to know. From that point on, Milton's only interest was the upcoming wedding of his good friend.

Maribeth and Bill were galvanized by Milton's phone call. They immediately relayed the story to Isabel and Tannenbaum. The four of them met for dinner and the only topic of discussion was how Preacher John turned into Joshua Best and what became of him. He had gashed their lives too deeply for them to feel any sadness at his passing. However, they were now able to put him in the past and forget him. They promptly did.

As Maribeth and Bill lay in bed that evening, Maribeth asked, "Honey, why do you think Preacher John changed the way he operated?"

"Maribeth, that's a question that only he can answer. I would guess that when he fled Milan he was scared to death of Motorcycle Man. He undoubtedly took the stolen money and went into hiding, maybe in some small tourist town out west. I'm sure he decided that he must remain anonymous so he chose a different way to make money. He picked a good one; it is easy for large sums of cash to flow under the guise of charity. In fact that's similar to his previous occupation. The only thing that tripped him up was his constant lust.

"No matter the flock to which he belonged, the angels or the atheists, Preacher John was a black sheep."

From that point on, memories of Preacher John, or Joshua Best, evaporated like water on a hot sidewalk after a summer shower.

CHAPTER 11

The fortieth wedding anniversary of Maribeth and Bill Bruckner loomed on the horizon and it became apparent to them both that they were entering the senior citizen portion of their lives. As a rule, they did not feel they were in that category but, chronologically, they knew they had earned the distinction. They didn't fight against it; life had been very good to them. They were in good health, there had been no major family problems, and they were financially well-off. Moreover, they had each other. The "for better or for worse" part of their marriage vows had been for the better.

However, both were aware of aging. They noticed the generation ahead of them, Bruckner's mother, Isabel, and her husband, Tannenbaum, were slowing down. His mother was forgetful and Tannenbaum was physically fragile. At the same time, the generations behind them, their own children and grandchildren, were speeding up.

Maribeth's and Bill's personal relationship during their long marriage changed as their bodies changed. They went from just the two of them to a family of three children, and on to become the grandparents of six, with great-grandchildren in numbers yet to be counted. Their love, which started as a hot, passionate flame, became a steady, warm heat that reignited more often than their friends would suspect. What kept their bond so tight was the respect they felt for each other. They had separate minds and thoughts and each reached their own conclusions, many times ending up on opposite sides of a given situation. When that occurred, they simply accepted the other's disagreement and moved on. There was no chasm between them too wide to bridge.

Maribeth had become a handsome, matronly woman with many interests with and without her husband. She was a member of the Milan Historical Society, the Milan School Board, and still a faithful member of her beloved bridge club. She took yoga classes regularly and attended every event involving her grandchildren. Growing up with them was the major reason that she and Bill were not snowbirds who migrated to Florida.

Bruckner also kept busy. He dropped in on the family restaurant every few days, mostly out of habit. He had a small office set aside specifically for his use. He didn't intrude on business activities and he offered suggestions only when asked. He mostly talked family affairs with his son in the building where he earned his living for so many years; it was his comfort zone. He went to exercise classes and took walks with Henry Tannenbaum when he could get Tannenbaum to stir. He was active in Rotary Club along with being a member of the Downtown Development Authority. He spent much of his time volunteering at the Veterans Administration Hospital in Ann Arbor. He never forgot his own treatment when he came back from Vietnam.

The Bruckner's days were not a frenetic rush but a steady hum of activity. They had done their work penance and earned the right to retirement. They were pleased with their activities and their lifestyle.

In late February, Bruckner decided to go for a walk in Wilson Park. The weather, although cold, had been sunny for almost a week and he was sure that the asphalt paths were free of ice and not slippery. He got up before sunrise on Saturday, dressed warmly, and drove to the park. He walked beside the Saline River, enjoying the solitude and the early morning chill. As the day grew brighter, the stark contrast between the white snow and the black trees pleased him. The water made music by strumming against the icy river banks as it flowed downstream. The simple beauties of nature satisfied him. He bundled up against the wind and felt peaceful as he finished his walk.

Bruckner was nearing his car in the parking lot when he noticed a small, elderly woman walking about thirty feet ahead of him. He looked to see if he recognized her. At that moment, two large men suddenly appeared and grabbed her from behind. They tried to rip her handbag from her arms.

She screamed, "Help! Help!"

As Bruckner ran to her rescue, his boots slowed him down. One of the thieves hit her in the face and she fell, clutching her handbag. Bruckner caught up to the men and hit one on the side of his head. Both men immediately swung around to face Bruckner. One of them punched Bruckner while the other took a monkey wrench out of his pocket and swung at him. The blow hit Bruckner in the head and, even though his heavy parka deflected the wrench, he was knocked unconscious.

When he awoke, his head throbbed, he ached all over, and he was completely confused. He moaned, "Oh my god, I hurt. Where am I?" Immediately, he felt his hand being squeezed. Maribeth answered, "Darling husband, just lie still. You're in St. Joe Hospital. You were beaten up by two thugs in the parking lot. I have been praying for you, Love of My Life. You're going to be alright but you will need to be in the hospital for a couple of days."

"I'm in the hospital? Why am I here? I don't remember much of anything. I do know that my head hurts like hell. Hold my hand, Maribeth, I love you."

Maribeth squeezed her husband's hand a little harder. "The doctor will be back shortly to talk to you. In the meantime, just lie still and relax. I've been here waiting for you to wake up."

Bruckner still was totally confused and could not remember what happened. He asked a completely dumb question. "Maribeth, I didn't do anything that deserves a scolding did I?"

She leaned over and kissed his forehead. There were tears on her cheeks, "Silly Love, there's absolutely nothing to scold you for. You saved a woman's life. The doctor said you took a beating but that you will completely recover.

"I am so proud of you."

Just then, the doctor entered the room. He was a man of medium height, thin, with a shock of carrot red hair. He wore a white smock with his stethoscope draped around his neck. His voice was a low baritone and he radiated confidence. "Mr. Bruckner, I am Doctor Cornwallis and, yes, before you ask, it was one of my ancestors, a distant relative, who surrendered to George Washington at Yorktown. That was in the past; it is now the present and I'm on the side of the good guys. You are definitely one of them and I'm here to help you get better.

"Let me tell you about your condition. You have sustained a concussion. Your assailants hit you often and you were badly beaten, but you were fortunate to have been wearing heavy winter clothing. Your parka took the brunt of their kicks and punches. I know you ache all over, but I don't think you sustained any permanent damage.

"However, just to be sure, I think we should observe you for a few days while we run some tests. After that, we can release you and let nature finish getting you back to normal. Any questions?"

Bruckner nodded his head in agreement; he hurt too much to try to answer. The next three days proved the correctness of Doctor Cornwallis' diagnosis. The medical tests, the X-rays and the MRI's showed no permanent damage; his aches and pains eased enough so he could move his head and body without flashes of sharp pain. He began to think he would be able to leave the hospital.

During these three days Maribeth was in constant touch with Bill's mother, in Florida for the winter with Tannenbaum. Isabel wanted to know if she should fly home to be with her son. After Bill talked to her and reassured her that he was going to get well, Isabel was persuaded not to make a special trip back to Michigan.

The morning that he was scheduled to leave the hospital, Bruckner was cleaning up in the bathroom when two unexpected visitors tapped lightly on the door. Maribeth was sitting in a chair, reading the discharge instructions. She looked up and saw the men standing there. The first was a handsome black man of average height with a clean shaven head. His body was lithe, his brown suit neatly pressed. The second was slightly taller with blond hair and he wore a leather motorcycle jacket and black pants. He had a Van Dyke beard and dark glasses.

The man in the brown suit smiled at Maribeth. "Are you Mrs. Bruckner?"

She answered, "Yes."

Both men remained in the doorway. "We are detectives from the Monroe County Sheriff's Office. I am detective sergeant Frank Galloway and this is my partner, detective Lawrence O'Reilly. Here are our identification cards." They each handed Maribeth a plastic card that showed their photographs.

Maribeth glanced at the photographs and then looked at each man. She handed back the cards and asked, "Monroe County? Isn't the Washtenaw County Sheriff's Office doing the investigation?"

Sergeant Galloway smiled and answered, "Milan lies in two counties, Monroe and Washtenaw, so you can say that crimes are split, half in one county, half in the other. Wilson Park, where the attack took place, is inside Monroe County. This why our office is doing the investigation."

Maribeth nodded. "I assume that you are here to talk with my husband?"

"Yes, we have some questions and we need a written statement. Dr. Cornwallis wouldn't allow us access before today; he wanted to protect his patient. He called our office yesterday afternoon and said we could now talk with your husband."

Bruckner, who had overheard the conversation, said, "I have been wondering when someone from the sheriff's office would show up. I'll try to help you all I can."

Galloway and O'Reilly came in and sat by the bed opposite Maribeth. "Mr. Bruckner, we have the two suspects in custody and we have talked with the victim and the firemen who captured them. However, we still are not sure of a few facts and we're hoping you can fill us in on what happened."

"I didn't know that you caught those guys. I'll be glad to answer your questions but first, tell me, how is the lady who they attacked?"

"The only lasting physical injury she suffered is a broken front tooth when they punched her and knocked her down. However, she's badly shaken up and has moved in with her daughter. Incidentally, she considers you as the hero who saved her life.

"Now, if you would, tell us what you saw and heard during this attempted robbery."

Bruckner was surprised. "Me? A hero? Good Lord, no. I don't know as much as you may think. I was knocked out of action early. I was there to walk in Wilson Park that morning. As I headed back to my car, parked in the lot between the fire station and the park, I saw an elderly woman walking ahead of me. As I looked at her, two men ran up behind and tried to grab her purse. She screamed and I ran to help her. One of the thugs had a monkey wrench. After I spun him around, he hit me on the head with it. That's all I remember until I woke up here."

"Do you think that you could identify the two assailants?"

"Sergeant, to be perfectly honest with you, I don't think so. Both of them wore hoods and things happened so fast that I never got a good look at them. I didn't even see the face of the victim."

"Can you remember what you heard?"

"That wasn't much either. The lady screamed 'Help' twice and had just been thrown on the ground when I got there. Sorry, I'm afraid that I haven't been of much use to you but I wasn't in action very long. I'm glad they were caught. Can you tell me how you got them so quickly?"

Sergeant Galloway smiled as he replied, "This is an interesting case in the sense that both of you victims seem to have saved the life of the other. You interrupted one of the thugs just as he was ready to beat her with his monkey wrench. That probably would have killed her; she's an elderly woman and she didn't have a heavy parka or a hood covering her head.

"When they turned on you, she grabbed her purse, pulled out a can of Mace, and sprayed the eyes of the men who were beating and kicking you. She really doused them; they had hurt her physically and she was scared and furious. She kept spraying them and yelling for help.

"A group of volunteer firemen who were meeting at the fire station that Saturday came running to her rescue when they heard her screams. By the time they got to her, the two thugs were on their hands and knees, unable to see, pawing at their eyes, and begging for mercy.

"This is where the investigation stands today. We want to prosecute these two; they are dangerous and we want to get them off the streets as soon as we can build our case. Would you be able to write a statement within a few days and sign it?"

Before he answered, Bruckner asked for more information about what happened. He asked Sergeant Galloway, "What do you know about the victim?"

"Her name is Trina Lopez. She's an elderly woman who is retired; she worked at St. Joseph Hospital as a nurse's aide for about thirty-five years. She's a good, gentle person; she kind of reminds me of my grandmother. She didn't deserve to be mugged by those criminals. That's one of the reasons I want to close the paperwork and move on to the prosecution."

Bruckner promised to turn over a signed statement within a day or two and the officers left. Shortly after they left, there was another tap on the door. Bill and Maribeth looked up to see a woman standing in the doorway. She was wearing an unbuttoned overcoat and they could see a nurse's uniform underneath. She was olive-skinned, with black hair and a pleasant smile. She asked, "Mr. William Bruckner?"

He thought, "She is not one of my regular nurses," as he replied, "That's my name, but everyone calls me 'Bill.'"

She held out her right hand to shake his. "I wanted to talk to you before you left the hospital. My name is Sonia de Los Angeles and I came to thank you. It was my mother whose life you saved."

Bruckner felt embarrassed. It had not occurred to him that he had done anything heroic; he had tried to do nothing more than help someone in trouble. He thought of something that would help him over his awkward moment. "From what I've been told by the police, your mother prevented those thugs from beating me worse than they did by spraying them with Mace. She saved my life. She is a brave woman."

Sonia turned and addressed Maribeth, "We both have something to be grateful for. You have your husband and I have my mother. Things could have been worse."

Maribeth was taken with her sincerity. "You are right. Daughters and mothers understand how precious life can be.

"How is your mother doing?"

"Not too well, I'm afraid. Her mouth hurts where her front tooth was broken. She is so frightened about her experience that she has moved out of her apartment and is living with me and my three children. I am a widow and, of course, she is welcome."

Bruckner asked, "And how are you and your family coping?"

"We are managing. It's crowded at my house and it is sad to see an older person knocked off their feet. But she is alive and recovering from her injuries so I'm blessed.

"I have to go. I'm a nurse and I work in pediatrics. I need to be on duty shortly. I've been checking on you every day and I knew you were leaving today. I want you to know that my family and I prayed for you and are so thankful that you saved my mother.

"God bless you, Mr. Bruckner."

Bill Bruckner squirmed. He knew his visitor was expressing her heartfelt gratitude but he didn't feel that he deserved that much praise. To climb out of his well of embarrassment, he asked, "What was your mother doing in the park so early?"

Sonia de Los Angeles laughed. "Every Saturday morning my mother goes to the Milan Bakery early to buy a loaf or two of day old bread. Then she walks to the river and feeds the Canada geese. When the weather is good, she takes her grandkids; but, rain or shine, cold or hot, Momma has to feed her birds on Saturday morning.

"I asked her once why she has to do this every Saturday, even in weather that is so bad I won't allow my kids to go with her. She told me that while she feeds the geese to keep them alive she prays for the rest of the world. On Sunday, she goes to church to the earliest Mass, to make her prayers for the rest of the world more formal."

Her voice broke as she added, "Now, she seems so sad and afraid to leave our house. She keeps asking how you are doing.

"I only hope I can get her back to feeding her birds again."

Bruckner looked at her, in complete amazement, while she spoke. His mind flashed back to the two or three times that he and Henry had seen an elderly woman feeding the geese on their Saturday morning walks. He remembered that they changed their walking pattern on Saturdays to avoid all the squawking geese and their droppings. He thought to himself, "Boy, is Henry going to be surprised when I tell him that the woman we avoided is the woman who was attacked and who saved me."

His thoughts came back to the present. He looked at Mrs. de Los Angeles, then Maribeth. "Listen, Mrs. de Los Angeles, my wife and I would like to meet your mother. I want to thank her, and if we can help in any way we would be glad to. Your mother has been through an awful ordeal."

Sonia quickly replied, "Oh, Mr. Bruckner, my mother would be thrilled to meet you. She talks about you constantly. She would feel so honored if you came to visit her."

They exchanged addresses and phone numbers and a few days after Bruckner got home, they set up a time to meet. Bill and Maribeth drove to the de Los Angeles home on Mooreville Road. It was a small house, tidy and well kept. Mrs. de Los Angeles walked Bill and Maribeth into her tiny living room and introduced them to her mother. Bruckner was surprised to see how short and frail Mrs. Lopez was; he guessed that she would have to stand on a box to be over five feet tall. Her face mirrored years of living and hard work but her expression was one of peace and serenity. She had gray hair which was piled into a knot on top of her head, and she smiled as they were introduced. She, in turn, introduced her three grandchildren, polite and well mannered. She proudly talked about each of them before she dismissed them.

Sonia served tea and cookies to their guests and they began to chat. Maribeth and Bill noticed that Mrs. Lopez held her right hand in front of her face when she spoke. They assumed that she did not want them to see her mouth. Her guests let her lead the conversation by asking questions. She told them about herself; her mother had come to Michigan from Mexico as a widow. She was an only child who was born in Ann Arbor. She worked as a nurse's aide for thirty-eight years at St. Joseph Mercy Hospital. And, she worked hard so that her daughter would have a formal education. When Sonia became a registered nurse, Mrs. Lopez's dream had come true. Her daughter was going to have a job with more prestige and a much better salary than she ever had.

Near the end of their conversation, Mrs. Lopez appeared to feel more comfortable talking with them and Bruckner wanted to steer the conversation toward the attack. However, he didn't want to repeat questions that the police had already asked, and he didn't want to ask questions that seemed stupid, such as "Did you notice that you were being followed?" He was not sure how to begin. Finally, he decided not to ask any questions. He quietly said, "Mrs. Lopez, my wife and I want to thank you for coming to my rescue when I was unconscious. Your actions surely saved my life."

She took her hand away from her mouth to wave it as a stop sign. Bruckner could see the gap in the front of her mouth where her tooth was broken. He gathered that she was undoubtedly sensitive about her appearance. He wondered if it hurt.

She quickly responded, "Mr. Bruckner, it is I who is thankful. If those men had kept on hitting me, they would have killed me. I wasn't wearing a parka and they were so much bigger than me. As you know, any block of ice can be broken into cubes with a hammer. They surely would have gotten me if you hadn't stepped in."

She paused for a second and then continued, "But there was no way I was going to give them my purse. I worked hard for my money. Let them get a job and earn it like I did. After they hit me and knocked me down, I fished into my purse to find my can of Mace. I always carry it because I know there are bad people in this world. I was angry, they had hurt me. They were busy beating you and had forgotten about me. I was able to get real close before I sprayed them with Mace. Once they stopped to protect their eyes, I kept on spraying. I felt that it was my right to get even. They deserve what they got because they were doing bad things. The police tell me that I was swearing at them in Spanish. I guess that's true. They are scum who tried to rob an old lady of her money.

"However, you are the one who saved my life. For myself, my daughter, my grandkids, I thank you. I will pray for you everyday of my life."

The four of them chatted for a while but it soon became apparent that Mrs. Lopez was getting tired. She faded from the conversation and didn't talk much. She kept her hand over her mouth more often and she began patting her lips. The Bruckners noticed she was drifting away, so they said their goodbyes.

Driving home, there wasn't much conversation between them; they were each caught up in their separate thoughts and impressions about their visit. It wasn't until they were sitting at their kitchen table with pie and coffee, that Maribeth said, "You're awfully quiet, Bill. What are you thinking about?"

Bruckner leaned over and touched Maribeth on the cheek. "I knew you would ask. I'm thinking about Mrs. Lopez. You won't believe this but I have seen her before. When Henry and I walked on Saturdays, we occasionally saw her feeding her geese. It was very noisy, with a lot of geese flying all around her bench. We were concerned about being hit by goose poop, so we changed our Saturday route to avoid that area. What a strange twist of fate. I can hardly wait to tell Henry.

"She's so small, yet neither of those big bastards could pull her handbag away from her. It must have looked like elephants wrestling an ant, and the ant won the match. Good for her. What a feisty lady. She's not afraid to say what she thinks. I like her; she has a sense of humor. However, I am concerned. You saw her keep her mouth covered. Do you think she's in pain?"

Maribeth replied, "I'm not sure. Part of the reason she put her hand over her face could be vanity; she probably takes great pride in what she looks like in public. Like you, I also wondered if she was in pain. That was a terrible ordeal under any condition and, for a woman her age, it must have been especially difficult.

"You're right, she has been though the mill. She seems like such a good person. Can you imagine going to the park, feeding the geese, and praying for the world informally on Saturday. Then, on Sunday, going to church to pray for the same thing formally? She must have a heart full of love. Mrs. Lopez certainly does not deserve what happened to her."

Bill was quiet for a while before he finally said, "I feel responsible for her in a way."

Maribeth smiled. "Somehow, I knew that was coming. You are a pushover and I love you for it. I absolutely agree. We should try to help her but I don't know what we can do."

Bruckner suggested, "Well, how about getting in touch with her daughter and asking if she has any suggestions? That would surely tell us if we could be of help, don't you think?"

Maribeth called Sonia and set up a luncheon date within the next few days. Sonia came to their home and they quickly established the intimacy necessary to talk about her mother's problems. She told them that her mother had been so glad to meet them and how much their visit had meant to her. Sonia confided that she was worried about her mother. Mrs. Lopez was feeling some pain with her broken tooth, but that was not the reason she was hiding her mouth. Her mother was always proud of being fastidious and now she thought her appearance was ugly. She was ashamed of her looks and no amount of persuasion did any good. She was concerned that her mother was afraid to go to the park again. After a question from Bruckner, Sonia also admitted that her mother was not going to church on Sundays. Her mother's personality seemed to change since the assault and Sonia wondered if she would ever recover from the experience.

As they talked, it was evident to Maribeth and Bill that Mrs. Lopez's broken tooth needed attention. Sonia said that neither her mother nor she could afford dental bills right now. Worse, her mother wouldn't consider going to the clinic at the University of Michigan's dental school because, "She didn't need anyone's charity."

The Bruckners promised to visit Mrs. Lopez. And they did, once a week. They soon confirmed their impression that Mrs. Lopez was a down to earth person with a strong, simple character. She accepted no excuses for not working hard. She had insisted that her daughter get an education and not end up a nurse's aide. They also found that Mrs. Lopez was stubborn; until she had the money to go to a dentist, she would not go to the dental clinic.

After their third visit, Bill said to Maribeth, "She ain't going to give in gracefully, she's an obstinate lady. We need to do something."

"What can we do?"

"First, I'm going to call my dentist friend, Dr. Franklin Delano Roosevelt Rubin. Whoa, don't laugh at that name. That's what his parents called him after they emigrated to this country, Roosevelt was elected President and they became citizens. He's a Vietnam veteran like me and he's a good guy. He has been my dentist for years. I'll ask him to do whatever it takes to fix her teeth.

"Now comes a question for you. What would you say if I told you that I am thinking of paying Mrs. Lopez's bills?"

Maribeth waved her palm at him and laughed. "I would tell you that I'm not the slightest bit surprised."

"Well, would you object if I paid her bills?"

"Why would I object? You are trying to do good for someone who needs help. We can afford it financially and it's the right thing to do. I'll agree with whatever you wish to do for Mrs. Lopez. However, I'm not your problem, not by a long shot. Getting her to agree to see your dentist will be your problem."

Bruckner knew that his Maribeth was probably right.

At his first opportunity, Bruckner talked to Dr. Rubin and explained Mrs. Lopez's circumstances, Dr. Rubin told him that he would be glad to examine her and only charge for his actual expenses. If necessary, he would give Mrs. Lopez a very low dollar amount and collect the rest from Bruckner.

Bill and Maribeth held a strategy session with Sonia to discuss the best way to approach her mother. They all agreed that she would be stubborn and resist. Bruckner convinced them that he should talk to

Mrs. Lopez alone. That way, she wouldn't feel pressured by a posse into something she was reluctant to do.

On a day that was warm with sunshine and hinting of spring, Bruckner arrived at Mrs. Lopez's house carrying a plain Hershey bar. He handed it to her when she answered the door. She looked at him quizzically, accepted it, and asked, "Where is your lovely wife?"

"Maribeth couldn't come today, Mrs. Lopez."

"Well, come in Mr. Bruckner and sit down."

She served him tea from a pot; three teacups and some homemade cookies sat beside it. After he was served, Mrs. Lopez broke off a piece of the candy bar, put it in her mouth, and let it dissolve on her tongue. All the while she did not say a word.

Finally, with her hand covering her mouth, she said, "It is a little strange that you make an appointment to visit today and arrive not with your wife, but with a candy bar. If I was a suspicious old woman I'd say that this is a different kind of visit."

Bruckner thought, "She is sharp." Aloud, he said, "You are right, I do have something to say. However, before I tell you, I want to remind you that you saved my life and that you tell everyone that I saved yours. To me, this means that I'm involved in your life and you're involved in mine and that we care about each other."

He paused for a second, and then asked, "Would you like to be able to feed your geese again?"

"Yes," was the quick response.

"Then, why don't you?"

Mrs. Lopez didn't answer right away. Finally, she replied, "Because I don't want people to see my broken mouth. They will make comments or ask questions."

"Then why don't you get your 'broken mouth' fixed? Doesn't it hurt?"

Another long silence before she answered, "Yes, sometimes it hurts bad. However, I can't afford it and I won't stand in line at the dental clinic to accept charity."

Bruckner smiled at Mrs. Lopez. He admired her honesty, her simplicity; he considered them to be rare qualities. He would treat her the same way she treated him, hoping that she would accept his offer. He began by asking, "Mrs. Lopez, how long were you a nurse's aide?"

"More than forty years."

"That's a long time. And, during all that time, didn't your neighbors and friends come to see you to ask you questions about their health?"

"Of course, there were many sicknesses and diseases that I could help them cure without going to the hospital."

"Oh, so you can give charity to people who need help but you can't accept charity from people who want to help you?"

Mrs. Lopez looked surprised. She pointed at her friend and replied, "Hah, You are trying to trap an old woman. This is different. I need someone who has special skills and knowledge; my neighbors didn't."

Bruckner shook his head. "No, it's not different. Your neighbors came to you because they knew you did have special skills and knowledge. You were their doctor and you cared about them.

"Your daughter, my wife and I, want to help you in the same way you helped others. I have a friend who is a dentist and is willing to examine you to see if he can help. He wants to do that because he doesn't want anyone to suffer or be in pain. Like you, he considers doing good for others is the right thing to do."

"You told your dentist friend about me?"

"Yes, I did, because I don't want you having pain, if there's any way to fix your tooth."

Mrs. Lopez sat a long time without saying a word. Then she asked, "He will tell me how much this will cost before he begins? I don't want charity and I will pay."

"I'm sure he will."

She again sat quietly, thinking about accepting help. "Well, that's not charity and maybe I can make monthly payments. I would like to get my mouth fixed and have no more pain; I really hurt at times. I think I might go see your dentist friend."

She paused again before she added, "I'm glad that God sent you to me."

Bruckner made no reply to that statement.

It took several visits before Dr. Rubin finished the work on Mrs. Lopez's teeth. When he was done, it was impossible to see that tooth had been broken. His fee was low enough that Mrs. Lopez could arrange to pay it without any financial help from Bruckner.

However, after Mrs. Lopez's tooth was fixed, there still remained a problem. The attack had frightened her and she was afraid to go out by herself. Gone was the lady who walked freely through her neighborhood, talking to children and giving nonstop advice to their parents. Now she would not leave the house without her daughter or a friend accompanying her. She would go to Wilson Park only if Bruckner or Sonia went with her. Her horizon of happiness seemed blotted out by her attackers and she could no longer navigate without it. She was physically healthy but her joy of life was almost completely drained; Mrs. Lopez's spirit was crushed by her muggers. Bill tried to explain her state of mind to Maribeth. They sat on their porch drinking lemonade when he began. "While we were at her home, she was calm and pleasant. It was only when she and I and two of her grandchildren got to Wilson Park that she changed. As we got out of the car, she visibly froze; she tensed up. We walked to the Milan Bakery to get bread for the geese and sweet rolls for the kids. When anyone approached us, she moved close enough to slide into one my pockets.

"She has relaxed a little since that first time. Now Mrs. Lopez mostly watches the kids feed the geese. She isn't quite as tight as she was but she is far from relaxed. When I told Sonia how her mother acted, she was upset. Her mother had always been so happy going to the park with her grandkids. Now, one of her few remaining pleasures has been taken from her.

"Sonia is right. I don't know if Mrs. Lopez will ever enjoy feeding her geese again. Right now, she is scared to death.

"It was a sad afternoon."

Later, lying side by side in bed, straight as two carrots and holding hands, Maribeth said, "Bill, you have been quiet all evening. Is something bothering you?"

"My mind keeps going back to Mrs. Lopez. She's close to the same age as my mother. When I think about her like that she becomes very personal to me. I admire her. She has worked hard all her life to earn a living. With only a little education, she raised a family and she pushes her grandchildren to get the education she always wanted.

"Trina Lopez is not a cardboard cut out. She's an honest, forthright person who speaks her mind. She can be gruff; you can either take her or leave her. I find her delightful. If you believe in God, she has to be considered one of his bravest foot soldiers."

"Why do you say, 'bravest?'"

"Because she doesn't just wave the flag of Christianity, she actually lives it. She measures her actions by the Ten Commandments. You have to admire that."

Maribeth had to smile. "You really like her, don't you? Have you ever told her that you don't believe in God?"

"Yes, I like her very much and no, absolutely no, we have never discussed religion. I have never told her that I don't believe in God. She follows her beliefs the same way I follow my disbeliefs. There's no need for me to compare my thoughts with hers. I'm sure she would be surprised if she knew my views. Her views are much simpler than mine. I imagine her picture of an atheist is a person with horns on his head and his teeth filed to points, ready and eager to chomp on Christian children.

"In reality, thinking of her is where my problem starts. She deserves a lot better than she has received. She's in the twilight of her life and she should be able to enjoy one of the few things she loves so much—feeding her Canada geese at Wilson Park with her grandkids. Instead, she's afraid to leave her daughter's house. Mrs. Lopez has faithfully followed her Catholic beliefs all her life, why should this ordinary desire be denied her?

"As far as I'm concerned, she has been cheated by her God. You can tell me all about 'God's will' but I have a difficult time believing that, in his grand scheme of things, he can deny Mrs. Lopez the happiness she has earned. Doesn't that appear to be petty? She should be showered with happiness and joy instead of anxiety and pain.

"I think your God really gets a pass from his believers. When good things happen, everyone says, 'Praise God for the blessings He bestows.' When bad things happen, everyone says, 'It is God's will,' and they let the calamity drop there. If He is held responsible for the good things, He should also be held responsible for the bad things."

Maribeth didn't say anything right away. "You haven't said any of this to Mrs. Lopez have you?"

"Hell, no. I'm sure she would neither understand nor agree with me. These are my own thoughts and they have nothing to do with hers. I wouldn't interfere with her beliefs any more than I want her to interfere with mine.

"You will find that most atheists keep their thoughts to themselves because they feel they are in the minority. Many believers become hostile the minute they find out a person is an atheist. I don't know why. Religion treats us as devils with pitchforks with no morals or standards."

Maribeth patted his hand. "Listen, my love, I do not agree with you about God. I believe in Him, you don't. I can't rebut your disbelief any more than you can rebut my belief. So, I rely on my faith and you rely on your what—evolution, revolution, anarchy? I don't have the correct words to describe your idea of the universe.

"Honey, I'm not mocking your disbeliefs, I just have a hard time understanding why you think there is no God. I also can't picture religion as you envision it. You're intelligent, and I know you think things through before you make up your mind, so your beliefs, whatever they are, aren't just random thoughts."

Maribeth stopped talking for awhile before continuing. "You've seen the same events take place in this world that I have and you and I start with the same values of right and wrong. But, you interpret these events much differently than I do. Sometimes, I have to pray hard to keep my faith, no matter what the evidence. I completely agree with you that what has happened to Trina Lopez is awful. That doesn't mean I have lost my faith in God; it only means I have to try harder to be a better person during my lifetime and help the more unfortunate like Trina Lopez.

"Even though I disagree with you, you have struck a nerve. I will admit you raise puzzling questions; and they are not foolish. I have no answers concerning why Mrs. Lopez should have experienced such a bad time at her age. She's a lovely person and we both agree that she certainly deserves more than being traumatized."

This time, there was a longer pause. Then, Maribeth spoke softly, "I have lived many, many years as your loving wife, grateful to have you as my husband. You may not believe in religion but you follow the virtues that religion preaches. You are one of the kindest, most gentle persons I've ever known. Which makes me wonder why you haven't resolved your issues with God? You both seem to be on the same side."

Bruckner kissed his wife on top of her head and sighed "I am not too sure that God would agree that He and I are on the same side. I can agree with you that if there is a God, he would want nothing but the best for the species he created. However, I think that there is a disconnect between your God and the humans he is supposed to have created. Humans tend to cluster together in their individual religions and they forget his message of universal love.

"I didn't decide to become an atheist in the way you pick a meal from a menu. It's just that I found too much hate and unhappiness that went unanswered. I'm not talking about just America, your God is responsible for all of humankind in every continent on our earth. There are armies of starving, sick people—sick children—all over the world. Millions have been killed in unjust wars. They were innocent of any crime, except being in the wrong place at the wrong time. I've seen that myself. Take my word, it hurts to see such total suffering. Believe me, it's not right. That's not the way the world should be run.

"If your God created the human race, he either has lost control or has given up on his creation. How can poverty and pain ever be justified? The picture of kids with bellies bloated from malnutrition and flies all over their faces makes me sure that there really is no almighty power in control. I can't reconcile the heartbreaking moans of innocent people with the heavenly harp twangs that religions broadcast.

"I didn't originally choose to be an atheist and it isn't easy being one. You are constantly marching on your left foot while your friends and neighbors are on their right. And, I can't feel true to myself if I belong to a religion that believes it is the only way to salvation. First, I'm not sure there is such a thing as salvation. Second, why does each religion insist that it has the best ticket on the railroad?

"I backed into atheism because I see no other answer to explain why there isn't enough love and compassion in the world to offset all the hate, the disasters, and the accidents that slaughter the innocent. If others can derive personal peace from religion, good for them; I wish them luck. For me, I see no organized, orderly approach to our universe. You tell me that God doesn't have to reveal the hand he is playing to us humans and I reply to you by saying that I don't believe He ever dealt the cards.

"I realize that you put up with a lot from me and I feel blessed that you are my life companion. It has not been easy for you. However, I want you to know this. I have loved you with all my heart and soul from the time that I first met you. Your love has nourished me and made me aware that no matter how our universe is run, I am fortunate to have you for my wife. I am an atheist lucky enough to be in love with one of God's most beautiful creatures. I will go to my grave considering myself the most fortunate man in the world because I have been blessed to have you as my partner."

Husband and wife both realized that there was no more to say. Each believed what they believed and they knew they were in disagreement. However, both recognized the goodness in their partner and that their disagreement was not the same as disrespect. They loved each other fiercely and understood that only after death would they discover who was right or wrong. Until then, they had each other and what happens after life was a completely different matter.

In all their years of snow birding, Isabel and Henry Tannenbaum never followed a set schedule for leaving or returning to Florida. They relied completely on the weather and their personal whims. They would reluctantly leave Michigan only after the fall leaves faded and all the family reunions were finished. They would willingly leave Florida when the spring flowers in Michigan were beginning to bloom. This year they were more eager than ever to head home. They had not seen their friends or families during the winter and that made them antsy. Isabel was also extremely eager to see her son and reassure herself that he had completely recovered from the attack in Wilson Park.

Although she had been dissuaded from returning home after Bill was assaulted, Isabel kept worrying about him, Maribeth, and her grandchildren. They were so much on her mind that she decided to leave Florida weeks before they usually made the trip. Isabel and Henry arrived in Milan earlier than expected and completely unannounced.

Ordinarily, on the first Sunday after the Tannenbaums returned from Florida, there would be a big welcome home party. Isabel and Maribeth, would lay out a menu, cook too much food, and invite the whole family. Isabel's children and grandchildren would show up and tribal chaos would follow. That was Isabel's way of catching up and regaining contact with the family she missed so much.

No one in the family had any idea of the Tannenbaum's return. Only Maribeth, Bruckner, Isabel, and Henry came to the homecoming dinner. No one else in the family could make it; they all had previous commitments. The four of them tried a new recipe for John Marzetti that Maribeth and Isabel found on the Internet. They enjoyed themselves, ate too much, and everyone pitched in to clear the dining room table and clean the kitchen. They retreated to the living room to continue talking.

Only toward the end of the evening, after Isabel heard firsthand about the attack and was certain that her son had recovered, did the talk turn toward the other victim. Tannenbaum turned to Bruckner. "Bill, I was amazed when you called and told me that the woman who was attacked was the same woman we avoided on Saturdays. I don't remember what she looked like but I do remember her feeding the geese. What a mess that was.

"Anyhow, you told us about the attack on Mrs. Lopez and her immediate reaction, but we haven't heard anything since. How is she doing now? Is she making any progress?"

"Henry, I'm discouraged. After all this time, she is still frightened when she leaves her daughter's house. To some degree, she has withdrawn and it's difficult to get her to talk. That attack changed her and I don't know if she will ever recover. Her daughter is despondent. She feels that her mother has been turned from what Sonia calls, 'the neighborhood gadfly to the neighborhood ghost.' I'm not sure that she'll ever get over it."

Isabel said, "What a terrible thing to happen to her." They nodded their heads in agreement and sat quietly. There was nothing else to say.

Then, Bill spoke. "You know, for the life of me, I don't understand it. Here is a woman who obeyed all the rules and is a good person. Now, toward the end of her life, her world is ripped open. Why can't she be allowed to enjoy her remaining years and her grandkids?

"It bothers me; I've been thinking a lot about the attack on Mrs. Lopez. It raises the same issues that the four of us have discussed for years. We are right back where we started, except we are all much older. Maybe no wiser, but older. And, unfortunately, as we age, we get less flexible. If you don't believe me about flexibility, just stand up and try to touch your toes."

Bruckner paused, then continued, "That stiffness is not confined to our bodies, it applies equally to our thoughts and mental processes. We are entrenched in our previous positions. However, there is one good thing to be said for growing old. No matter how much we disagree, age gives us the wisdom to bow to each other.

"So, here we are, after all these years, right back to the same discussions and the same questions you keep asking me. You have never changed my mind and I have never convinced you. However, as far as I can tell, our differences never stopped us from talking to each other.

"I want tell you about my recent thoughts since the attack on Mrs. Lopez. And, I have some questions for you. I know that you will hop all over me. You have in the past and you will in the future. That's okay, at least hear me out and think about my questions.

The three of them nodded and, after a moment of thought, Bruckner continued, "Let me start by going from the bottom to the top. It will help you understand how I came to be the black sheep in the family.

"When I was younger I attended a heck of a lot of religious services. That includes many of the Protestant and Catholic churches and the Jewish temples around this area. Some I liked, some I didn't. That depended on which way the sermon pointed me, toward heaven or hell. However, the one feeling I got from all of the visitations was the warmth these people showed each other within their congregations. The building was filled with love and respect for their own kind. That feeling was transmitted to any newcomer who attended their service. Hospitality was extended to me, an unknown visitor, at whichever service I attended. It was an exciting feeling. For people going to their respective churches, religion is alive and pleasant.

"However, as you go up the chain—from the local level to where religious policies are made—the feeling of goodwill fades. Remember that besides being a way of life, a church is an institution that needs funds to survive. That may be one reason why each church claims to be the only way to salvation. Whatever the reason, each religion claims its faith is the only way.

"And, this is the place where my problem with religion starts. The hierarchy associated with each religion seems more intent on format than on faith. Why can't Catholics, Jews, Protestants, and all other believers, have the same rewards in the afterlife no matter which path is followed? They all practice love and peace; this they have in common even if they express their religions differently. For a simple mind like mine, one God per universe is enough. If God loves one race or one color more than the others, why did he bother making second bests? That puzzles me.

"There are many more things that puzzle me. If they happened to meet, what would God and Allah say to each other? For that matter, what would Jesus and Muhammad talk about?

If Jesus appeared as a tourist in any holy Christian site, what would he think? In Jerusalem, would he be disappointed at the distrust and anger that hangs like urban smog over everything? In the Vatican, would Jesus condone all the beautiful art work and edifices or would he want those riches turned into fishes and loaves and distributed to the poor and needy? I don't pretend to know the answers.

"Another question based on population. I know that you three believe that goodness and love is not contained to just one religion. But, let's say there are eight billion people living in the world today. And, let's say that Christians, including all Catholics and Protestants, are about two billion of that population. Now, if Christianity is the only way to heaven, as Christians are told, that leaves three-fourths of the world's people damned to perdition. Even if my figures are not accurate, my point is, by having this minority vote, most people alive today are doomed. I don't believe that any God, no matter what religion, would deliver such an ultimatum.

"So, that's where I am, confused about formal religion but not the slightest bit concerned about it. My personal opinion, and I'm speaking only for myself, is that there is no God above us humans who could put our universe in harmony. I wish there were. I keep going back to a question that I have no answer for—why can't religions unite people in love instead of dividing them in hate? I wish I knew the answer. Religion is either a handmaiden that helps the faithful or religion is a whore that religious bigots try to sell to everyone.

"Whether or not my atheism puts me in the bad person category is, I think, a separate question."

With that, Bill Bruckner held up both arms in a surrender position. "Now I'm ready to face the slings and arrows of you who disagree with me. However, before you launch either, I could use something to drink and maybe another cookie."

His mother walked over and patted him on the shoulder. "I will fix us all a snack. You certainly deserve that much before your sentencing." Maribeth followed Isabel into the kitchen. Bruckner and Tannenbaum didn't say a word until they returned.

After everyone finished their snacks, Henry put down his coffee cup down and began, "Bill, I can't speak for the pope but I can answer you as a friend. We have known each other for what, more than forty-two years? During all this time I have been a devout Catholic while you have been struggling with your conscience.

"First, I will tell you that I don't always agree with my church. I think that women should be able to be priests and I think priests should be allowed to marry. In spite of my disagreements, I believe in God and Jesus Christ. My faith carries me through any differences with the church.

"You raise questions that are provocative and for which I have no immediate answers. However, I know in my heart that Jesus is the Prince of both Peace and Love, and that no innocent person should ever be wrongly judged or condemned. Again, I believe this based on my faith.

"Faith seems to be the major difference between us. I believe that my reward for trying to live a good life will come after I die; you don't believe in life after death. As we both sit here, neither of us can convince the other that one of us is wrong. So, as it has been from the start, neither of us will know the answer until we die.

"In the meantime, I will say that you are one of the nicest people I have ever met. You claim to be an atheist but you show as much goodness as the most pious priest in my church. To me it's strange but true; you follow religious values but claim no religion at all. I'm sure there is a place for you in heaven but I'll be damned if I know exactly where. That will be up to Saint Peter and his committee to decide. However, I do intend to have a talk with him about you.

"Until then, let's all enjoy ourselves for the persons we are and the love we share with each other."

Later that evening, Maribeth and Bruckner hugged each other in bed, she suddenly patted his cheek and said, "I didn't say anything tonight but Henry is right about you, you are a good man. I would say that your head is a little screwed up but your heart is in the right place. You are a good husband and a wonderful father.

"Do you remember how you and I used to dance at the Crossfire every night after we closed? We were finding each other then. Those were such sweet nights. I can still remember the very first time I heard Ed Ames sing, "My Cup Runneth Over." I was dancing with you. That song was so beautiful I adopted it as our own. I still get goose bumps whenever I hear it.

"That was the night you told me that you had seen enough death, pain and misery, and all you wanted was peace and harmony. I cried for you because I knew then that you cared for the world and I knew that I would marry you, if you asked me.

Later, I was completely surprised to find out that you were an atheist. I'm still not sure what that really means because you have the same moral values that I have. In many instances, yours are better than mine. You can be more forgiving than I could ever be. So, I don't care what you call yourself, I know who you are and I love you for it."

There was no reply from Bruckner. After a long period of silence, Maribeth continued, "Bill, I know you're not sleeping, aren't you going to say anything?"

"Honey, I don't know what to say. I'm not a philosopher or a deep thinker; I'm only a person who was always more interested in making a living than in solving riddles. I have thought about life and death as much as you. As an atheist, I'm as human as you who believe in God. I just drew a different conclusion. That doesn't make me any more right or wrong than you.

"What I try to do is bumble through life loving those who are closest to me and trying to do the best I can for everyone else. I believe in trying to do good because it makes me feel good. I guess that is my religious creed. I can't explain it any different from that.

"However, there is one fact that I do know. The smartest, happiest thing I ever did in my life was to marry you. I consider you as my reward for trying to live an honest life. I am deeply thankful that you are my wife.

"Now, if you don't mind, I'd like to try to go to sleep."

CHAPTER 12

Michigan is the largest state east of the Mississippi River. However, Michigan is not one continuous land mass. It is a state consisting of two large, independent peninsulas connected by a bridge that is almost five miles long; the bridge connects them at the Straits of Mackinac. Because of these two peninsulas, Michigan is bounded by four of the five Great Lakes and has the longest freshwater coastline in the world. The informal name for each peninsula is easy to remember. The more northern area of Michigan is referred to as "The Upper Peninsula," while the larger southern area is called "The Lower Peninsula."

Although both areas together form the state of Michigan, there are distinct differences between the two. Each have their own climates, cultures, economies and lifestyles. The Upper Peninsula, with its vast undeveloped areas and sparse population, has a more bucolic, laid-back way of life. The Lower Peninsula, with its larger population, maintains a much more robust, cosmopolitan environment that includes commercial centers and factories.

The relationship between the two sections, although united through proximity, politics, and taxes, is sometimes strained. Their ethnic and historical backgrounds are so different that their impressions of each other, even though jocular, are not particularly flattering. The area north of the Mackinac Bridge is seen as a territory different from the area south of the bridge and, sometimes, both sides act as if they were sorry that the bridge was ever constructed and opened. They act like long-time dance partners, each hoping upon hope, that a third dancer will be kind enough to cut in.

The Lower Peninsula is a little contemptuous of the "Yoopers," a term for the Uppers. The Yoopers refer to the area south of them as "Troll Land" or "Da Mitten." The Trolls, the people who live under the bridge, think the Yoopers are a little slow and wonder why any sensible person would want to live through the harsh winters that the Upper Peninsula endures. The Yoopers think most Trolls are aggressive, self-centered, and don't appreciate the tranquility of living in a peaceful, natural environment.

Despite the misunderstandings, the two Michigan land masses seem to work because they have more in common than they have differences. As a political unit, they rely on each other. There is no personal anger in their thoughts; they are rather amused by their partner's perceived shortcomings. They leave it at that; for both the Upper and Lower peninsulas coexist and life goes on.

However, within the state of Michigan there is a rift wider than the distance between the two peninsulas. This split is longstanding, it completely divides the state, and is far more complicated and emotional than simple geography. It raises emotions, both good and bad, to a fever pitch. From a logical point of view, these emotions are almost irrational in origin. The state divides its loyalty between its two biggest educational institutions, Michigan State University and the University of Michigan. A Michigander, whether a Yooper or a Troll, passionately roots for either one school or the other.

The University of Michigan was founded in 1817. At first, it was established in Detroit as a "Catholepistemiad, or University, of Michigania." However, the name was so ridiculed that, in 1821, it was officially changed to the University of Michigan. In 1837, after Michigan became a state and the city of Lansing was chosen as its capital, a group of businessmen in Ann Arbor sold their land to the state for use as a university. This association had previously purchased forty acres in the expectation that Ann Arbor would be the new state capital. Because their plan failed, Michigan moved to Ann Arbor and evolved into the institution it is today.

Years later, in 1855, the Agricultural College of the State of Michigan was established, the first agricultural school in the United States. In 1886, the name was changed to the State Agricultural College. As an institution of learning, Michigan State University expanded its scope and enhanced its educational capabilities resulting in name changes over the years: Michigan Agricultural College, Michigan State College of Agriculture and Applied Science. Finally, in 1964, the college took the name Michigan State University. It had met all the criteria necessary to be a full-fledged university. As an institution of learning, MSU is every bit as proud and famous as its sister Big Ten university, the University of Michigan.

There has always been a rivalry between the two schools. Because the schools were founded under such different standards, that was a normal reaction. The older school, the University of Michigan, has a feeling of superiority over its "cow college" younger sister; at the same time, Michigan State feels that people from Ann Arbor are arrogant snobs, too sure of their self-importance. When both were smaller, the University of Michigan touted itself as the more cultured institution. Over the years, as both universities grew in size and stature, the differences between the two dwindled. They are now both considered important centers of learning, teaching, and educating.

Although both universities have a large pool of graduates living in Michigan, many Michiganders think of these two schools only in terms of their athletic accomplishments. Because college athletics are now big business, with budgets and profits in the tens of millions of dollars, this rivalry has intensified almost to the boiling point. In the emotional extremes of partisanship, families have splintered, marriages have broken up, and friendships have fractured, all because of loyalty to "the other team."

Both universities have added fuel to the fire by enlarging their football stadiums. MSU has a stadium that seats over 75,000 people while U of M prides itself on its "Big House," the largest stadium in the United States and the third largest stadium in the world; it has a seating capacity of more than 114,000 people. The sizes of these stadiums indicate just how huge collegiate athletics has become. Universities need winning teams to make money; football coaches can be hired or fired solely on their record of wins or losses. Finance has diluted the flavor of amateur athletics.

What makes this rivalry even more intense is that both universities compete for the same student athletes within the entire state of Michigan. Angry questions are raised when a young man announces his choice of schools. The losing school's fans immediately suspect the recruiting process is corrupt and some alumni are willing to break the rules so that their alma mater maintains a winning team. Alumni can be insidious; many of them keep beating the drum even when they are no longer in the band. Each game played, no matter what the sport, fuels a hotbed of emotion long before the contest has begins. The academic ideal of sportsmanship is supplanted by the profane spirit of winning at any cost.

All these factors play into the choice a fan makes when he or she elects to cheer for either Michigan State University or the University of Michigan. And it is not a fainthearted commitment; it is a loud, noisy endorsement. Its importance is not short-termed; loyalty is usually a decision that is never changed or revoked. Once a Michigander decides to root for either the Spartans or the Wolverines, it is almost unthinkable to change alliances. Their commitment can border on rudeness and disrespect for the rejected university. Unfortunately, this scornful attitude exemplifies the sports scene at all of today's big universities.

When Maribeth and Bill first met, Maribeth had studied at Michigan State while Bill had gone to Michigan, but school loyalties were never part of their discussions. They both were too busy trying to keep the Crossfire from closing. It was an exhausting period, and they had little time to think of anything else. It was only when they began to turn the restaurant business around, and after they had fallen in love, that the subject of the two universities arose. They each continually reminded the other of their poor choice of loyalty. The continual bantering about their respective schools became one of the strands woven into their marriage nest.

Their collegial loyalties started to heat up when, on a cool, crisp Sunday in early fall, Bill and Maribeth played hooky from work. The restaurant business was picking up and they had not taken any time off for weeks. When Maribeth came to work that particular morning, Bill kidnapped her and drove to nearby Lillie Park. They walked the paths until they reached an overlook on Turtle Rock Pond. They sat there, awed by the moment. The sun warmed their faces and bodies as it enhanced the brilliance of the red, yellow, and orange of the leaves. The coolness of the air was like perfume for them as they watched the birds flying over their heads, flitting and fluting. The couple slipped into the contentment that rises when stress dissolves and nature is in harmony with itself.

They remained quiet for a long time. Suddenly, Maribeth asked, "Bill, do you think that your team has any chance of beating my team next Saturday?"

Bruckner was startled; he came back from his reveries. The question puzzled him. He answered by asking his own question. "You're talking Michigan and Michigan State?"

"Of course. They're playing at the Big House on Saturday and State is a ten point favorite. Are you willing to bet against that ten point spread to help your team and make me rich?"

"Huh. What you really are betting on is that your gang of gorillas will eat bananas faster than my gang of gorillas. I'm not sure that I want to encourage gambling, it leads to other bad habits."

Maribeth almost snorted. "If Michigan was favored by ten points you wouldn't be on a soap box preaching about gambling. You'd be looking for suckers to make money."

"Isn't that what you are doing?"

"Of course not. I'm giving you a chance to show your loyalty to those misguided, young lads who are trying their best to embarrass the earnest student athletes of Michigan State."

Bruckner rose to the bait, he jeered, "See, you are adding fibbing to your list of transgressions. These so-called 'earnest student athletes' will only show up if their parole officers allow them to. Just the same, even though you want to take my money, I'm willing to accept the ten point spread to show that my team of Rhodes scholars will do their best to thwart your team of high school dropouts.

"How much do you want to bet?"

That question opened the door for some lengthy negotiations. After haggling over money, both Maribeth and Bill decided to switch to other forms of payment. Neither of them was interested in punishing the other; what they really wanted was mischief. What they settled for was that the loser of Saturday's game would have to sing the fight song of the winning team to the restaurant staff, just before opening the following Tuesday.

This started a custom of rooting for, and betting on, their own teams. After a few years they changed the loser's penance to wearing a baseball cap with the winner's logo on it for a full week.

The interest in the bet became so popular with the restaurant staff that Maribeth and Bill considered incorporating the Michigan/Michigan

State rivalry into the barroom side of their business. They had tried to make the bar at the Crossfire more profitable and they noticed that no matter what sport was being telecast—football, baseball, basketball, or hockey—the bar was always filled with sports fans. They eventually built a portable dividing wall that split the room between teams. Michigan State fans could view their team on one side of the room while Michigan fans were viewing theirs on the other. Each section had, along with a giant television set, a huge, bulletin board where rooters could post individual notes. To keep some semblance of good taste, the bulletin boards were out of reach of the customers and all comments were screened by the bartenders before being posted.

Over time, the back bar of the Crossfire became a sports bar that held a special interest for both Michigan and Michigan State fans. They came prepared to have a good time, rooting for their own team and bashing their opponent. For the most part, it was a raucous, good-natured crowd that didn't get too rowdy or out of control. As it turned out, their trifling with each other about their respective schools turned into a cash cow for the owners of the Crossfire.

CHAPTER 13

The theory is that, as humans age, their wisdom increases and they become role models for younger generations. Living for a long time is supposed to make seniors more tolerant, more understanding, and more reasonable. It is not important whether or not their wisdom is because they have learned what is important for happiness or because they are approaching the end of their time and want to leave graciously. What is important is that the elders are supposed to guide their youngers into leading harmonious, productive lives.

Unfortunately, the theory does not take into account the many different facets of human nature. By the time many people reach old age, they are battered and beaten by their life experiences and have reacted poorly. Some elders are as sour as kosher dill pickles. Some are frozen in prejudice, some are bitter about life, and resort to living in the past. A few are even past their individual "use by" date. There are less older people setting good examples than there should be. Like every human category, elderly people can always be lumped together to fit into some kind of statistic necessary to prove some point. However, it is a fact that attaining old age does not automatically guarantee wisdom and grace.

The year after Bruckner's assault, on an early Sunday morning in

May, Maribeth and Bill were eating breakfast on their porch. The phone rang and Maribeth answered it. She listened to the person speaking to her for a few seconds and suddenly said, "Wait, I want to put this on the speakerphone so Bill can also hear you."

Before she punched the telephone button she looked across the table, waved her finger at her husband, and spoke in a sharp tone. "This is your mother."

Maribeth switched to the speakerphone. "Okay, Isabel, we both can hear you now. Tell Bill what you were saying."

Isabel sounded as if she was crying when she spoke, "Bill, I need you and Maribeth to help me. Henry has broken his right ankle. We are supposed to return to Milan this week but he's not going to be able to drive our car."

This news surprised them. They knew that Henry and Isabel planned to drive home from Florida shortly but this was the first they had heard of Henry's accident. "Mom," Bruckner cried, "that's terrible. How did Henry break his ankle? Is he in much pain?"

"We were on our usual morning walk when we came across a fallen tree. Henry slipped as he was climbing over a branch. It's a bad break; they had to put pins in his ankle. It hurts quite a bit and he absolutely can't drive. He is hobbling around with the aid of crutches. If you can't help us I'm not sure what we'll do."

Maribeth spoke up, "Isabel, don't worry. Of course, we'll help. That's the least of your worries. Tell us what you need and when you need it, we'll take care of whatever you want."

Bruckner added, "Of course, Mom. Just tell us how we can help."

"Well, I would like to keep to our schedule and get back to Michigan as soon as we can. After we are home, I'd like Henry's doctors to see him. I feel better when we see the doctors we've been going to for years.

"Could you come down to Florida and drive us home?"

Maribeth looked at Bill, waving her hand at him to signal him to reply for both of them. "Sure Mom, no problem. When do you want us to come down?"

Personal arrangements were discussed, flight plans were made, and arrival details were planned. Two days later, on Tuesday, Maribeth and Bill landed at the Sarasota-Bradenton airport in late afternoon. They walked to the baggage claim area and Bruckner looked at the mob of people in the terminal. He had not flown in a long time and had forgotten what an ordeal it could be. There were mobs flowing with them, there were mobs flowing against them; worse, there were mobs, on both sides, trying to flow through the steady stream of people. No one could stop without being buffeted from all four directions. He told Maribeth, "Good Lord, this is an ant hill run by humans. I hope we make it."

They retrieved their bags, spotted Isabel standing near the main entrance, looking anxiously for them. They waved to her and made their way to her side. Her son was struck by how much his mother had aged since he last saw her. Her spine was more curved and her shoulders more rounded than he remembered.

She vigorously hugged and kissed them both and, after asking how the flight was, she said, "I'm so glad to see you. I drove to the airport; Henry stayed home. That's why I'm late. I hate driving, so here are the keys."

After Bruckner took the keys, she added, "From here on, you will be the designated chauffeur. Henry can't and I won't. I hope you don't mind."

"Mom, I don't mind at all. Denny the Driver is at your service."

They drove from the airport to his mother's condo and she detailed her husband's accident. They were walking on a footpath they frequently used for exercising when they came across a fallen tree. Tannenbaum had helped Isabel step over the downed trunk but he slipped and fell as he followed. As he was falling, his ankle was suddenly jammed in the fork of one of the branches and it took the force of his fall. He was stunned and in pain. They had forgotten their cell phones, and he lay there until another walker on the trail called 911. He was taken to the emergency room; the doctors operated on his ankle and told him it would be a long process of recuperation. Since his accident five days ago, he was still in a lot of pain and depressed about not being able to drive. Maribeth and Bruckner said they could easily understand his feelings.

When they arrived at the condo, they found Henry sitting with his right foot elevated, impatiently awaiting them. He tried to rise to greet them but Maribeth went to him, kissed him on the cheek and pleaded, "Henry, don't get up. Isabel says that you are to stay off your foot and keep it raised. We have come to help you get back to Milan—you really don't have to move. Please sit down."

Tannenbaum settled back in his chair and Bruckner shook his hand and tried to make light of the situation, "Hi, Henry. I'm sorry about your accident. It couldn't come at a worse time for you and Mother. Maribeth and I are glad to help out. All you have to do is tell Maribeth what you want and she will order me to do it.

"How are you feeling now?"

"Actually, the pain seems to be lessening each day. I feel very stupid for having this accident just before our trip back to Michigan. I'm pleased that you and Maribeth came down to rescue us but I'm embarrassed. I hope this is not too great an inconvenience."

Maribeth shook her head. "Henry, after all the years that you made yourself available for Bill and me, don't even go there. This is not an inconvenience. We're glad that we can return to you some of the many things you have done for us. Now, let's get on to eating, I'm starved; only pretzels were served on our flight."

There followed a joyful reunion. The four of them hadn't seen each other in almost six months. Henry listened but he didn't do much talking. Although, toward the end of the evening, he did begin to join in on the conversation. They spent the evening chatting, catching up on family news and Milan events. Finally, they discussed in detail what had to be done before they could leave. It was decided that they would start early on Saturday morning for the trip back.

After they were in bed, Bill asked Maribeth, "Honey, how do you think my mother and Henry look?"

"Well, Henry looks thinner and he is much quieter. Maybe it's because of his pain. Still, he doesn't appear as animated as he usually is. Your mother is worried about him and she seems distracted. I'm glad we flew down here to help them out."

"My mother seems to have aged since the last time I saw her. Don't you think so?"

"You may be right, Honey. She does look tired, but don't forget, she is in her mid eighties. Henry's accident has frightened her. Just before we came to bed she told me that she's concerned because Henry is so depressed and unhappy. Between the two of us, we will have to cheer them up and help them get ready to leave; it looks as if we have our work cut out for us."

In reality, it turned out to be an easier time than they expected. Isabel and Henry were hungry for the love and support of their family; they responded by perking up. They became less fretful and more cheerful. Their first day, Wednesday, set the pattern for the next three days until their Saturday departure date.

The mornings were spent sitting around the condo talking, visiting, and reminiscing. After lunch, Bill and Maribeth would go sightseeing. They visited the Ringling Museum and the Selby Gardens. After each visit, they ended up prowling around St. Armands Circle. They realized it was a tourist trap but the weather was so invigorating and the circle so alive and fascinating that they could not resist the temptation; they had to partake in the activities. Friday, their last day, they toured Longboat Key, Siesta Key, and again finished the day at St. Armands Circle.

They were happy just to be outside in the gorgeous weather and joined with the high-spirited visitors milling in and out of the unique shops.

They reveled in these afternoon outings. Their evening entertainment was not quite as joyous. It turned into an onerous duty. Isabel and Henry had six or eight friends over every evening to say goodbye and meet Bill and Maribeth. They both were happy to meet the older couple's friends, they found them intelligent and friendly, although the topics the guests discussed took them by surprise.

After they went to bed on that first night, Maribeth looked at her husband. "Well?"

"Well, what?"

"Don't 'well what' me. I saw your face; you didn't talk much or smile all evening. What was wrong?"

Bill sighed. "The conversation. It was all about aches and pains and symptoms and medicines and doctors and what parts of their bodies were not functioning and what parts were still working. I almost thought I was a doctor in the emergency room."

"It wasn't quite that bad."

Bruckner carried on. "You may think that way but I don't. I tried changing the subject a couple of times but no one was buying it. They each wanted to be sicker than the other."

"Bill, you are absolutely exaggerating."

"Okay, I could be. Even so, you'll have to admit that the people here tonight were obsessed with either their health or their lack of it."

Maribeth responded, "I would call it preoccupation, not obsession. Don't forget that the people we met tonight are retired and they moved here to relax for the rest of their lives. They're not too active, and they have been neighbors for a long time. They have time to sit around, keep track of their bodily functions, and try to outguess their doctors. In its own way, it's really kind of sad."

"Maribeth, you're right. It is sad. But, from a spectator's point of view, it's annoying. Privacy is a privilege that, once violated, can't be restored. I don't want to hear about their ailments any more than I want to tell them about my sex life. I'm sure you will have no trouble agreeing with that."

His wife laughed, "I can easily and readily agree with that. However, let's wait and see how we act when we reach their age."

With that, they closed the subject and went to sleep. However, Thursday evening, with a different set of guests, the conversations were similar to the night before.

When they were alone again, Bill groused to Maribeth even more than he had Wednesday evening. "Honey, one more night of this and I'll be able to pass all the tests necessary for becoming a general practioner. I can't believe people can spend so much time communing with their insides. There is life outside of their bodies, why don't they go live it?"

"Bill, did you enjoy our trip to the Selby Gardens this afternoon?"

"Yes, I had a good time at both the Selby Gardens and St. Armands Circle."

"Then, judging by your present mood, Isabel's and Henry's friends really got to you this evening. You're usually much more patient than I am when it comes to dealing with people. You are out of sorts; what's bothering you?"

"I'm not sure. To me, it seems like a waste of time to come together to bid farewell to your friends and then do nothing but talk about how your body is falling apart. There's not much anyone can do to stop from aging. Why revel in it? Go out and live it up."

"I feel the same way, Sweetie; but that's my life and yours, not theirs. You and I have no right to judge them. As you often tell me, 'it ain't any of our business.'"

Bruckner agreed, "I guess it isn't but it sure is irritating to listen to. I want to get my mother and Henry back to their home in Milan. That will be better medicine for all of us, much better than listening to everyone describe how they are slowing down. Hearing this all the time is damn depressing."

Maribeth couldn't disagree with her husband because she felt the same way. However, she was apprehensive about how Bruckner would react on Friday, the last night before the return to Michigan. She fretted over it even as the final group of guests arrived. The conversations were almost identical to the other two nights, except that Bill entered the conversations more than he had before; he seemed to be having a good time. When he offered to make everyone a Viagra Margarita, Maribeth knew he was enjoying himself. She was puzzled at the change in his behavior.

Later, she began her inquiries by teasing him with his own ploy. "Well, Beauregard the Bartender, what would you have done if anyone accepted your offer of a Viagra Margarita?"

"Simple, I would start mixing a regular Margarita and then I would announce that I was sorry but I just remembered that we used up all the Viagra last night and I needed to get more."

"You are absolutely impossible."

"Maribeth, you know how I love compliments, I will gladly accept them from anyone, especially from you.

"Seriously though, I thought about what you said and I agree. These friends of my mother and Henry have reached a point where they do little about living except to think about themselves. It's sad that they're not pulling on their oars anymore; I hope you and I never get to that stage, but that's beside the point. This is where my parents' guests are and it's up to me to accept it, not evaluate it. It's none of my business. I'm not at all pleased when someone intrudes on my business. I owe them the same courtesy. If that's their choice I should nose out.

"So, if I can't beat them, I decided to join them. For the last two nights they gave me an extensive medical education whether or not I wanted it. Last evening, I applied my training as I listened to them. Hearing of their many symptoms gave me an idea. The results of this idea are going to make us, you and me, rich. Very rich. We will become millionaires with this new business that we will start."

He stopped, waiting for his wife to make some comment. Maribeth thought a moment before she answered. "Listen, I'm not going to spend any of my money until I understand our new business. I would like to hear all the details on how I became so rich."

Bruckner waved his arm expansively. "You certainly deserve to know. I noticed that each person described his or her problem in detail and then there was a discussion whether or not their medications helped. Those who could express themselves well made their problems dramatic; those who had trouble describing what was wrong with them didn't earn much sympathy or much attention.

"So, I thought, 'Why not help older people who want to be noticed? Why not start a Malady of the Month Club?'"

Maribeth was startled, "A what?"

" A M.O.M. A Malady of the Month Club. The last week of every month we will mail our members a detailed list of symptoms for them to have for the next month. It will give our subscribers instructions on how to present their problems so they get all the sympathy they are looking for. We will also mail them the necessary medications to relieve these monthly symptoms. The medications will be placebos, of course, but not just ordinary placebos. They will be big, gaudy pills that glow in the dark and be very tasty. Naturally, the dosage will be taken three or four times a day. Our members will be able to pull out their pills, bright red, blue, yellow or whatever color and attract attention when they take their medicine.

"Then, the following month, they'll have an entirely different set of symptoms and a different colored medicine to alleviate these medical problems. Our prices will be reasonable—say about $52 dollars a year for all these extraordinary and delicious symptoms.

"We will teach our customers how to smartly guard their symptoms. We are on our way to the Kingdom of Wealth."

Maribeth laughed and then volleyed. “To get to your Kingdom of Wealth you will have to travel through the State of Sanity and, believe me, you will be detained at its borders.”

Bruckner feigned injury. “Now why would you say that? Our lifestyle is about to change and you’re acting as if you don’t believe me. You will feel foolish sitting among all the basketfuls of money accumulating in our living room.”

Maribeth shook her head. “Before I spend any of the money in those baskets, answer me this. What are you going to do when everyone who signs up for your Malady of the Month Club shows up at a gathering with the same symptoms and the same gaudy medications?

“It will look like an epidemic has struck.”

Bruckner was surprised. “Hmm. Good thought. I hadn’t planned on that, but this is going to be such a success that your scenario just might be possible. However, you, as our marketing manager, will insure that no individual zip code is overloaded with one of our patented maladies. You will have so many symptoms, ailments and happy pills at your disposal that we can protect all zip codes from epidemic outbreaks. Come to think of it, we can use this to our advantage. We can promise that, under no condition, will any of our medicines cause weight gains. You, in your new position, can list all the health benefits of our pills.”

Maribeth went along with Bruckner’s fantasy. “Just a minute there. I’m not signing on as your marketing manager or any other job until you tell me what my pay and my benefits will be. This sounds like a Ponzi scheme to me. It’s not that I don’t trust you, it’s that I want to know what’s in it for me. After all, you did say that this is a scheme to make baskets of money.”

“Well, it is; but it will also render a service to those who want to draw the attention of their peers to themselves. What better way to be noticed than to have some of the most unusual symptoms your friends have ever heard of?”

Maribeth had to laugh again. “Honey, you are an absolute nut. If your company ever is successful you can franchise all over the world and become a billionaire, not a millionaire. You could also start up other companies, like a Religion of the Month Club or a Politics of the Month Club. You could be famous as 'the King of Clubs' and I will be able to tell people that I knew you before you became famous.

"In the meantime, please don't start any of these moneymaking operations until we get your mother and Henry safely home. You can surely wait until then before you make your fortune."

Bruckner sighed; he knew the playful part of their conversation was over. He and Maribeth were back to reality, the job of traveling from Florida to Michigan with two elderly people. "I don't expect we'll have any real problems," he said. "We won't make the trip as fast as if it were only you and I traveling. However, there is really no rush. We'll set a pace that is comfortable for Mother and Henry. We have a planned itinerary, we will follow it, and we'll get home when we arrive at their driveway. Their comfort is what will be important.

"As far as my businesses are concerned, I'm not sure that I want to start a new enterprise at my age. I'd rather relax and enjoy life. I'm sorry to disappoint you by not offering you a share of the company and a large salary; I'd much rather have you as my wife than as my marketing manager."

Maribeth moved close to her husband and kissed him. "I'll take that as a compliment. Let's stop chatting and fool around. We have an early rise and a busy day tomorrow."

CHAPTER 14

The four of them began discussing the details of their return trip to Milan as early as Wednesday morning. Bill and Maribeth had assumed that, because of Tannenbaum's injury, it would be a direct trip home. That would be less than a 600 mile drive with frequent pit stops and exercise breaks. They were surprised to find that Isabel and Henry were thinking about sightseeing before heading to Michigan. The first few minutes of their conversation were a little confusing because the two couples seemed to be at cross purposes. Finally, Bruckner said, "Mom, Henry, we are not on the same wavelength. I thought, because of Henry's ankle, we were heading straight home. Where are we going before we head home? I'm not objecting, but it would help me to know where you want me to drive."

Both Henry and his mother grinned sheepishly. Isabel said, "Bill, I guess we didn't tell you this last night. Henry and I are in the process of selling our condo. We both love it down here but we miss being with our friends and families. Truthfully, even with all the good weather and all the activities available, it can get boring. If you don't move around, you get stuck in a rut; people down here love to talk about themselves. We miss young people with young attitudes. We miss our family.

"In past years, we've always driven straight down and straight back, never stopping to visit. When we sell the condo there is a good chance we won't ever get back to this part of the country. Before Henry's accident, we talked about going to places we both want to see and would like to visit. Last night, after we talked with both of you, we decided that, if you and Maribeth agreed, we would still like to do some sightseeing. Henry thinks he can manage to walk, as long as he uses his crutches. Would both of you be willing to do that instead of heading straight home?"

Maribeth and Bruckner liked the idea of traveling and the conversation quickly changed from driving straight home to selecting places they would like to visit. The list got so large that the four of them had to stop and regroup. It was soon obvious they would never get home if they visited all the suggested sites. Each morning, until the day they left, they spent hours deciding what to see and how long their trip would take. It was an exercise in constant confusion which they enjoyed immensely. By the time both couples were ready to leave, they thought they had a solid list of places to visit and an accurate idea of their travel time.

They were wrong. The very first day they lost track of time and never regained it until they drove into their Milan driveway. They started to go astray when Isabel read a roadside billboard near St. Augustine. She muttered, "Oh, my!"

Maribeth quickly asked, "Isabel, is something wrong?"

"No, Dear, I just read an advertisement about visiting St. Augustine, the oldest city in our country. It was founded in 1565. I had completely forgotten about St. Augustine. Wouldn't that be fun to visit?"

They talked about it, saw many more billboards enticing people to stop at St. Augustine, but no one answered Isabel's question. They drove in silence. However, when Bruckner reached the road sign directing the way to St. Augustine, he veered off interstate 95 without saying a word. When the detour was noticed, everyone was pleased with the decision.

They lost a day and a half but gained a sense of history in an area that existed centuries before any of them were born.

So went the entire trip. They stopped whenever something caught their fancy. Savannah was added to the list when Maribeth realized how near to it they would be driving. During their two and a half days in Savannah they toured the city, asked questions, enjoyed the rich culture and reveled in each other's company.

By the time they got to Charleston, the first stop on their original list, they were a little tired but—more important—emotionally ecstatic. Traveling released them from the bonds of ordinary worries and cares; they were free to let their thoughts flow completely. They understood each other so well that, when they had discussions, they could giggle about serious subjects and pontificate over silly ones.

Charleston was an eye opener for three of them; Tannenbaum was the only one who had been there before. They did all the normal tourist activities: toured the city, visited Fort Sumter, the Citadel, and Fort Moultrie, overate at the local restaurants. What completely caught their interest was the time spent looking at the *H. L. Hunley.* They were amazed at the bravery it took to volunteer for duty on this primitive submarine after it sank twice before torpedoing the Housatonic, losing thirteen of its eighteen crewmen. They were surprised to find that, even though the *Hunley* was built close to two hundred years ago, it still was constructed with some of the modern features of today's submarines.

On the last day in Charleston, they sat looking out at Fort Sumter and spoke of how the history and culture of this beautiful area affected them. They enjoyed delving into the history of the city and could easily understand the feelings of those who had lived through its traumatic era. Charleston brought them face to face with the fact that, although the Civil War was over, the lessons of that war were still important. They agreed that any country that does not pay attention to its past will mortgage its future.

The four left Charleston, slowly making their way to one of their original destinations, Appomattox Court House. Tannenbaum had read extensively about the Civil War and was fascinated by its significance to our country. He visited many of the battlefields when he was younger and now felt he had to see what he thought were its two most important sites—where the war began and where the war ended.

Appomattox Court House gave them a much different feeling than the city of Charleston. It was not commercial, it was not developed. It just quietly sat in the location where the anger and the hostility had officially ended. They slowly moved around McLean House, listened to the park ranger's words and tried to appreciate what Lee and Grant both must have felt when they met in the parlor.

Henry insisted on limping over to the field where the Confederate soldiers laid down their arms and their regimental banners. It was a cool, cloudy morning as they looked out at a field smaller than they had expected. No one spoke for a while. Henry broke the silence. "How sad. How magnificent. These men tried to kill each other for four years and now the defeated had to lay their weapons on the ground in front of their enemies, the victors. After that, they were free to try to pick up their lives. What were their thoughts as they marched up, threw down their guns and proud banners and then walked away?

"And what about the soldiers they surrendered to? Were they any better off? What were their thoughts when General Chamberlain ordered them to salute their former enemies as they surrendered and they obeyed? They must have been just as eager to go home to their families as the rebels were."

They spent hours reading pamphlets, asking questions, crisscrossing between buildings, and soaking up the atmosphere of that quiet shrine. They left in a subdued mood; nobody talked much about what they had seen or felt. It wasn't until after the long drive to their hotel in Richmond that they began to share their feelings.

They next day, they were sitting together in a secluded part of the hotel lobby and sipping wine from a large bottle they shared, when Isabel said, "Henry, thank you for suggesting that we visit Appomattox Court House. I can't remember when I have been so moved by such deep feelings. I'm overwhelmed when I think of all the ironies that surround that small village. The war starts in McLean's front yard and ends four years later in his parlor; Grant is so generous in his terms to Lee; Gordon acknowledges Chamberlain's salute and responds with a salute of his own. Twenty-eight thousand men pass by in defeat. History is filled with heartbreak and heroics. I don't know what to say or do. I don't know how I feel. My mind is churning with what I experienced yesterday."

Maribeth entered the conversation. "I feel the same way. I've never felt so overwhelmed in my life. We visited a location where a war ended almost one hundred and fifty years ago. Tens of thousands of young men lost their lives in that conflict and millions lost their way. It stands open to the public so that we can see what our forebears went through. But I don't know if we can imagine exactly what they had to endure. Why don't people pay attention to the past? Why do we keep making the same mistakes?"

A quietness settled in as they sipped the wine and brooded over their thoughts. Then, Bill spoke, "When I was a young man, the Vietnam War was being fought. When I approached the time I was going to be drafted, my Mother didn't want me to go into any of the services. She thought the war was unjust. I, being all of eighteen years old and being sure that I knew better, wanted to be drafted; I looked forward to being in the army. My life forever changed. Since then, good things have happened to me and bad things have happened to me. What might have happened, if I had avoided the draft, I will never know. What I do know is that the course of my life changed because of the Vietnam War.

"As I stood where those rebel troops surrendered their weapons, I kept hoping that all of them, along with the union troops, made it back to their homes safely. Even though they saw combat years before I was born, I felt as if I knew them as fellow soldiers. We were cheered into battle by older men who were supposed to be wiser than us. After all the battles were fought, veterans have been neglected by the same men who were supposed to be wiser than us youngsters."

Bill turned and patted his mother on the hand before he made his final remark. "It turns out that my mother was smarter and wiser than the older men that I listened to."

Henry smiled and said, "Here. Here." There was silence for awhile and then he continued, "I have lived through a lot of wars, the Second World War, the Korean War, the Vietnam War, the Iraq War, the Afghanistan War, and Lord knows how many skirmishes like Panama and Haiti. Too many, too many.

"What makes it seem so useless is that it seems people can get together and be friendly to each other without any government being involved. Isabel and I have traveled all over the world. Besides the different societies and cultures that we enjoyed, what we also remember is that the people we met were similar to us. Mothers loved their children no matter what continent we were standing on. So why do governments have to destroy each other to have their way? Why is war so addictive to those old men who control the destiny of their countries?

"If I had the power, I would force every elected official in Washington, D.C. to come to Appomattox Court House and spend two days learning the meaning of what happened at this sacred place. I want them to think, not just react, every time our country faces a crisis.

"Now, I'm getting down from my soapbox."

They were a tired group when they disbanded to go to their rooms a few minutes later. After they were in bed, Maribeth snuggled against Bill and said, "Freedom and love, love and freedom. I guess those are the two most important intangibles in our lives. We are still fighting for them today just like we were during the Civil War. Maybe that's why I feel like I do right now." She stopped talking.

After a pause, Bruckner asked, "And how is that?"

"I'm not sure. It's a little funny that I was not prepared for the emotions that hit me. Of course, I knew about the Civil War. I've read about it and heard about it but I didn't expect to get caught up in it like I did. It was like pouring boiling water on dried soup; the smells and flavors immediately come to life. I felt the emotions of both sides. What those people lived through. There has to be a better way to solve problems; killing more of them than they kill of us is not an answer."

Bruckner held Maribeth closer to him to console her. "You're right, Honey. There should be a better way but every generation has to find its own answers and that's the problem. They usually make some sort of emotional decision before they find wisdom; that leads them right back to the mistakes of the past. Occasionally, we get it right and we take a step forward.

"I don't know in what direction the world is presently headed but I can honestly tell you that I'm nervous about its future."

After seeing Richmond they left for their final destination, Washington, D.C. Three days were spent rubbernecking the buildings, visiting galleries, libraries, statues and monuments, all of which had been paid for by their taxes. In contrast to their previous destinations, there was no introspection to interfere with their sightseeing; they just toured and enjoyed themselves.

Their last day in D.C. was much different; the couples split up after lunch. Isabel and Henry went back to the Smithsonian Institute and Maribeth and Bill went to the Vietnam Veterans War Memorial.

Bill didn't say a word as he and Maribeth, hand in hand, approached the Wall. He hesitated and seemed reluctant to move forward. Finally, to gain time, he went over to look at the statues of "The Three Servicemen" and the "Vietnam Women's Memorial." After that, Bill and Maribeth walked to a visitor's kiosk and gave the park ranger the name of the soldier he wanted to locate. Following the instructions he was given, they slowly walked down the face of the Wall searching for the engraved name of his dead brother.

Maribeth was terrified to see the listing of the names of 52,282 men and women. As they walked, their figures reflected off the black marble wall. The thought of the sheer number of Americans who sacrificed their lives clutched at her humanity. Maribeth wept. She couldn't help but wonder what her beloved husband, Bill, was going through. It was eerie.

Bruckner found the panel he was looking for and he knelt on the ground. He rubbed his index finger back and forth across his friend's name. At first, tears welled in his eyes. Suddenly, Bruckner buried his face in his hands and broke into uncontrollable sobbing.

Maribeth's heart broke at the sight of her husband rocking and crying. She knelt beside her husband and cradled him in her arms. She squeezed his hand to let him know she loved him. Bill did not respond. He eventually calmed down. They got up and walked over to a bench. Maribeth handed Bruckner a couple of tissues, he blew his nose and dried his eyes. They sat holding hands without saying a word.

When Bill regained his composure, he returned to the visitor's kiosk and repeated the procedure for locating the name of another brother. This time when Maribeth held him, he didn't speak but he did return the squeeze of her hand. They sat at the Wall for a long time before returning to their hotel.

The couples didn't meet again until they sat down for dinner that evening. The three of them were quiet, waiting for Bill to speak. They realized how important this day was for him and they were anxious to hear his thoughts. When each had a glass of wine, Bill raised his glass and, with his voice cracking, said, "I propose a toast. To my brothers, who I talked with today. I am at peace. I can only hope they are, too." He cried as he finished speaking. They all raised their glasses and drank in silence. Then he continued to talk, "There were four of us that clung together just to survive. There was Sam Cutler, who you all knew. There were my two brothers who were killed in action. Dan Goldman and Shorty Beaumont. Dan was a Jewish kid who could imitate voices and make everyone laugh. Shorty was Beaumont's nickname because he was over six feet, black, and was an excellent athlete. When the four of us got to Nam we weren't fighting for democracy versus communism. We were fighting to keep ourselves alive. Two of us lost that fight.

"When I first came home, Dan and Shorty were in my nightmares every night, dying and asking 'Why me?' I couldn't answer them then and I can't answer them now. 'Why me?' they would ask and I would wake up and scream, 'Why them?' I still don't know.

"What I do know is that I talked to the Wall today and told them that I had not forgotten them. I will never forget them. They are still my brothers and I will remember them until the day I die. I told them about Sam Cutler, and Maribeth—my beloved Maribeth—and my family. I apologized that it took me so long to get to the Wall to talk with them and I promised that I would be back. That is a promise I intend to keep.

"I can't explain why I feel so good right now, but I do. This is our last night in Washington before we head home. Let's eat."

And they did so with great enthusiasm. Afterward, sitting with their wine, Bruckner again began to talk. "I'm sorry if I'm monopolizing the conversation tonight, but I feel like the genie who has been let out of the bottle. Does anyone object to letting me ramble for a few more minutes?"

When nobody said a word he continued. "We just finished visiting some of the most historic sites in our country's history. I was reminded of how brutal the Civil War was and how each succeeding generation needs to be alert in defending our constitutional rights. I really understood and related to what happened at Charleston and at Appomattox Court House.

"However, that was about 150 years ago. My mind was always engaged but my emotions were not active. It was different today at the Wall. While I was talking to my brothers it dawned on me that I was not speaking about past history. I lived through what that monument memorializes. My name could be inscribed on the Wall, just as well as Shorty and Dan.

"Bullets are blind on a battlefield. Until you're hit you have no idea where they are or what they will do when they hit. It is the cruelest game of Russian roulette ever laid on our young. It is the battlefield that bonds us so closely together, no matter what our race, religion, or color. I wish that my brothers had survived. I would give anything to be able to talk with them in person and not to their names on the Wall.

"Anyhow, our sightseeing is over and tomorrow we head home. This trip has made me more aware of how fortunate I am to have you as my family. Whether by design or by chance, I realize that I am a blessed man."

They stood, faced each other and held hands as Henry spontaneously spoke. His words reflected his faith. "Lord God, thank you for your protection during our journey. Thank You for showing us what our forefathers went through to give us the freedoms we now enjoy. We hope You will continue to bless us and protect us as we drive home. I ask for Your guidance and Your favors in the name of Your only son, Jesus Christ, who died for us." Bill, who participated in this blessing, didn't say a word.

They hugged and kissed each other, went to bed, and fell into deep sleep.

The 600 mile trip from Washington, D.C. to Milan was uneventful. However, it took them almost two days to complete the journey. Not only did they have their normal pit stops, there were also additional delays as Henry's ankle began to swell and ache. They turned off at the nearest rest plazas to let him elevate his foot. When the swelling went down, they would continue driving. After they reached home, Bruckner drove Tannenbaum to the Emergency Room at St. Joseph Hospital. The diagnosis was an infected ankle. He needed to take antibiotics, keep his ankle elevated, and remain off it until the swelling went down.

Isabel, Maribeth, and Bill were relieved with the doctor's diagnosis but Maribeth and Bill thought that taking care of Henry could be a problem. They thought that Isabel was too frail to have the responsibility of caring for her husband by herself and Maribeth couldn't guarantee she could be at Isabel's house to help. Isabel argued for awhile but then admitted that Maribeth and Bill were probably right. The three of them discussed their options in hushed concern until Bill suddenly said, "What about asking Trina Lopez if she could help us?"

Maribeth immediately asked, "Could she? She may not be able to, she may not want to. It is a good idea but we have to find out how she is doing and if she would be willing."

Bruckner called Sonia De Los Angeles for a brief update about her mother and asked her if she could come over that afternoon. She arrived just after Isabel got there; they both recognized one another from Sunday service at the Immaculate Conception Parish. Bill introduced his mother and Sonia to each other, and when they were comfortably seated, Bruckner asked, "Sonia, how is your mother doing? Has she gotten back to feeding her Canada geese on Saturdays?"

"Mr. Bruckner, she is about the same. She is not as anxious as she was immediately after the attack but she's far from what she used to be. She seems almost listless. We can't seem to motivate her."

"Well, how is she physically? Could that be part of her problem?"

"No, I don't think so. She still is strong and active; she's always cleaning and dusting and polishing inside the house. She just doesn't like to go outside on her own. She will sometimes go to feed her geese on Saturday but only if the grandkids or an older person goes with her. I still am concerned."

"Sonia, this may sound a little odd but do you think your mother is capable of working?"

"Working?"

It was Isabel who answered her question. "My husband has a broken ankle that has become infected. The doctor wants him to be stationary.

He can take care of himself, perform his own toiletry, move about when he needs to. My son and his wife don't think I can do all that is necessary to follow the doctors orders. I don't like to admit it but, they are probably right.

"We need someone to give him his medicines, to make sure he is comfortable, and to be available to help him. We wonder if your mother would be able to help us. If she is capable of handling these duties, we would like to hire her. It could be a good thing for her and us."

Her daughter sat quietly. Then she thought aloud, "My mother, go back to work? There is no physical reason she couldn't and it might do wonders for her self-confidence. It is a possibility."

She turned to Isabel. "She wouldn't be required to do any heavy lifting or strenuous activities?"

Isabel replied, "No, your mother would be there mostly for companionship and to take care of my husband's requests when I'm not at home. I will be here most of the time and Maribeth will be in and out. Your mother's major job would be to give him his medicines and just help him. Isn't that the same work that she did for years?"

Mrs. Lopez's daughter answered, "Yes, among other responsibilities, that is what she did. This might be a good idea."

She stood up, thanked them and promised that she would go home and talk it over with her mother. She wrote down Isabel's phone number and assured her that she would hear from either herself or her mother very shortly.

Isabel returned home and within two hours her phone rang. She quickly answered it.

A woman's raspy voice asked, "Mrs. Tannenbaum?"

"Yes, this is she."

"I am Trina Lopez. Your son saved my life; I want you to know that. I am happy to meet you. Your son also helped me get my teeth fixed; he is such a good man. You should be very proud of him. "

"Mrs. Lopez, I am very proud of him."

"Good. My daughter says that you want to hire me to look after your husband, Mr. Henry Tannenbaum. Is this true?"

"Yes, we need someone with your nursing skills to help him until his ankle is healed."

"Would I be responsible for feeding, washing him, and changing his linens? Don't forget that I am an old woman."

"No, no, Mrs. Lopez. He can physically take care of himself. He's only required to elevate his foot and stay quiet. You would be there to make sure he takes his medications on time and to help him if he needs or wants something."

"And I would be paid for this? How much are you thinking?"

"I don't know, Mrs. Lopez. We will probably pay you the same hourly rate that you earned at the hospital."

"That is too much because I won't be doing all the duties I was doing when I worked."

Isabel smiled at Mrs. Lopez's honesty. "This may be true," she answered, "but, we are hiring you for your skills whether you perform all of them or not."

They negotiated her wages, working hours and transportation to and from her house. Mrs. Lopez was concerned about showing up for work; she didn't drive anymore and she wanted to make sure she was always on time. It was finally worked out that either Bruckner or Maribeth would drive her to and from work. When every detail was settled, Trina Lopez rejoined the workforce; she was anxious to meet her new patient.

When Mrs. Lopez and Maribeth showed up at Isabel's house the next morning, she was wearing the uniform she wore at St. Joseph Hospital. Isabel met them at the door and escorted Mrs. Lopez through the house to show her where everything was located. The three of them then went into the kitchen for Isabel's coffee and sweet rolls. They talked; first, about what would be needed for Tannenbaum's recovery and then about themselves. They became comfortable with each other and began using each other's first names. Trina told them how glad she was to be back at work and helping the people who had rescued her. She was grateful and would take good care of Mr. Tannenbaum. Isabel said that she was happy Trina accepted the job. Before introducing Trina to Henry, she said, "Trina, my husband has been out of sorts the last two days. He usually has a sweet disposition. Please be patient with him if he seems a little cross."

"Isabel, my experience is that people who are in pain act differently until their pain subsides. I will help him feel better. You have nothing to worry about."

Comforting Henry Tannenbaum proved harder than Trina Lopez expected. The first three days, he hardly spoke a word to her. She would greet him with pleasantries and encourage him to talk about himself. He would answer her in monosyllables when she spoke to him and would not willingly engage in any conversation. He would take his medicines when Mrs. Lopez gave them to him but he would not talk. The lack of communication between them bothered Trina.

The morning of the fourth day, as she handed Tannenbaum his medicine, she said, "Mr. Tannenbaum, are you angry at me?"

The question caught him by surprise. He immediately answered, "I'm not angry at you, Mrs. Lopez. Why would you even ask a question like that?"

"Because I'm here to help you get well. But, you do not tell me how you are doing and you do not talk to me. You must be unhappy with something."

Tannenbaum did not answer quickly. When he did, he spoke slowly. "Mrs. Lopez, I am not angry with you. However, I am angry with the rest of the world. My ankle throbs, my medicine makes me feel sick, and I'm not sure It's going to heal properly. I'm close to ninety years old and I don't know how much longer I have. I'm afraid of ending my life in pain."

Mrs. Lopez immediately replied. "Mr. Tannenbaum, in all my years of nursing I have never lost a patient due to an ankle injury. I know you are in pain and there is medicine for this. You and I are the same age, I understand your fear."

Had Mrs. Lopez stopped there, she would have done her job. But, in her attempt to change her patient's attitude, she added, "Pain and fear are emotions that you have to fight. If you want to get better, you need to act stronger than you are now."

That last statement angered Tannenbaum. He already was suffering pain and in fear. He didn't want advice, he didn't need advice, he hadn't solicited advice. What he wanted was sympathy and he didn't feel he was getting any. His anger made him do something he rarely did. He quickly lashed back by asking, "Like you have so that you can feed your geese every Saturday?"

Mrs. Lopez looked at him with widened eyes and her mouth sagged open. Tannenbaum felt a deep shame. He had tried to make her feel bad only because his own feelings had been hurt. Her experience was worse, much worse, than his. She had been beaten and brutalized. She was still recovering. He had absolutely no right to taunt her.

Henry Tannenbaum immediately tried to apologize. "Mrs. Lopez, I'm sorry. I shouldn't have said that. I spoke completely out of turn and I'm embarrassed. I am so sorry. Please forgive my stupidity."

Mrs. Lopez sat down beside Tannenbaum, thinking about what he had said. Finally, she pointed her finger at him. "Mr. Tannenbaum, there is truth in what you spoke. I can solve your problems and you can solve my problems but our strength has to come from inside us. Without strength, there is no end to the problem. I still have great fear. I have no right to tell you to be strong when I am so weak. I think I should leave. You and your wife should get someone else to help you. Someone who is stronger than I am."

Tannenbaum banged the tip of one crutch heavily on the floor. "No, Mrs. Lopez, I don't want you to leave. You were trying to help me and I spoke completely out of turn because I was angry. My pain made me say something stupid.

"You are a fine nurse. I need you and I want you to help me. Please, please, accept my apology and stay. I will do whatever you ask and I will be a good patient. Honestly, I really need you. You can help me find my strength."

Mrs. Lopez thought for a long time before she replied. "Well, maybe we can help each other. Working again makes me feel good. I'm a person again and not an old biddy sitting on the shelf. I will stay and help you get well and, then, maybe you can help me feed my geese."

Their mutual agreement worked for both of them. For almost two months Mrs. Lopez came to work five days a week, giving Tannenbaum tough love and encouragement. She bossed him around. "You are the patient and I am the nurse. If you follow my directions you will get better much faster." She made sure he took his medicines on time and followed the doctor's instructions exactly. Slowly, the pain eased and the infection was contained. He began to heal. With physical therapy, he regained almost complete use of his ankle. He had only a slight limp as a result of his accident.

Tannenbaum realized how important Mrs. Lopez was to him; he not only respected her abilities as a nurse, he grew quite fond of her as a person. During this period, Isabel asked Mrs. Lopez and her daughter to stay for dinner several times. Maribeth and Sonia would help Isabel prepare the meal and there would be high spirits and loud talk across the dining room table. Henry would insist he was being held captive by the worst nurse in the world and Mrs. Lopez would claim that he was the worst patient she had ever been asked to help. There was love and the celebration of life at their dinners.

Toward the end of his physical therapy, Tannenbaum walked around his neighborhood accompanied by Mrs. Lopez. He hadn't started driving yet so they would walk in the neighborhood around his home. Mrs. Lopez was relaxed during these trips, far different from the attitude she had when she and Bill Bruckner went to feed the geese. After the assault she was afraid for her life. Now, working again had restored her confidence and she could walk almost anywhere and enjoy herself.

When Tannenbaum started to drive, he wanted to walk in Wilson Park to see if Mrs. Lopez would be comfortable returning to the place where she was attacked. He asked if she would accompany him. After a moment of thought, she agreed. He didn't mention feeding the geese; he left it to her to bring up the subject. He parked the car and they crossed the bridge spanning the small river and walked along its bank. It was a pleasant day and there were others strolling along the river.

At first, Mrs. Lopez appeared tense. When an unknown man approached them, she quickly put one hand inside her large purse until the stranger walked a safe distance away. Tannenbaum assumed Mrs. Lopez had a can of Mace ready, if necessary. Soon, she was more relaxed in her reaction to other pedestrians coming close. She still had her hand inside her purse, but she was less agitated and not nearly as nervous.

They sat on a river bench and watched the ongoing parade pass in review. Mrs Lopez said, "You know, Mr. Tannenbaum, working with you has made me feel good. Helping you get better and earning money makes me want to do the things I have always done. If we can come here tomorrow, I'd like to feed my geese. I'm sure they have missed me and I have missed praying with them.

"Can we do that?"

Henry was quick to respond. "Mrs. Lopez, I'm glad to hear you say that. Yes, tomorrow we'll walk here and feed those damn geese you like so much. I consider them a nuisance because they drop so much poop all over the park. However, if you want to feed them, so be it. That's what we will do."

The following day, Mrs. Lopez bought two unsliced loaves of stale bread. When their walk was finished, she sat on a bench, broke off pieces of the bread, and threw them on the ground. Immediately, they were swarmed by twenty or thirty geese, eager to take advantage of a free lunch.

Tannenbaum could only shake his head as they were surrounded by squawking, hungry geese. However, he was overjoyed to see Mrs. Lopez's reactions. She was throwing chunks of bread as far as she could and laughing with her birds.

Henry Tannenbaum had accomplished his part of the bargain with Mrs. Lopez. She was again enjoying the responsibility of feeding her geese. She would always be aware of who was near her but she had overcome the fears associated with being in Wilson Park. He was delighted with the results of their walk—even though he had to be careful where he stepped, so as not to get any goose poop on his shoes.

CHAPTER 15

Even though the term "old age" is commonly used, it is a category that is difficult to define. There is more to the definition of "old age" than the calendar. Obviously, senior citizens are automatically included in the definition; however, most of them are not quite ready to accept that honor without protesting.

Some seniors are much younger than their years and there are some youngsters who are in the "old age" category long before their calendar time. Physical health, mental acuity, and strength of disposition all factor into the definition of "old age."

However, when a person does get old, the winter of their existence is upon them and they understand that their life span is nearing an end. The wondrous spark of life will soon be extinguished from their earthly bodies. They become aware that, whether they wish it or not, the mystery of life after death will be revealed to them. Some resist the thought of death, some resign themselves to the thought of death, while a few welcome the idea of death.

We humans are puppets who can only speculate about our puppeteer. We really don't know the answer until we cross the boundary that separates life from death. It is possible that once we cross the boundary we still will not know.

Isabel and Henry Tannenbaum were starting into their ninth decade of life, their third decade of marriage. As they aged, they moved more slowly, but they were far, far from their dotage. They retained their mental capacities, their sense of humors, and their enjoyment of life. It was the lifetime of wear and tear on their bodies that was aging them.

They had married late in life and they were grateful that each had saved the other from the bitterness that loneliness brings to old age. They were not carbon copies of each other. They were more like team players. They had the same moral standards but different personalities. In thirty years of marriage they learned that give and take was more effective and more fun than head-butting. They were an ideal couple, easy going and fun to be around. Outside of slowing down and clinging more to each other, they were still Isabel and Henry Tannenbaum, the elders of a clan.

Of course, each had changed in personality but not their personal values and beliefs. Isabel was afraid of falling. She was careful where she walked and would hold Henry's hand on uneven terrain. She prepared uncomplicated meals for them and Henry had no problem with that. His tastes were simple and he always thought the food in front of him was the best meal that he had ever eaten in his entire life. Isabel would lock all the doors in their house at night before retiring. For some reason, she became wary of burglars. Her big difference from Henry was that she was more conservative in her attitudes. Anyone who opposed something she was in favor of was no longer automatically granted their stance; they had to prove why they were right. Part of this later attitude was due to the cultural change taking place in her country. She did not approve or like what was taking place in Washington, D.C.

Henry was having trouble with the ankle he broke. It was arthritic and forced him to limp. He refused to use a cane and, as a result, walked much slower. Similarly to his beloved mate, he had become more conservative for the same reasons that she had.

They would spend hours trying to figure out where their fellow humans and their country were headed. Hardly anything made sense to them. The educational system bothered them. The knew that children are born inquisitive and eager to learn. That has always been a human trait. So why is our educational system failing its duty to teach? And why our are college graduates leaving school with their futures heavily mortgaged?

The two of them bemoaned the decline of newspapers and the growth of pretty looking television commentators explaining, in detailed and demeaning attitudes, what was happening in the world. They were especially bemused with the instant gratification, instant information, demands of the young, technical generation. They were old enough to know that life took its time to unfold. Tweeting, face-booking, and texting allowed for communicating, but people seemed to be talking much more and listening much less. Isabel and Henry wondered if instant communication wasn't contributing to the decline of respect that they were witnessing?

They both realized that older generations are always worried about the ideas of the generations that follow. And they could be wrong; so they kept their thoughts to themselves. They tried to be open-minded and not look down their noses as the world spun around them.

Isabel and Henry did simplify their lifestyle. That began shortly after they attended Sonia De Los Angeles's wedding. She married a Mexican doctor she met on a visit to Cancun. Trina Lopez was so happy for her daughter that she got tipsy at the wedding. That evening, Trina Lopez passed in her sleep.

After the funeral, Isabel and Henry began to think about all their friends and companions no longer alive. They decided to huddle even closer together. They didn't turn into recluses but they did try to conserve their energies. A good night for them was to sit in front of the television watching the Public Broadcasting System, drinking hot chocolate, and eating homemade oatmeal and raisin cookies.

Henry and Isabel ran all their outside errands together and made local trips for their enjoyment. They would admire babies and talk to young children when they were out and about. This invigorated both of them. One of their favorite jaunts was to go to Ann Arbor on Saturday mornings to shop at the farmer's market in Kerrytown, a historic section of the city. They enjoyed the communal atmosphere among the buyers of fresh fruits and vegetables and the farmers selling their produce. It was a celebration of daily living that makes both buyers and sellers feel good. The farmer's market turned ordinary activities into memorable pilgrimages. Isabel and Henry examined the fresh produce, flowers, and baked goods. They talked with strangers, exchanged recipes, and gave suggestions freely. The crowds, the hubbub, and just having a good time excited them. However, parking was a problem. The Tannenbaums arrived early and got there before the market opened to make sure they could park nearby. Spending more time driving than shopping at the farmer's market was not uncommon and it was not something that either of them wanted to do. There was also a hint of conceit in their visits to the farmer's market. They enjoyed being pointed out as a striking pair of senior citizens.

One Saturday evening, they were sitting watching television when Isabel said, "Henry I'm tired. Today's trip completely exhausted me. My age is beginning to catch up to me. I wonder how much more time I have."

Henry quickly came over and sat down beside her. He took her hand and replied, "Isabel, we have both lived for a long time. All of us are only here temporarily. I guess that's why we look forward to our future time in Heaven."

"Maybe so, Henry, but I do enjoy my time. I have you, my children, my grandchildren and my great grandchildren. I have so much to be thankful for, I don't want to leave yet."

Henry kissed her on the cheek. "Isabel, My Love, we still have plenty of time left, so let's not fret. We'll just enjoy the time we have and leave our future in the hands of God.

Henry Tannenbaum was deceived. They did not have much time to enjoy each other. Fate had other plans.

On a warm, summer day Isabel was in her garden doing what she enjoyed, planting flowers. As she stood, she felt a little dizzy, so she sat down on a wooden garden bench. She misjudged the height of the seat and, instead of sitting gently, she landed hard enough to jar her head and slam her back against the bench. After sitting and resting, for a few minutes, she went into the house to fix lunch. That evening, and for the next few days, Isabel complained of a backache that eased only when she put heat on it or took Tylenol. The relief was temporary; her backache kept getting worse. Finally, despite her protests, Henry called 911 and Isabel was taken by ambulance to the hospital. After X-rays, MRI's, and examinations by the doctors, the diagnosis was that Isabel had crushed one of the vertebrae in her spine and that she needed an operation.

This presented a problem because she was on a blood thinning medicine. The surgeon could not operate until the blood thinner was out of her system. She was given medications to speed the process of purging the blood thinner and preparing her for surgery. She was confined to bed for a few days until she was ready.

During the wait, Isabel turned ninety-one. To celebrate this important milestone, Henry threw a surprise party in her hospital room. All her friends appeared and Henry showed up with a large sheet cake that read, "HAPPY 19th BIRTHDAY." Isabel was delighted with the party and she joked about the reversal of the numbers. Friends, neighbors, and the members of the 1:15 Club showed up. Many of them brought pictures of the flowers in her garden that they wanted her to see. There was an air of happiness and optimism at her party.

The operation went smoothly. However, a problem occurred almost immediately after the operation. Isabel could not swallow food or drink liquids. She could retain nothing. She would gag, choke, and throw everything up. Doctors examined her throat to determine if the anesthesia tube had caused a problem. They found nothing that would explain her violent reactions to food and liquids. She was examined by specialists trying to determine what was causing her swallowing problems. Nothing appeared to be medically wrong, so Isabel was transported to a nursing home for short-term rehabilitation.

That was not to be. Her swallowing problems got worse and, after a few more days of not being able to eat or drink, Isabel was transported back to the hospital. She was examined in the emergency room and was immediately returned by ambulance to the nursing home.

The medical staff at the nursing home called the hospital and angrily asked for an explanation why she had been sent back to the nursing home. They had expected the hospital to keep her for more tests to determine what was happening. Isabel was finally readmitted to the hospital but the damage had been done. The surgery wound had become infected. She asked Henry to make sure that no one came to see her. The only person she wanted to see, outside of Henry and her immediate family, was her minister, Father Frank. He was as much her friend as he was her priest and he came to visit her almost every day.

Isabel had not eaten in almost three weeks. She could not swallow any food, the wound was infected, and her doctors were concerned. She was in pain, weak, and despondent about the outcome. A feeding tube was inserted through her nose. She was now being given antibiotics, nourishment, saline, blood thinner and pain relieving medicines through intravenous feedings. Her arms were purple from her shoulders to her fingers from the bruising she received when the nurses and doctors tried to puncture her veins. Still, the doctors could not determine, with any certainty, the cause of her medical problems.

After another week of tests, tubes, and torments, Isabel could not stand the torture any longer. She was in constant pain and the uncertainty of her future scared her. She called her husband to her bedside and said, "Henry, I can't take this any more. I want to die."

He almost screamed as he said, "Oh, Isabel, please don't say that. I need you to live."

"Darling Henry, I love you. However, I'm in so much pain. They don't know what is wrong and, even if they did, does it do me any good? There's no guarantee that I won't crush another vertebra the day I leave here. I've lost all my dignity. Someone has to wipe my bottom to keep me clean and it can be either a man or a woman. I can't go through this again. I'm going to ask them to remove all these tubes and just let me die.

"I have been thinking about this for a while and I'm at peace with my decision."

Henry was devastated. He needed her to live. He loved her. He relied on Isabel for his own life. She was his mother lode of happiness. He couldn't stand the thought of her being in pain, but he didn't want her to die. However, Henry was completely aware of how Isabel was suffering. He had prayed constantly for her to recover.

He thought about what she had just said. He decided that if she was in so much pain he couldn't fight her decision. Her pain was tearing him apart. No matter how much he loved her, he couldn't fight her. She had been in such agony over the last three months. He hated her decision but he wouldn't try to change her mind. She was the person carrying the fears and the physical pain. He lowered his head and sobbed.

The medical profession is barred from helping a patient take his or her own life. However, they are also legally and ethically bound to keep a patient comfortable. The hospital can legally and ethically allow a patient to die with dignity and as free of pain as possible. The decision to die must be the clear, absolute, and final choice of the patient.

During the next few days, four or five doctors, including her surgeon, an infectious disease specialist and a psychiatrist, had discussions with her. They had to be certain she understood that if her decision were carried out, her future was irrevocable. She would die.

Isabel told them all the same thing. She completely understood the consequences. She was ninety-one years old and had had a good life. However, she was now in constant pain and, even if she recovered from the operation and the infection, she could easily crush another vertebra. She would always be afraid of falling whenever she was walking. She was at peace with herself; she was ready to pass. It was her decision to make and that was what she wanted.

As Isabel ordered, all the tubes, the needles, the monitoring devices were removed and she was transferred from the hospital to a hospice. For Henry, pessimism turned into numbing despair. He was roasting on the spit of hopelessness.

The hospice was an attractive building, far off the road, surrounded by large flower gardens and trees. Isabel's room was spacious and pleasant with a single bed, a convertible couch, and a large bird feeder outside the window. There were no drip poles or hospital equipment in the room. Isabel's first comment to Henry was, "This is more like a bridal suite than I expected."

The difference between the hospital and hospice was immediately apparent to Isabel and Henry. Hospitals are for curing. They keep the patient busy with medical appointments, medicine schedules, routine taking of vital signs, and the constant, redundant asking of the same questions. There is continual bell ringing and people being paging over loudspeakers. The major concern is healing the sick.

Hospices are for comforting. They are tranquil and quiet with as little activity, apart from caring for patients, as possible. They are aware that their patients have come to die and they want them to be as comfortable and worry free as possible. They also try to console their patients, as well as the patient's family. Their major concern is to ease the end of life's journey.

Once Isabel arrived at the hospice, Henry's daily routine changed. In the hospital and the rehabilitation facility, he had visited her from early morning until mid evening. He would then go home, try to get some rest, and return early the next day. He was her only visitor because she didn't care to see anyone else.

Now that he knew she would to die, he stayed in the room with her every night, sleeping on the couch that made into a bed. It was uncomfortable but, every time she asked, he lied and told Isabel that it was fine. Either Maribeth or Bill would come so Henry could go home, clean up, check the mail and the bills. He would return as soon as possible to be with Isabel. She wanted him by her side constantly and he insisted on being with her.

A week after Isabel was admitted, there was a tap on her open door and a man entered. He was of average height, slender, with a blond, trimmed beard and thinning blond hair. "Mrs. Tannenbaum," he said. "I don't know if you remember me but I am Dr. Concannon. I interviewed you when you first arrived."

Isabel replied, "Dr. Concannon, in the last two months I have met almost every doctor who practices in the Ann Arbor area. Yes, I remember you because I told you that I can't take any pain medication orally and you agreed that all my medications would be through the picc line implanted in me."

He answered, "Well, I think that is working well. We don't have to keep bruising your arms looking for veins. That is good. The staff tells me that you are getting low doses of morphine for your pain. However, they also told me that you're not eating or drinking anything. Aren't you hungry?"

"Not really. It's so painful for me to throw up that I would rather not take the chance of eating and I have lost my appetite."

"Well, what about drinking? I can see that your lips are dry and chapped. You must be thirsty?"

"Yes, I am thirsty; but, I'm so afraid of throwing up that I'd rather not try to drink anything."

Dr. Concannon shook his head. "Mrs. Tannenbaum, there are ways to relieve your thirst. You can take a cold, wet washcloth and suck on it or you can sip water.

"I want to make you as comfortable as I can. You do not have to torture yourself. Does that make any sense to you at this point? Please think about trying to eat or drink. Why should you suffer needlessly?"

Isabel didn't reply. However, she did close her eyes and, after a few minutes, tears welled. Dr. Concannon stood up and said, "Please, Mrs. Tannenbaum, think about it." Then, he patted her hand and left the room.

During this conversation, Henry was sitting on the other side of the bed, stroking Isabel's arm with his fingers. After Dr. Concannon left they both sat silently. Isabel quietly spoke, "I'd like to try a cold washcloth." Henry jumped up immediately and soaked a clean washcloth in cold water and handed it to Isabel. She put a corner of the washcloth in her mouth, sucked on it for a minute or two, and gave it back to Tannenbaum. Then she drifted asleep. When she woke up, she asked for another wet washcloth. Henry suggested that she try to eat something but she totally refused.

The following day, instead of asking for a wet washcloth, Isabel asked, "Henry, do you think I can have a little root beer?"

Tannenbaum went to the nearest store and returned with a large bottle. He poured root beer into a plastic cup filled with ice and handed it to Isabel. She took her time sucking it through a straw but she drank all of it and asked for more. She said, "This root beer tastes delicious." During the rest of that day, and the next, she drank cold root beer constantly. She would drink it in little sips. However, Isabel still refused to eat.

It was on the third day that she quietly turned to her husband. "Henry, if they have some strawberry ice cream, I'd like to try some." He asked the nurse and shortly he was feeding Isabel strawberry ice cream from a small cardboard cup. From that point on, all Isabel would eat and drink was ice cream and root beer. She enjoyed both and they gave her body a little sustenance. Not enough, however, to fight the infection that was invading her wound. She was getting weaker and she and Tannenbaum both were aware of this.

The little she did eat seemed to change Isabel's attitude toward her imminent death. She spent a lot of time with Father Frank and her husband going over details of her funeral and the disposition of her most valued personal items. Father Frank came twice a day to pray with Isabel and his visits always ended with his blessing; Isabel always asked him to recite the Twenty-third Psalm. When Bill was there, he would hold hands with Henry, Father Frank, and his mother and silently listen to the prayers.

The prayer sessions, the root beer and the strawberry ice cream revived Isabel; she changed her attitude about seeing her friends. She asked to see the members of her bridge club. She had Henry and her son scurrying around her home locating specific personal items that she wanted to give her three card-playing friends. They came at the appointed time, spending over three hours laughing at their past adventures and misadventures. The three of them left, kissing and hugging Isabel goodbye. They each had tears streaming from their eyes as they left her room. They knew they were not saying, "Goodbye until we meet next week for bridge." They were saying to their beloved friend, "Farewell forever."

Within a week's time, Isabel had three other meetings with her most intimate friends. Her room was filled with laughter, old stories were relived and past memories were resurrected. She told everyone that she had lived a good life she was thankful for that. She would waggle her index finger at her husband and her son and admonish them if they said anything she disagreed with. She said that she intended to leave the world laughing. When she wasn't in pain, she was coherent and witty.

It was after this brief period of enjoying her friends and family that Isabel's infection began to eat her life. Isabel required more opium to conquer the pain. She was more subconscious than conscious, her frail body became even more gaunt. She occasionally said, "I want to go home and see my flowers," or "I want to die." Both statements cut deeply into her family who were now by her bedside in a constant vigil. They were terrified at the thought that Isabel was in pain and couldn't ask for more morphine. For the last forty-eight hours of her life Isabel lay unresponsive in her bed, her grieving family constantly at her side. Without ever regaining consciousness, Isabel died.

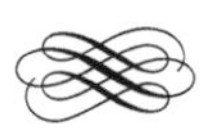

A memorial service for Isabel was held a week later at the funeral home that handled her cremation. Father Frank conducted the service, more a celebration of her life than a burial ceremony. The room was packed with people who had known Isabel at some time during her long life. There were voluntary testimonials from those whose lives had been touched by her. The service was a show of love for a person who believed that respect and kindness was the right of every person in the world.

Less than three months after the service, Henry Tannenbaum was found dead in his home. His death certificate read that he died of natural causes but Maribeth and Bill knew that he died of a broken heart.

They saw him go from a hopeful sunrise when he first learned of Isabel's spine to a crushing sunset when he realized she would die. His despair defeated his capacity to live. They watched him shuffle aimlessly, day after day, from room to room in his empty house. He absolutely refused to stay with them; Henry said he wanted to be left alone with his memories.

The Bruckners had brought Henry a hot meal the night before he passed. He didn't eat anything and when they again urged him to come home with them he said, "It doesn't make any difference where I am or who I am with, I am totally alone. Being alone is not the same as being lonely; being lonely means you have memories that console you. My memories do not help me, so I am alone. My wife of thirty years is gone and my memories are drowning me. I can't help myself.

"Isabel, my beloved wife, is no longer with me. I don't want memories. I want her. I want to be with her. We can't be united in this world so I will go to the next world to be with her. That is the only way out of hell.

"I am looking forward to our reunion."

Tannenbaum got his wish later that evening.

He was cremated and his ashes were interred beside Isabel. Both of them remained alive in the hearts and thoughts of their families.

Isabel was under medical treatment over four months before she died. From the very beginning, when she was first diagnosed with a crushed vertebra, Tannenbaum was convinced that she would recover and come home. Between his belief in God and his love for Isabel he was sure that nothing bad was going to happen. He was always cheerful and positive when he and his wife talked between themselves.

When Isabel couldn't swallow and went to the nursing home, he was concerned but not worried. He prayed harder and more often. He didn't realize that his life would be changed until Isabel went back to the hospital. Suddenly, he found himself asking God to intervene as he prayed for a miracle. When his heart was pierced with the knowledge that his wife was dying, he told God that he didn't understand why she was being taken from him and everyone who loved her. He told God that they needed her more than He did and he didn't want Him to take her so soon. After he got no answer, Henry prayed for Isabel's comfort, her soul, and her entry into heaven.

Not once did Henry lose his faith. Even though he didn't understand why this personal tragedy was happening, he couldn't renounce God. He had believed in Him all his life. It never entered his mind to question God's way. He just prayed harder that Isabel suffer no pain and receive her due reward when she reached heaven.

When Isabel passed, the ache in his heart reverberated like a huge gong being struck again and again. He missed her wit, her charm, her physical presence so much that, when he was home by himself, he cried for hours. Bill tried to console him, Maribeth tried to console him, his friends tried to console him. All efforts failed. There is no way to comfort the aged when their partner passes; the survivor loses not only a spouse but also the will to continue.

Henry Tannenbaum was stunned. He was not prepared for his loss. His wife, the most precious jewel in his life, was gone. The complete reality of her death didn't sink in until he returned to their empty home. Then his loneliness emotionally crushed him. Every room in that house had memories and events from their past; he sobbed as he realized that his wife was forever gone. He lost his taste for life and gave up. Shortly before he died, he told Bill and Maribeth that he knew he would be reunited with Isabel in heaven.

During Henry's memorial service they both prayed that his prediction was correct. They wanted him to be with Isabel. Maribeth and Bill wept for them both.

Maribeth took Isabel's death extremely hard. Isabel had long ago become Maribeth's adopted mother as well as her best friend. They shared their personal and their family lives together. Maribeth couldn't imagine who could fill the void of Isabel's absence.

Before her operation, Maribeth sat by Isabel's bedside and they reminisced about the past. Maribeth told Isabel that she remembered her help and guidance when she first started working at the family restaurant. Isabel told Maribeth how fond of her she was and felt she could confide in her about her wayward son who had just returned from Vietnam. Later, when Maribeth and her son were married, Isabel was delighted to have her as her daughter-in-law.

Maribeth cried when she realized that Isabel's medical problems were getting worse. She saw that Isabel was failing. She knew Isabel was embarrassed when the hospital aides, male or female, cleaned and washed her. It bothered Maribeth that Isabel thought she had lost her dignity. No one as sweet as Isabel could ever lose her dignity. Maribeth tried to console the woman she so loved.

When Isabel's physical condition started to decline, Maribeth prayed for divine intervention. She told God that her mother-in-law was needed on Earth; Isabel was precious and special to all those who knew her. Maribeth promised to be more faithful in her prayers and her religious duties if He would spare Isabel for a few more years. Whenever Isabel rallied and felt better, Maribeth thought her prayers were answered. However, as Isabel weakened and began slipping, she realized that Isabel was going to die. That truth hit her hard. She sobbed as she despaired and wondered if God even heard her urgent prayers. Certainly she had had no sign from Him that He had.

It was not until months after Isabel's passing that Maribeth began to again think about her personal relationship with God. She was not ready to give up her belief that there was a God. She concluded that she should not have questioned His decision to call Isabel to His side. She would just have to do better on a personal basis, to have more faith in Him.

This was her consolation and the way she fought through her deep sorrow.

However, a gap developed between Maribeth and Bill. They both lost their way inside the daze that surrounds grief. Neither of them discussed how they each felt. Bruckner would not talk about his feelings. He didn't say a word about the deaths of his mother and Henry. There was no need, Maribeth knew he was hurting as much as she.

Bill Bruckner's reactions to his mother's medical problems were the opposite of those of Henry and Maribeth. Because he didn't believe in their God he could easily blame Him for what was happening. That is precisely what he did. When he found out about his mother's crushed vertebra, he was concerned. Having a major operation at her age could be risky. He was wary. Then, as her medical problems multiplied, he became worried and angry.

By her bedside, Bill was extremely nervous, anxious. He flinched, mentally and physically, at the thought that she was in pain. He would continually ask her how she felt. It was at this point that he began talking to God. "Why are You doing this? My mother is one of Your most beautiful creatures on earth. She has faithfully followed Your rules all her life. She is truly a good person. Why are You putting her through this torture?" As his mother's life slipped away, Bruckner became even more scared, more disturbed, more angry. He watched his mother's health deteriorate and could do nothing about it. He became increasingly bitter at what he thought was such an unjust ending. Watching a parent die is a cruel form of punishment. Although he seemed calm and reasonable to everyone he talked with inside, he was a boiling caldron bubbling with fear and hate when he thought of the future.

During the final days of Isabel's life, lying unconscious and barely breathing, Bruckner became unhinged. When he was in her room he would sit and watch her for hours. He would hold her hand or rub her shoulder and, when she stirred or moved her head, he would agonize over the question, "Is she in pain?" He could not leave that question alone.

When he returned home from his vigil Bill drank heavily to stop his thoughts so he could sleep. He became paranoiac. The night before his mother died, Bruckner drank almost half a bottle of bourbon. He staggered into his backyard and shook his fist toward the sky. "God, You son of a bitch, You bastard. Why are You doing this to my mother? No one has ever loved You more or tried to follow Your teachings more than my mother. Is this the way You reward her for her devotion?

"You bastard, if You are angry with me, take Your revenge out on me. Me. Not on someone I love and who loves You. If You want to punish me for not believing in You, go ahead. That is Your right. I would have no complaints. But, if You are a just God, spare her, reward her, and do her honor for believing in You."

Later that evening, Maribeth found Bill passed out in a chair in the backyard. She was aware of how deep his pain for his mother was. She helped him into bed without making a fuss or saying a word about his drinking. That night, she sobbed herself to sleep.

After the memorial services for Isabel and Henry, Maribeth and Bill began to reassemble their own lives. Their schedules had to be altered because there were now large voids to fill in their daily routines. They had spent much more time with Isabel and Henry than they realized. Along with the grief that drowned all thoughts of happiness were empty time slots that had been filled with activities they engaged in together. New pursuits and interests had to be found to substitute for what never could be replaced.

What was different this time, though, was the fact that neither Maribeth or Bill talked about their personal feelings. They each kept their emotions hidden and sampled only for their own grief. They first had to reconcile themselves with the reality that they had lost two of the most important and beloved people in their lives. Their grief was deep and frozen inside them; it not only blocked their thoughts, it also numbed their vocal cords. They had to wait—defrost and examine their emotions before they could discuss them. It took a long time for this to happen.

CHAPTER 16

The ebb and flow of coastal tides are ceaselessly working to cleanse the beaches over which they wash. The flow tide floods the beach, the ebb tide carries the dregs out to sea. In the same way, the ebb and flow of daily life works to help humans overcome their most heartbreaking experiences. It is not an easy transition and it takes a long time for the pain to ease. We never forget the past and there are moving episodes remaining in memory never to be fully erased.

In a sense, this is good. Once a person can recall the past without wincing, the hurt and pain are bearable. This allows good memories to flow without the continual ebb of tears and sorrow. Memories provide continuity from one generation to the next. Without continuity, we would have no history, and without history, there would be no humanity.

Neither Maribeth or Bill thought a sea change could purge the sadness of their losses. They continued grinding out their lives as best they could, never discussing the deaths of Isabel and Henry. At first, it seemed too sensitive a subject for discussion. After they adjusted to life without the two people they loved so dearly, neither one wanted to talk about it. Their everyday routines continued and time kept rolling along.

It was not until their third great-granddaughter was born that the subject of Isabel and Henry came up. Even then, it was broached indirectly. They eagerly went to get their first glimpse of the latest addition to their family. They spent a long time cuddling and studying their new family member closely. Instead of driving home when they left the hospital, Bill said to Maribeth, "Listen, it's such a beautiful day and we are so lucky to have a healthy new great-grandchild, let's celebrate."

"How?" Maribeth asked.

"Well, we are close to Lillie Park. Let's get hot pastrami sandwiches at that delicatessen we like and have a picnic at the park. We haven't been there in years. Today we have a lot to be thankful for."

They bought their sandwiches and sat in the pavilion overlooking one of the lakes; it was a gorgeous day and they were the only people in the pavilion. Enjoying her lunch and the pleasant view, Maribeth remarked, "What a happy day, and isn't our new family addition a beautiful baby girl?"

Bill chewed on his sandwich for a few minutes. "Maribeth, I've yet to see a baby that you didn't think was beautiful. However, in this case, I have to agree with you. That child is one of the cutest sausage links I ever saw."

Maribeth was a bit surprised by his description of their newest addition and she was not at all pleased. She sharply replied, "What do you mean, 'sausage link?' That's no way to describe my new, beautiful, great-granddaughter."

Bruckner chuckled. "Whoa! That's not my description, it was Henry's, and he meant it as a compliment. He maintained that each generation was a sausage link, connecting the previous generation to the next generation by the sausage casing."

Maribeth was not mollified. She sniffed, "That does not sound very gracious."

"Gracious or not, that was Henry's idea. I told him that I didn't believe it was right to think of humanity as sausages and time as sausage casings. However, Henry said . . ."

Suddenly, Bill stopped speaking because he saw Maribeth staring at him with an odd look on her face. He asked, "What's wrong?"

She leaned across the picnic table to pat his hand. "Sweetheart, nothing is wrong but this is the first time I've heard you mention Henry's name since he passed."

Bruckner sat silently for a while before he squeezed Maribeth's hand and grinned sadly. He said, in a low voice, "I miss him. I miss my mother. They have been gone over two years but I'm reminded of them every day. Someone will say something that bounces in my ear like an echo or I will see something that flashes me back to the past and when that happens, I fade from where I am and find myself thinking about them.

"Isn't that weird?"

"No, it's not weird. I miss them so much. They were a huge part of our lives and now they are gone. Why should we forget our feelings for them and what they meant to us? If we did that, it would dishonor them."

Bill smiled at her. "You are so wise. You make me feel good when I talk with you." He stopped for a few minutes, then continued. "You know, Henry used to say, 'All of us living here on this earth are only temporary. We will be replaced by the next generation.' I never really paid much attention to his statement until after he passed. He's right. You and I are getting old and we are probably next in line."

Maribeth spoke right up, "Well, thanks a lot for that happy prediction. How soon is this going to happen?"

Her husband patted her hand. "Honey, I don't mean we're going to stop breathing immediately. We're healthy and we have a lot to be thankful for; we will enjoy ourselves as long as we can. However, you have to admit that our time is coming—our new great-granddaughter is proof of that."

Maribeth didn't answer him but silently, she agreed. They finished their picnic quietly and went home. The rest of the day and into early evening, neither of them had much to say. Maribeth finished cleaning the kitchen after supper and went to the den to talk to her husband. He wasn't there and the television wasn't on. She quickly went through the other rooms in the house searching for him. She still couldn't find him. Finally, she looked toward the glass doors leading to their backyard and saw him sitting outside on a lounge chair.

She joined him outside. "I didn't know you were out here. I looked everywhere for you and you were nowhere inside. I wondered what happened to you."

"I'm sorry. It looked so pleasant that I just wandered out here without telling you. Now that you're here, sit beside me. I need to talk with you." He patted the cushion next to him and moved a little so she could join him. When they were both comfortable, Bill spoke. "Isn't this a beautiful evening? Maybe it has been given to us through the courtesy of our new great-granddaughter."

Bruckner was correct about the evening. The air was cool without a chill, there was no breeze and the moon was full, not a cloud in the sky. The pale, yellow light magically clung to whatever it touched, painting everything a pleasing color and disguising all blemishes. It was a night to inhale deeply and smell your dreams.

After a while, Bruckner reached out and held Maribeth's hand. "Darling wife, the one constant I have in my life is you. You have given me happiness in good times and solace in bad times. Don't think that I didn't realize how you got me to bed the night I got drunk, the night before my mother died. You never said a word, you just helped me. The next morning I never felt so alone and ashamed of myself." He stopped talking.

Maribeth finally replied, "What was there to say? I knew why you had been drinking. You needed comfort, not criticism. Isn't that what love and marriage is about?"

They both gazed at the backyard, with its bushes and gardens, and tears streamed from their eyes. Maribeth's husband snuffled, wiped his tears away and said, "I am becoming a complete candy-ass, crying all the time. Before you came out, I was thinking that a newborn makes every person think about what life means. That small bundle of squirming humanity, our great-granddaughter, absolutely demands that we feed her, love her, and protect her. We gratefully do so, and that forces us to examine our lives to see who we are, who we love, and if we could be a better person. I want that child to be proud of me when she grows up.

"My mind keeps going back to the death of my mother. When she decided to stop all medical treatment so she could just pass away, I was completely stunned. I totally disagreed. I wanted her to continue fighting and get better. I wanted her to live. To this very day, I don't know whether or not she made the right decision. From her point of view, what would the quality of her life be if she had survived? Would she have recovered enough to enjoy life? Would she always be afraid of falling or crushing another vertebra? I can't answer those questions but I kept asking them to myself as I watched her fade away.

"The last week was the worst. She lay there, unconscious as her body began to shrivel, but still she fought for life. She would moan or, as it sounded to me, try to sing a song. She tried getting out of bed a few times, to say she wanted to go home. I couldn't tell whether or not she was in pain. The only thing I did know was that she was dying. My heart was ripped open by my terror. I have no doubt that her pain deranged me.

"I must have been out of my mind. I started to drink to get rid of my fear. That night, before you finally put me to bed, I did something that I now regret and am now bothered by. I screamed at God. I regret it now because I know that my mother would not have approved of me. She would have asked me to respect Him just as she would have said that He respected me. Today, I would agree with her, but the pain I was bearing at her bedside was too much. I wanted Him to account for his actions. He didn't and I'm ashamed of myself. I showed Him, if there is a Him, no respect; and that means I didn't show any respect to my mother. This is the main reason that I haven't talked to you about my mother's death. I am so sorry for what I did and there is no way I can make amends. Every memory about her death is like placing a red hot coal in the palm of my hand."

Maribeth asked, "And now?"

Bill answered his wife by asking a question of his own, "Have you ever noticed how old people react when they see babies or young children? They absolutely come alive. They show deference, they carry on a conversation and they listen while the child talks. It's as if they regain their own youth, spending time with youngsters.

"That's how I felt before you joined me. I was remembering how much my mother loved beauty. I've never known anyone who enjoyed looking at the clouds and watching the sunsets as much as she did. She was the same way about birds. She would talk to them, as if they were her children, while they ate at her feeders.

"My bad memories about her death were beginning to fade, even before today. I am going to try to put these thoughts out of my mind now and I will stop hugging the thorn bush. My great-granddaughter is going to receive all the love I can pour into her. Even though she never met my mother, I am going to tell her about the wonderful person my mother was. This is the best way to honor Isabel: teach her offspring what goodness and love really are."

They watched as a cat silently stalked across their yard hunting prey and not succeeding. It walked off in a fit of disdain. The cat's antics brought a smile to Maribeth's face as she asked, "Does this mean you now believe in God?"

"No. It means that I shouldn't have been rude to Him. I think that He put my mother through extremely cruel and unusual punishment. No matter what I think, I know that you believe in God as did my mother and Henry. I will respect your image of Him. Swearing at Him is a direct insult to three people I love very much. I should honor your respect. My love for all of you must include respect for your beliefs even if I don't share those beliefs. You have no idea how deeply I feel about my love for you."

Maribeth leaned against his shoulder. "Oh, yes I do, my darling atheist husband. I feel the same way about you. I remember the first time I saw you looking through your father's desk. When you stood up, I saw a tall man whose face was hidden behind a full beard and whose hair was in a long pony tail swirling down his back. Your father told me about some of the family problems and I wondered if you were dangerous.

"After your father passed, I came close to not working with you. I wasn't sure who you were or how I would be treated. However, I figured I owed it to your father and my parents to try to work with you and revive your restaurant. That was the smartest decision I ever made in my entire life. I found that behind that shaggy exterior was a man with a sweet interior. The first day you showed up for work looking like a human being and not a Neanderthal, I was shocked and shaken. I had to go back to my office and catch my breath.

"All these years later, you still take my breath away. You are a person who cares about other people. It amazes me that even though we disagree about God, we share the same moral values. In theory, we are a complete mismatch.

"I guess we're proof that love can flourish despite what the head tells the heart. I am thankful that I followed your advice and didn't resign immediately after your father died. You are my reward for trying to live a good life."

They sat close, holding hands and letting their eyes, ears, and noses carry them through the beauty of the night. Bruckner didn't respond for so long that Maribeth finally asked, "Sam the Sleepy, you are awake aren't you?"

Bill's reply was without a tag name for Maribeth; he was serious. "Yes, Honey, I'm awake. I was thinking of how odd life is and how lucky we are. There are thousands and thousands of generations that have preceded us, billions of people who passed through this world before we were born. We could have lived in different parts of the world and never have met. The odds in favor of us being alive at the same time and finding each other are almost nonexistent. Yet, we did. How did we beat the odds?

"I'm confused by fate. I'm thankful we are together but I don't understand how it happened. It's not logical and I'm as baffled as I was in my diaper days; I just can't make sense of the world.

"I give up, I'm not a philosopher, I'm just someone who loves you.

"It is so peaceful out here but it's getting chilly. Are you ready to go in the house?"

"Yes, my love, I am."

Even though both said they were ready, neither of them moved. They were content to stay where they were and bathe in the peace and tranquility of the evening. Bill broke the serenity. "You know, Honey, you and I have never discussed our funeral arrangements. Do you have any thoughts or preferences?"

Maribeth leaned against her husband. "Other than being with you, I have no preferences. I don't think I want to be buried in the ground. What do you think?"

Bill sat and meditated. "I've never really given it any thought. I guess it's the kind of topic that people don't want to pay attention to; maybe they think it's morbid. Well, we owe it to our family to have everything planned so that, when we pass, they won't have the extra burden of straightening out our affairs. We owe them that, don't you agree?"

Maribeth snuggled with her husband. "Yes, I remember when my parents died, first my father, then my mother. It was a nightmare straightening out their funeral and financial arrangements. Doing business while grief stricken was the worst experience of my life.

"To answer you, no, it is not morbid to make our own final arrangements and, yes, we do owe it to our children to make our wishes clear so there is no confusion. It is something that we need to decide and take care of."

Bruckner patted his wife's shoulder. "You reminded me that there is more to this than just funeral arrangements. We haven't had our wills brought up to date in years. We definitely want to avoid probate court. I'll make an appointment for us with our lawyer. We'll get our legal documents all squared away.

"As far as funeral arrangements are concerned, I've no preference between being buried or being cremated. My only concern is the same as yours, I want to be with you. If you don't want to be buried, then we will be cremated. So, I guess that's the answer; we will both be cremated. Is that okay?"

Maribeth nodded her approval and they both sat silently for a while before Bill spoke again. "There is something else that I want to ask you about. I have been thinking about Henry and Sam; the older I get, the more I meditate.

"Anyhow, the other day it struck me that I'm not going to the V.A. hospital as much as I used to. I want to; I see and read about these kids who have been through Iraq and Afghanistan, some have had four or five tours, and I cry for them. We grind them up, make misfits out of them, and then abandon them. There are so many that need help. They sleep under overpasses, they panhandle, they commit suicide."

Bruckner paused, got angry, and spoke bitterly, "Goddamn it, don't we ever learn?"

After a short silence, he continued, "Honey, I'm sorry about being on a soapbox. I feel so bad for these youngsters. What I'm getting to is that I would like to have one or two of these veterans over for dinner maybe once a month or so. It won't cure their problems but it would be my way of showing these young men and women that someone does care for them. Knowing they are not alone is important to them—it was to me. I take it as a way to honor Henry and Sam.

"Would you object to us doing that?"

Maribeth choked a little as she replied, “You are a silly old fool. Why would I object to such a kind gesture? The meals won’t be fancy but they will be nourishing with plenty of leftovers for our guests. We owe so much to them.

“You make me very proud of my choice of a partner.” It was her turn to be quiet for a while, then she added, “You have put me in a mood. Let’s go in the house, now.”

With that, Maribeth and Bill both stood up and put an arm around each other’s waist. They inclined their heads toward each other until they touched and then slowly walked into the house, down the hall into the bedroom.

As in everything else in life, practice makes perfect.